# RIDE

### WITH THE

## T.K. RIGGINS

**How To Set The World On Fire Series:**

Book 1:  How To Set The World On Fire

Book 2:  Money Jane

Book 3:  Next Level Hot

Book 4:  Outlaw OTP

Book 5:  Questbeats

Book 6: Ride with the U

*For the Roughriders,*
*Winning is our aim.*

# Table of Contents

# Prologue

Ashlyn heard a faint cry in the distance. She searched the forest, peering through the trees to see what it could be. After a few moments of silence, she returned to studying the mushrooms at her feet.

The creamy tops were splattered with purple highlights, as if painted by a five-year-old artist. Ashlyn thought of her own daughter's beautiful finger paintings. Although the colour seemed random, Ashlyn knew there was a method to Mother Nature's artistic madness.

Ashlyn picked a few of the mushrooms, then noticed a delicate gutheriea at the base of a tall oak tree. The flower's petals reached towards the sunshine—that is, until a louder cry echoed through the forest. Then the gutheriea cowered, pulling its petals inwards like a fist, as if it were getting ready to defend itself from an oncoming threat.

But Ashlyn wasn't threatened; this time, she'd determined which direction the cry had come from. She tucked her mushroom sac away and ran towards it.

The forest bed was covered in short shrubs, moss, and dead branches, which made it a perfect habitat for fungi and medicinal plants. Ashlyn had been carefully searching for potion ingredients, but now she trampled over the terrain without a care. Being close to the ocean made everything wet and slick, which caused her to slip and crush a few more plants in the process.

After ducking under a broken tree trunk, Ashlyn noticed a clearing in the foliage above her. It looked like a piece of the sky had fallen through the trees, breaking branches and toppling over small trees in its path. Instead of a giant piece of blue sky lying in the wreckage, however, she noticed a young unicorn caught in the destruction; it was pinned to the ground by the fallen trees.

"Oh my," Ashlyn gasped.

The black unicorn let out a weak cry. Its head bounced around as if it was in a daze.

"It's okay, I'm here!" Ashlyn tried to sprint to the scared little creature, but she kept slipping on the loose, wet branches. She used her hands for balance, and crawled like a cat across the rough forest floor. When she reached the unicorn, she brushed its short mane away from its eyes.

The black unicorn let out another, soft cry. Its eyes fluttered closed.

"It's okay, little one," Ashlyn said. "My name is Ashlyn Garrick. I'm going to help you out of this mess."

Ashlyn pulled out her wand. She held it loosely in her right hand while she kept her left on the unicorn's mane, just beside its golden horn. She concentrated on her magic focus, channelling her power through the wand, and then felt the connection she was searching for. A soft, white glow shone from her open palm.

She felt the pain and fear of the young unicorn, but it was faint. Ashlyn didn't detect any head trauma, but as her glowing palm moved down the unicorn's neck, she felt his pain increase.

There were a few shallow lacerations on the unicorn's side, but the cuts got deeper where a log rested on the animal's ribcage. Ashlyn felt that both of the unicorn's wings were broken, along with its right hind leg, but that wasn't the worst part. The unicorn was so hungry and parched that it would soon die from dehydration.

"How long have you been here?" Ashlyn muttered. She quickly healed the unicorn's scrapes and minor cuts, but it would take much more of her magic to heal broken bones and any internal injuries. The light faded from her palm.

The unicorn didn't answer.

In order to save the unicorn's life, Ashlyn needed to move him. She stared at the tree trunk that lay across the unicorn's belly, reaching up and beyond the log that the unicorn was pinned against. Any movement of the trunk could hurt the unicorn more, and Ashlyn wasn't strong enough to simply lift it off.

"What would Dom do?" she asked. Her husband was a scholar, and knew how to solve the most difficult of problems. He wasn't physically strong either, but was always able to use or build something to gain an advantage. An axe would be useful to divide the trunk into smaller pieces, but the crew she was with didn't keep any weapons with them. Would a wheel help roll the trunk? Or maybe a rope could be tied to each end to slide the trunk out of the way? Those options would still require physical work.

Ashlyn snapped her finger. "Leverage!"

Dom always talked about teaching their son the ways of the warrior. While some battles could be won through direct strength, others could be won by choosing a quick, well-placed blow. When outmatched by a bigger foe, leverage was Dom's key to gaining victory.

Ashlyn looked around for the right tool. She might be able to use a large branch to lift the heavy trunk off the unicorn, much like a seesaw. There weren't any branches close to her, but when she stood, she noticed a few on the other side of the fallen debris.

She took a few steps, and the unicorn cried out again.

"It's okay." Ashlyn dropped back down to pet the unicorn's black mane. "I'm not going far. Here, I'll leave this with you so you know I won't disappear." She placed her wand next to the unicorn, spinning it until the etching on the base faced up.

"Truth." Ashlyn ran her finger along the etched word. "I have a young son, and I've taught him that we are only as good as our word. Know that I speak the truth when I say that I won't abandon you."

The unicorn snorted, and then closed his eyes.

Ashlyn climbed over the fallen log that the unicorn was resting against and searched for a suitable lever. Some branches were thick enough, but too long. Another seemed perfect, until further examination revealed some cracks. She finally found one that was long enough, but not quite as thick. It would have to do.

She dragged it up and over the trunk, and then placed the base of her lever beneath the log on top of the unicorn. She pushed the branch as far as she could into the soil that was just below the unicorn's hooves, and then steadied herself. "Here we go," she said.

Ashlyn pulled down on the lever, but all it did was fall to the ground. She shook her head. "I forgot the counter."

She heard another snort.

She looked around and found a short, thick, broken trunk. She rolled it to her lever, propped it underneath the branch, and then pulled the branch down until it was snug. "That's better," she said in satisfaction. She looked at the unicorn. "I'm going to lift the log that's on top of you, but I don't know how much it will move. I need you to slide out, okay?"

The unicorn didn't respond, but his eyes were open and staring at her.

"On three," Ashlyn said. She counted down, and then pulled on the lever with everything she had. The fallen log lifted up a few inches, but nothing else happened. The unicorn remained motionless.

"C'mon, I can't hold this!" Ashlyn gritted. She didn't want to let the log fall again, because it might crush the unicorn even more. She needed the animal to move. "One hoof at a time. Just pull yourself forwards. You can do it!"

The unicorn still didn't move.

Ashlyn yelled in frustration. She jumped up and wrapped her legs around the lever. Her weight caused the lever to fall to the ground, pinning her on her back. It also forced the pinning log to roll past the hind legs of the unicorn.

The unicorn snorted.

Ashlyn pushed the lever off her torso and rolled towards the unicorn. She grabbed her wand and examined the animal again. Her glowing touch healed a few more minor wounds, but the damage under the surface was still immense. She'd have to get the unicorn to safety in order to help it further.

She knew she couldn't carry the unicorn back to her crew's cart, so she looked around the forest for more supplies. She gathered some twigs and branches, collecting them into a pile. She used some of the material from her shirt to fasten together the wood, creating a makeshift stretcher.

The unicorn's front legs were both still strong, so she pulled the unicorn by them onto the stretcher. She used her coat as a cover, to keep the unicorn warm, and then dragged the animal through the woods. She had to rest a few times, and checked in on the unicorn; she didn't feel like she was hurting him at all. So she tried to focus on getting him to safety.

After an hour or so, she'd finally made it back to her crew's cart. All three were loading their sacs and crates of plants into the back of it. None of them noticed her until she dropped the handles of her stretcher and tried to catch her breath.

"What happened to you?" Karley asked.

Ashlyn looked at her arms. They were muddy and scratched. "It's been a long day," she admitted. "Can you help me lift this in?"

"Sure." Karley moved to the other end of the stretcher. "What is it?"

"A young unicorn," Ashlyn said. She pulled the jacket down, revealing the black unicorn's face. It was fast asleep.

"What?" Karley peered at the stretcher. "Aw, I can't see it."

"Maybe once it gets better," Ashlyn said. "He's in rough shape. I'd like to get him home before we drop all our other items at the lab. I promised him I wouldn't abandon him."

"And you're a woman of your word," Karley said, nodding. "Let's get him secure."

Ashlyn and Karley picked up opposite ends of the stretcher, and they laid the black unicorn at the end of the cart. Ashlyn climbed in and rested beside the unicorn, using her magic to perform another quick evaluation. She could feel a steady heartbeat, but it was faint.

Karley sat up on the bench beside Milo and Anthony. Milo grabbed the reins, and the group trotted away. They travelled down a dirt path through the forest, which led to the closest portal gateway. By the time they arrived, the sun was beginning to set.

When they reached the twenty-foot-tall, triangular stone doorway, they stopped. Anthony inserted the correct amount of Aileron into the keystone, and then calibrated the doorway for the capital city of Kimroad with a pulse of light. As the doorway panels slid to the side, disintegrating into the stone frame, a glimmer of their destination could be seen through the doorway. They trotted their horses through and teleported to the other side.

It was a little darker in the city, since Kimroad was east of the forest they'd come from. Milo steered the cart through the busy cobblestone streets to the quaint home of the Garricks. When they stopped in front of her house, Ashlyn realized how stiff she was. She couldn't wait to clean herself up.

Karley raced to the back and helped Ashlyn unload the unicorn. Milo and Anthony held the open side of the stretcher as best they could, and they all shuffled to the front door. When Ashlyn opened the door, an embarrassing mess welcomed the group.

"Over to the fireplace," Ashlyn ordered. She pulled the group into the living room, clearing a path as she went. There were books and papers scattered across the area rug, dirty mugs on the short table, and a couple of blankets draped over two kitchen chairs. Ashlyn shoved one of the chairs with her foot to make room for the unicorn in front of the fireplace.

"This is perfect," Ashlyn said. She guided her helpers to lower the stretcher and gently place the unicorn on the floor. "Thank you all so much. Would you like to stay for tea? I think I have some desserts somewhere." She pulled the blankets away from the chairs and met the gaze of her two-year old son.

"Scuffles?" Kase asked. His beautiful smile dimpled both of his pudgy cheeks.

"Where did you come from?" Karley bent over and pinched Kase's cheeks.

"I'm hiding," Kase whispered.

"We should get our supplies back," Milo said. "I found some blue flysnappers that I should get into some water."

"And I have a jar of purple wingworms that I need to make a home for," Anthony added.

"Maybe next time," Karley said. She rubbed Kase's cheeks with the back of her hand.

"Okay, I'll see you at work tomorrow." Ashlyn led her team out of her house, and closed the door behind them.

She rushed back to the living room and bent over the unicorn. She pulled her jacket back from the unicorn's head, but it was still sound asleep. She stroked its mane gently, thinking about what she should do next.

"Horsey," Kase said. He had one of the blankets draped around his head.

He crawled over to Ashlyn and reached out for the unicorn's snout.

Ashlyn was surprised that her son could see the unicorn, since none of her crew had been able to. Unicorns were selective in who they revealed themselves to, and she wondered why the black unicorn had singled her and her son out.

"He's a unicorn," Ashlyn said. "See his horn? What colour is it?"

"Yellow," Kase said. He reached for the horn, but Ashlyn grabbed his hand. She helped Kase pet the unicorn on the mane instead. "He's sad, mama."

Ashlyn was shocked by Kase's description. It was as if he felt the unicorn's emotions, like a wizard. He'd never shown signs of being a wizard before, and since he was the size of a potato sac at birth, she and Dom assumed he was born to be a warrior.

"This unicorn is hurt, but we're going to help," Ashlyn said. "We need to be gentle with him. Keep his hair out of his eyes, and let him warm up by the fire."

"You found me!" Her husband's voice echoed from down the hall.

Calista laughed.

Heavy footsteps raced down the hallway and into the living room. Dom picked Calista up and tickled her. She giggled some more.

"Shh," Kase scorned.

"Sorry," Dom whispered. "What's going on?"

"I found a unicorn," Ashlyn said proudly. "He's in pain, but we're all broken from time to time. I know I can fix him. Can you see him?" She gestured to the stretcher.

Dom knelt down, shifting Calista to his lap. "No," he said. "Can you see him, Cali?"

"See who?" Calista asked.

Ashlyn pulled Calista's hair away from her face. The wavy strands were dull and dirty. "I thought you were going to take a bath today," she said.

"I did, mama," Calista said.

Ashlyn dropped Calista's hair and looked to Dom. He looked away. "Don't lie to me, Calista Elizabeth Garrick," she said sternly, turning back to her daughter. "We talked about this. If you want to bathe on your own, you have to stick to a reasonable schedule. You said you could do it."

Calista's eyes watered. She always led with her emotions before explaining herself, especially when she was lying. "But … mama … we were just …" her mumbled words became inaudible as she started sobbing.

Ashlyn kept her gaze on her daughter. She knew that it would take a few moments, but Calista would gain the strength of her voice. Ashlyn looked back towards the unicorn, which was still being tended to by her lovely son. Kase and the unicorn both seemed oblivious to the dramatic scene around them.

"It's my fault, Cali," Dom said.

Ashlyn spun her head around and glared at her husband. She wished he wouldn't bail out their daughter.

"We played hide-and-seek after dinner instead of taking a bath," Dom continued. "I'll help you out, though. I'll fill the tub with water while you get everything else ready. Then while you bathe, I'll sit outside the room and read you a story. How does that sound?"

Calista sniffled. "Okay," she said.

Ashlyn continued to glare at Dom, but his smile was getting to her. She didn't need to stay mad at her husband, even though he'd let Calista get away with a lie. He stood up and carried their daughter towards the hall.

"You shouldn't spoil her," Ashlyn warned.

"I'd tell you I won't anymore, but you know I lie like a ghost." Dom smirked. "You can see right through me!" He continued down the hall.

Ashlyn couldn't help but smile. Dom's cleverness was one of his best qualities. She turned back towards the unicorn and Kase. The unicorn's eyes were open, but Kase was still being the gentle caregiver. She ruffled Kase's hair. "You'll never lie to me, right, son?"

"No, mama," Kase said. "The unicorn is hungry."

"I have just the thing." Ashlyn stood up. She brushed her clothes, but then realized her hands were still dirty. She needed to wash up too. "Can you stay with him while I fix him something to eat? You're doing such a great job taking care of him already. I'll just be in the next room for a few moments. Why don't you tell him a story?"

"Okay, mama," Kase said. The unicorn followed with a soft snort. "Once upon a time—"

"Ooh, a perfect start," Ashlyn said. She smiled at her son, but didn't pay attention to how his story unfolded. Instead, she raced to the kitchen, which was more of a mess than the living room. There were dirty plates on the table, food all over the place, and a fire still under the cauldron. She couldn't even piece together what Dom had made the kids for dinner, but at least they'd had something.

She washed her hands at the sink basin, and then felt the kettle that had been left on the counter. It was still warm. She rustled through the cabinets, searching for ingredients suitable for giving strength to a young animal. She tried to think of what a unicorn might like, but in the end settled for classic medicinal herbs.

She grabbed some dried gingko, echinacea blooms, and zebra lily leaves. She found a freshly-cut pomegranate on the counter and squeezed the juice into a mixing bowl. She added the herbs and poured in some warm water from the kettle. Her final ingredients were a pinch of salt and a dab of honey.

She tasted the mixture and was satisfied with the result. It was a good first step before trying to feed the unicorn solid foods. He needed to gain some energy for the long healing road they were going to travel together.

Instead of spoon-feeding the unicorn, Ashlyn searched for an old leather canteen that she knew she had stored somewhere. The mouthpiece had ripped off, so the canteen wasn't used that much anymore. Dom had promised to fix it, but instead of waiting, Ashlyn had just bought a new one. The ripped canteen would be perfect in this situation, because she'd be able to get the pouch into the unicorn's mouth a little better.

After searching through almost every cupboard in her kitchen, she finally found the old canteen behind a few jars of pickles. She washed it out and poured her mixture into the open flap. She filled it to the brim, gripped the loose leather where the mouthpiece used to be, and headed back to the living room. She also nabbed a few scuffles to reward her caretaker son.

When she returned to the fireplace, she found Kase whispering to the unicorn. "What are you telling him?" she asked. She showed the plate to her son, who instantly sat up and grabbed a scuffle. He didn't respond: he just smiled and shrugged.

"Secrets between friends?" Ashlyn chuckled. She knelt down beside Kase. She ruffled his hair as he grabbed a second scuffle. "You should give him a name if you're going to be friends forever."

"His name is Turanus," Kase said. He bit into his dessert.

"Turanus," Ashlyn repeated. "What a beautiful name. How'd you come up with that one?" Kase always came up with the best names. Her favourite was the name for his stuffed dragon, which he'd named Billy Do-Dance.

"He told me," Kase said. He grabbed the third and final scuffle from the plate.

"He told you?" Ashlyn stared at the beautiful dark eyes of the unicorn. She didn't know unicorns could talk, but in the moment, she understood the bond that Turanus shared with her son. "Okay, Turanus, I made a wholesome drink for you. I'm going to pour it slowly into your mouth, okay?"

Ashlyn moved the ripped canteen to Turanus' snout. He obediently opened his mouth, so Ashlyn forced the broken flap as deep as she could without choking him. She gently tilted the canteen. Turanus gulped away.

"I think he likes it," Ashlyn said. She winked towards Kase.

Kase reached over and grabbed his blanket. He draped it across his shoulders and then lay on the floor, between Turanus and the fire. He combed the mane of his new best friend.

When Turanus was finished, he took a few deep breaths. He snorted a couple times and then closed his eyes. Ashlyn pulled out her wand, and evaluated the unicorn again. She could feel the warmth in his belly, but his bones were still broken. His wings and the weak muscles around his ribcage were also sore.

"That's it; now it's time to rest," Ashlyn said. "In the morning, when you have a little more strength, I will heal your bones. But just rest for now."

"Just rest, Turanus," Kase echoed.

Ashlyn combed her son's hair. They shared a smile.

"Is Turanus going to be our new pet?" Kase asked.

"I don't think so," Ashlyn answered. "Unicorns roam free. Hopefully when Turanus is better, he'll fly away and be with his family. I'm sure his mother is worried about him. But maybe he'll come visit us once in a while. Would you like that?"

"Yes, mama," Kase answered with a yawn, closing his eyes. Turanus added a snort.

Ashlyn felt a growl in her stomach. She didn't want to disturb her sleeping beauties, so she got up as quietly as possible and tiptoed back to the kitchen. She sat at the table, making up a plate of the cool mystery leftovers, and happily ate in peace.

It felt good to help an animal in need, and even better to involve her son. It was also a humbling experience, as Ashlyn reflected on the safety of those she loved. As much as speaking the truth was important, her family was even more so. She could hear Dom reading a story to Calista. She leant over to find Kase and Turanus fast asleep.

She was lucky to have such a wonderful family.

# CHAPTER 1

# Then I Look At You And The World's Alright With Me

Kase pulled his bowstring back. He had the giant buck in his sights, but there was some brush in the way. He needed the buck to lift its head just a little so he could get a clearer view of its neck. He knew a precise shot would mean a quicker death.

The bucks in the Kingdom of Moiras were a little tougher to kill than in the rest of the realm. They were five times as large as a normal deer and twice as fast. Not only would a perfect shot pierce its thick skin better, it would also help buy Kase some time to hide and avoid getting trampled in the process.

He felt the breeze from the east tickle his cheek. His scent carried back and away from his target. He held his bow, kept his breathing steady, and waited for the perfect moment.

In the blink of an eye, a black langara crashed down from the treetops. Her powerful hind legs gripped the back end of the buck, her giant claws digging into her prey's thick skin. The buck hollered and tried to pull away, but the langara was too heavy. Her giant fangs clamped around the back of the buck's neck, and the buck fell to the ground.

Kase sighed and lowered his bow. He heard some branches break behind him.

"She's too fast," Maxim said.

Kase turned around to face his friend. The white langara towered over him. Her wings were tucked in, and she was staring at the bloodbath that her mother had caused. She tilted her lioness head back and twiddled her whiskers.

"I had a chance to win, I just didn't have a clear shot," Kase said. He put the arrow back in its quiver.

"Maybe next time," Maxim said, bumping his shoulder with her head.

Her words weren't audible, but were sent to Kase telepathically. His heightened magic power granted him the ability to speak to a large array of animals, but he found that he only shared a telepathic bond with unicorns and langaras. It was advantageous when Kase hunted with the langaras, even if it didn't lead to him making the kill shot.

The black langara, Raiden, roared. Kase looked back and saw the blood that dripped down her giant fangs. The golden langara with the red mane had already joined her, and took a bite of flesh from the buck.

"Lunch time," Kase said.

Kase and Maxim jogged through the brush and joined the feasting langaras. Kase waited for his turn, and then drew a short sword when Raiden gave him permission. He cut a slab of meat suitable for him and his friends to enjoy a roast for dinner.

He wrapped the meat in a special cloth that his sister had made to transport food, and tucked it in his matching sac. He also grabbed a bone shard that had been dislodged by the hungry predators and slipped it into his pocket. He'd use the bone to bring the buck back to life in a few days.

He walked to a log that had fallen in the forest and grabbed a seat while the other langaras rushed in to eat. When Maxim was full, she pranced over to where Kase sat. The white fur around her mouth was drenched in blood. "Is it time to head back?" she asked.

"I don't want to take away from your feeding time," Kase responded. "If you're finished, then we can go."

"I'm pretty tired," Maxim said. "I'm looking forward to an afternoon nap. We're hunting again tonight."

The langara life was not that glamorous, but Kase appreciated the time he spent with them. They taught him how to be patient, and how to keep focused while on the hunt. He learned about the habits of their prey, and which of those habits were most advantageous for a quick strike. He also learned the appreciation that the langaras had for the creatures they fed on from where they sat atop the food chain.

Kase climbed onto Maxim's shoulders, grabbed the tuft of hair at her neck, and held on tight. Maxim took a few powerful strides before she jumped to a tree branch, launched higher, and flapped her wings. Kase ducked so none of the foliage would hit him, but Maxim soon shot through the treetops. She rose higher into the air, soaring over the Kingdom of Moiras.

Mountain ranges surrounded the frontier, but the kingdom was a secret jungle in the heart of the realm. Protected by a magical barrier that had been created thousands of years ago by the ancient realm's king, it was a safe haven for the inhabitants of the palace, the creatures of the jungle, and a powerful relic known as the doorway of life.

Kase and his friends had found pieces of the doorway in other parts of the realm, and then brought them to the secret Kingdom of Moiras to reassemble it. No one from their past knew of their whereabouts; not their families, other friends, or their enemies. The kingdom was both their new home, and their refuge from any danger.

The leaders of the Triple Crown had blackmailed Kase into finding the magical doorway for them, but with the help of his friends, Kase had thwarted their plans. High Scholar Sheese, High Warrior Mac, and High Wizard Zuke— who was really the notorious criminal Mardious Hood—were obsessed with the power of the doorway. But even they hadn't discovered the information that Talen, Cali, and Kase had uncovered. Unaware of the final location of the doorway, their enemies were on the hunt for Kase and his crew, but the kingdom was safe—for now.

Maxim headed straight for the ancient palace, and after a short trip landed in an open patch of grass beside the armoury. Kase looked for signs of his friends, but none of them appeared to be up yet; they all had a bad habit of sleeping past noon.

Kase dismounted, and then petted Maxim before she left. She liked scratches behind the ear the most, which worked out well this time since her face was covered in blood. Kase waved good-bye as she took off the way she had come, flying high above the palace towers and disappearing against the soft white clouds.

Since Kase had fresh meat, he should have headed to the kitchen first, but he decided to check the armoury, just in case. His duty to be a warrior professor wasn't until the afternoon, but his student wasn't that demanding in terms of scheduling. She was just the best part of his day.

He passed the kilns on the outside of the building, opened the side door, and entered the auditorium-like armoury. There were racks of weapons to his right, and the tools needed to make the weapons to his left. Curtis, Talen, and Lenia had spent some time getting a few of the furnaces working. One of their hobbies was blacksmithing, but none of them were really good at it yet. Kase had more interest in testing their weapons rather than creating them.

"Roar!" Kase yelled. He tapped his heart twice, kissed his fingers, and pointed to the sky. It was the warrior salute that he and Lenia used, since the one used by the rest of the realm didn't sit well with Kase anymore.

He didn't hear a response, so he left the armoury. He crossed the garden and entered the main palace. He didn't see any of his friends on the way, so he hoped they were all having brunch in the kitchen. When he arrived he saw only Lenia, who was sitting on a stool at the counter, nibbling on some berries.

"Good morning," Kase said, knowing it was already the afternoon.

Lenia smiled. "Hey, you," she said. She stared at Kase for a hot moment. "How was your hunt today?"

"I almost won," Kase replied. "Raiden is still too good, though." He pulled the meat from his sac and placed it beyond where Lenia was leaning. He leant on the counter next to her, but didn't sit down.

"I'm guessing you haven't changed your rules yet?" Lenia asked.

Kase shook his head. He could use his magic to control the giant bucks, but he didn't want to give himself an advantage over the langaras. They weren't really competing, because they were on the same team, and it felt better when Kase got a victory by hunting more like a langara than a wizard.

"If I went hunting with you, I'd definitely break my rules to win," he said.

Lenia laughed. "No you wouldn't. Not with me." She stretched her neck out. "Maybe you would with the others. But it's okay; I like it like that." She puckered up.

Kase leant in close, but stopped an inch away. "You have strawberries on your lips," he whispered.

Lenia pulled back, eyebrow raised. "So that means you don't want to kiss this?" She waved her palm in front of her lips. "Suit yourself." She chuckled.

"I still want to." Kase moved closer. "I just thought you—"

Lenia laughed, grabbed Kase's shirt, and tried to push him away. "Don't kiss me; I'm hideous." She laughed again. She grabbed another strawberry with her free hand and smushed it on her lips.

Kase pressed his lips together and made kissing sounds. He leant into Lenia, but with her arm locked, the momentum forced her backwards. She laughed, but then lost her balance on the stool. She let go of Kase's shirt before falling to the floor

"Ow!" Lenia landed with a thud. She clutched her ribs, but not on the side she had landed on.

Kase quickly leant down beside her. "I'm sorry, I didn't mean to …" He placed his hand on hers.

"It's my fault," Lenia said with a laugh. "I'm okay, though."

Lenia brushed Kase's hand away, but Kase had already felt the pain she was in. His power let him feel her wound, and it wasn't something she would have gotten from falling off a stool.

"You're cut," Kase said.

"Really?" Lenia said. "I don't feel …"

Kase rolled up Lenia's black shirt to expose her belly. She didn't stop him. At the bottom of her ribcage was a deep gash. It looked like it had already started to heal on its own, but since Lenia couldn't heal herself completely like Kase could, the wound had reopened.

"You didn't notice this?" Kase asked. "How did you … your shirt isn't even ripped?" Kase rubbed his thumb on the material.

"Fine, you caught me," Lenia said. "I was practicing some swordplay this morning, and accidentally cut myself."

"You practiced, cut yourself, then changed and came here to eat?" Kase asked.

"I wasn't wearing a shirt at the time," Lenia said. "I was in front of the mirror, practicing some swings, trying to be like my childhood hero Roman Garrick, and … have you never practiced shirtless in front of a mirror?"

"No." Kase chuckled. It was his dream to be like his grandfather, not Lenia's. He liked her ambition, though. He'd never really had a mirror big enough when he'd practiced by himself on the farm, but it could have been useful while training. "I wish I could have seen it."

Lenia smiled, then tucked her chin down and moved her eyes to the left. "It's embarrassing." She chuckled. "Are you going to heal me, or are you going to punish me, Professor Garrick?"

Kase smiled back. He placed his palm on her wound, and a soft glow shone around his hand. Now that he was able to bring others back to life, healing was a breeze. He absorbed her pain quickly, felt the gash on his own ribs, and healed her wound without leaving a scar. He gripped the edge of her shirt to roll it back down, but stopped.

"Are you sure you only have one cut?" he asked. He rolled her shirt a little higher.

"Maybe you should check me out, just to make sure," Lenia said. She arched her back to make it easier. "I'd use my lips if I were you."

Kase grinned. He gripped her shirt a little tighter, which rested just above where her gash had been. He kissed her belly softly, just above the navel.

Lenia giggled. "Maybe a little higher," she said.

Kase kissed her again.

Lenia arched her back a little more. "Higher," she said.

Cali cleared her throat. Lenia opened her eyes and reached for her shirt. Kase helped her push it back down. He looked over his shoulder to see his sister with her hand over her face.

Cali peeked through her fingers. "I didn't mean to interrupt, but we eat here," she said.

Talen stood beside Cali. She held a book with both arms crisscrossed in front of her torso. She didn't seem disgusted like Cali, but then again, Talen rarely showed her emotions.

"Sorry," Lenia said. "Kase was healing me, and we got a little carried away." Kase stood and helped Lenia to her feet.

"Oh," Cali said, dropping her arm. "Are you okay?"

"You should see the other guy," Lenia joked.

Kase laughed, but Cali and Talen didn't seem to get it. "We should get going," Kase said. "It's a beautiful day for training." He grabbed a few strawberries from Lenia's plate and a roll from the breadbasket.

"I'm glad everything is okay." Cali nodded to Lenia. "Before you go, we wanted to talk to you two about something important."

"Just us two?" Kase asked. "What about Aura and Curtis?"

"It's about Aura's birthday," Talen said. She placed her book on the counter. On the open page was a birthday heading with a list of supplies underneath. "She's washing up right now, so it's a good time to plan."

"Curtis is already checking his wine supply," Cali said. "He's pretty sure he has a good bottle ready for a special occasion."

Kase nodded. Curtis took pride in being a competent winemaker, and he'd gotten better since he and Talen found some information in the palace library. Unfortunately, he seemed to enjoy drinking wine more than making it lately.

"So what can we do?" Lenia asked.

"Well, it seems like our present for Aura isn't quite complete," Cali said. "We have a list of ingredients that you need to purchase on your next trip tomorrow."

Talen ripped a page out of her notebook, folded it, and handed it to Lenia.

"Roar," Lenia said. She tapped her heart twice, kissed her fingers, and pointed to the sky.

Since Lenia was presumed dead, she didn't have a bounty on her head like the rest of the crew. The Triple Crown had branded Kase, Cali, Talen, Aura, and Curtis as criminals, so their faces were plastered on wanted posters all across the realm. Even though Kase didn't like the idea of Lenia travelling beyond the Kingdom of Moiras on her own, he was outnumbered in opinion by the rest of the group. Luckily, his unicorn friend Turanus was a good escort.

Lenia had been able to sell some of the jewels they'd found at the palace in exchange for Aileron. With acceptable currency, she was able to purchase some commodities that the group couldn't find or make in their kingdom.

She was even able to keep tabs on the crew's families, and ensure that they were still safe. The Triple Crown had been monitoring most of their family members through task forces and new surveillance sage mirrors. Lenia was sure to keep her distance so no one would recognize her.

"What do you need me to do?" Kase asked.

"We need you to catch the main course for dinner," Talen said. "We were thinking of salmon, since you mentioned that there were some in the western river. I found a recipe that explains how to grill the fish outside. But since Lenia is allergic to seafood, we wanted to clear it with her."

"I appreciate you looking out for me," Lenia said. "If some salmon slips onto my plate somehow, and I have a reaction, Kase will heal me."

"Just not in the kitchen," Kase joked.

Cali covered her mouth and pretended to cough something up. "Thanks."

"I guess we can go now?" Lenia asked. She nodded to Cali, who nodded back.

Kase and Lenia made their way outside, leaving Talen and Cali in the kitchen. They spent some time stretching on the grass, and then warmed up with a light run down one of their usual trails outside the palace walls. They laughed, talked, and joked around on their run, but kept their focus on the work they were doing.

Over the last nine months of isolation in the kingdom, Lenia had improved her strength, speed, and endurance to help with her base warrior skills. Kase didn't credit his ability as a professor for how much Lenia had improved. She was an excellent student, and not only practiced hard, but studied hard too. She'd read a few of the books in the palace library that had information on combat techniques. She tried to make a few of the ancient weapons that the old king had designed. She even practiced some of his ancient magic to keep up her wizard skills.

Lenia was dedicated to being the best she could be, and Kase was proud of her. He enjoyed growing with her, teaching her what he knew, and learning the new things that she discovered.

The time they spent together was the best part of his day, which made every day a lovely day in the Kingdom of Moiras.

CHAPTER 2

# The Sweeping Insensitivity Of This Still Life

Aura turned the card upside down. "Is this a butterfly?"

Kase slumped in defeat. "It's a fairy," he replied. "I know you like them, so I drew one using some books from the library for reference."

Kase glanced at Lenia, who was pinching her lips, trying not to laugh. He was proud of his drawing, but it hadn't been clear enough. He felt a slap on his shoulder.

"It's your best one yet," Curtis said. His honest critique stung Kase a little more. Curtis took another swig of wine. "Read the inside out loud!"

Aura smiled and cleared her throat. "Happy Birthday Aura," she started. "A gentle touch, a soothing whisper; a heartbeat steady through fall and winter. You care for us through acts of service, but today we show our love in reverse. Love Curtis, Talen, Kase, Lenia, and Cali."

"The poem was my addition." Curtis beamed.

Aura closed the card and held it to her heart. "Thank you all for celebrating with me," she said. "The food was delicious, the wine is perfect, and the company is special. It's been an interesting year, but here's to another." She raised her glass of wine and they all toasted in appreciation.

Aura was at the head of the table, with Lenia to her left. Kase was beside Lenia, as always, and Curtis was opposite Aura. Talen and Cali were on the other side. They had set the table with fancy dinnerware and décor from the castle, but their giant feast was now finished. Used dishware cluttered the table, along with a couple of empty wine bottles, mostly closer to Curtis. Aura had a box in front of her where her plate used to be.

"Open your gift!" Lenia said.

Aura placed her card carefully beside her present. She undid the bow, but paused before lifting the lid.

Kase leant in closer from his seat, trying to get a better view. He had been tasked with making the card with Curtis, but Lenia, Cali, and Talen had prepared the gift. There were slats in the box, but he could only see straw on the inside. Based on Lenia's excitement, he was curious to see if it was a weapon that Lenia had fashioned with her newfound love of blacksmithing.

Aura lifted the lid and peeked inside. Her mouth dropped open, and she slammed the lid down on the table. She lifted a white wig from inside the box. "It's beautiful!" she shrieked. "How did you make this without me knowing?" She turned the wig around and then placed it on her head. She combed her fingers through the fake hair.

"Is that from Maxim?" Curtis asked.

"Yes, I clipped some hair from her back," Lenia said. She stood and nestled beside Aura. "There are some other things in there, too."

Lenia held up a couple of clips and bands and positioned herself behind the birthday girl. Aura lifted the wig while Lenia quickly adjusted Aura's real hair.

"Here's the best part," Cali said, dipping into the opposite end of the box. She pulled out a small, cylindrical container and what looked like a thin piece of skin. "While Kase was studying fairies, I was learning how to make appendages. This one is for your nose, and then we have some paste to help make wrinkles."

Aura clasped her hands together and seemed to hop in excitement. "It's just like I imagined," she said.

"Once we get you fitted up, you and I can go to town together." Lenia said. She struggled with Aura's wig. "Okay, just a little—"

"Wait, what?" Kase said. Not only was he unaware of Aura's gift, but now it also seemed like Lenia and Cali had been planning something dangerous behind his back. "You can't go to town. We all agreed—"

"It's time, brother," Cali said. "We've all been cooped up in this kingdom for too long. It's a paradise, but it's still our prison." Her hands, still holding

Aura's makeup, started shaking. She dropped them below the table. "We need to start taking turns getting out there. Besides, two of us getting supplies will mean fewer trips for Lenia to go alone."

Kase shook his head. He couldn't believe that Cali had kept this secret from him. He understood her desire to leave, and wanted to think through her reasoning, but the betrayal he felt kept clouding his thought process.

"Isn't the Triple Crown still hunting us down?" Curtis asked. "Will some paste and different-coloured hair really fool everyone in the realm?"

"Mardious Hood was able to convince the realm he was High Wizard Zuke," Cali said. "Considering he didn't get caught while taking on such a high-profile role, it's safe to assume that sneaking through the streets as fugitives is feasible."

Kase felt his breathing get sharper. Curtis was obviously not in on the plan, and it hurt that the two of them weren't consulted. Aura was surprised by the gift, and Cali and Lenia were dressing her up ... he looked at Talen to see what side she was on. "Tal?"

"The risk isn't quite as high for us right now," Talen said. "Thanks to the Unicorn Knight."

Cali and Lenia stopped tending to Aura. All three stared at Talen.

"Who's the Unicorn Knight?" Curtis asked.

"The most wanted criminal in the realm," Talen said. "Kase used to hold the number one spot, with us being his accomplices. But now the focus of the Triple Crown's manhunt has become the mysterious Unicorn Knight, because of—"

"His posters are plastered all over the towns Lenia visits," Cali added. She nodded towards Lenia.

"They only show a silhouette with the criminal's trademark unicorn helmet," Lenia said. "He's described as being a dangerous vigilante that must be avoided at all costs, but any information leading to his capture will be rewarded."

"I think you're underestimating the Guardianship," Kase said. "They're capable of hunting multiple high-profile criminals at a time."

"Well ..." Curtis said. He took a sip of his drink. "It's like fishing for sport. If you know there's a big fish in the area, you're going to concentrate on reeling that one in, because it gives you more glory. If the Unicorn Knight has the more impressive rap sheet, then I would be more focused on him if I were still a Guardian. His capture would earn respect from cohorts, a possible raise, and maybe even public appreciation from the Triple Crown. What's he wanted for?"

"Breaking and entering, grand larceny, vandalism, and murder," Talen said. "The Triple Crown might see our group as a bigger fish, but publicly we're only wanted for aiding and abetting. Kase is wanted for murder."

"Murder of me," Lenia said. "And nobody cares about that."

Kase's feelings of betrayal turned to guilt. Lenia's family, community, and colleagues didn't know that she was alive. It was too risky to let anyone in on the secret, because they might be seen as accomplices too.

"So you think that because the local Guardians are focused on this vigilante, you can take others to town in costume?" Kase was still worried about Lenia exposing herself, and now they wanted to risk others too? "Is there anything else you're keeping from me?"

"No, brother," Cali said. "You now know everything that we know."

Even with all the facts laid out, it didn't make Kase feel better. "Do we all get to vote on this, or did you just assume that you'd out-vote me again?" he asked.

"We were going to test how it went with Aura before making disguises for everyone," Cali said. "I'm sorry, brother, but it all happened really fast. We wanted to show off an example before making a decision. Should we vote now? All in favour of moving forwards with this plan?"

Everyone but Kase raised their hand.

Kase rested his elbows on the table. He tried to think of ways to explain the risks involved. He didn't have an analogy like Curtis, which he understood, even if he only fished for food, and not for sport. He knew that if any one of them got caught, the Triple Crown would use truth serums to extract information. Each one of them would be exposed, the secret kingdom would be found, and Kase's power of bringing the dead back to life would be abused.

"Have some tea, my dear," Aura said with an older woman's accent. She grabbed the kettle by the handle, walked over to where Kase sat, and poured him a cup.

Aura prepared tea every night after dinner, and it was a routine that Kase enjoyed. She filled Kase's teacup to the brim, and then gently pushed it towards him. He didn't mean to cause a stir on her birthday, but he couldn't shake the bad feeling in his stomach. He took a sip, but he didn't feel any better.

"Turanus will be with us," Lenia said. "I already told him about our plan, and even though he doesn't speak to me the way he speaks to you, I know we'll be safer."

Kase nodded. With Lenia's skills improving as a warrior, the new disguises and accents that they had, and Turanus watching over them to teleport them away at a moment's notice, it wasn't a terrible plan.

"I'm sorry I got upset," Kase admitted. He took another sip of tea. It was beginning to make him feel a bit better. "I just want to be involved in these decisions, rather than being surprised with them."

"We didn't want to ruin the surprise for Aura this time by telling you and Curtis." Cali went back to sorting through the box, keeping her hands busy. "I guess I didn't want to spoil it, because it's almost too good to be true."

"That's probably for the best," Curtis said. "I get talkative when I drink." He slammed back his wine, which he had refilled while they were talking.

"Honest Curtis," Talen joked. It was a sarcastic nickname that the crew had given Curtis in jest, because his honesty wasn't always pleasant. Sometimes his truth hurt.

"Thank you all for my card and gift." Aura giggled. "This is the best birthday ever! I can't wait to try this disguise out. Should we go to my room? I need a mirror, and I want to change."

"Yes, let's go," Cali said. She placed the items she was holding back in the box. "Kase, Curtis, can you clean up?"

"I can help too," Talen said.

"No, we need your help with Aura's … makeup." Cali placed the cover back on the box. "Lenia, can you grab the other end?"

Lenia put her pins and bands in her pocket and grabbed her side of the wooden box. Aura skipped away from the dining area while Cali and Lenia hauled her present. Talen shrugged, dabbed her napkin on the corners of her lips, and followed the costume artists.

Kase and Curtis gathered a few plates and hauled them back to the kitchen. Curtis started on cleaning the dishes, which included emptying the wine glasses directly into his mouth. Kase made several trips to and from the outdoor dining area, and joined Curtis with more tea instead of wine. Cleaning up after dinner took a little longer than normal with just the two of them, but they were still able to get everything done as a team.

Once they finished, Kase felt exhausted. He strolled through the castle on his own, longing for his bed. He had to climb one of the tallest castle stairways, since the rooms the group had picked were all in the tallest tower. It seemed to wind forever this time, and his legs got more tired with every step.

The sun hadn't set yet, but he was ready to sleep. He gained a little energy when he heard chatter from Aura's room. Her door was normally open, but he knocked anyway, thinking she might be dressing.

"Coming," Cali said. The lock sounded before the door cracked open. "Hey, brother. All done with the dishes?"

"Yes, mother," joked Kase. Cali didn't laugh. "Are you done with the disguises?"

"Almost," Cali said. "Come see!" Cali swung the door open. Lenia sat in front of the mirror in the corner, while Aura braided Lenia's brown hair. Kase barely recognized the smiling face that was being reflected.

"That looks amazing," Kase said. He walked with Cali to the old-looking women.

"Thanks, my dear," Aura said in her granny voice. "I'd smile, but the paste needs to set around my lips. So please try not to make me laugh."

"You never laugh at his jokes anyway," Lenia said.

Aura stopped braiding Lenia's hair. She was giggling, but covered her mouth. "I said don't make me laugh." Her voice was back to normal.

Lenia stood from her chair and turned to Kase. The paste made her forehead wrinkly, but the skin around her eyes, nose, and mouth was puffy and droopy. There were dark lines that added roughness to her skin, and even a few fake moles that had hair coming out of them.

"Don't I look beautiful?" Lenia asked. "Kiss me." She grabbed Kase by the waist, puckered up, and closed her eyes.

Kase laughed. "I don't want to kiss you like this." He tried to push her away, but she grabbed him tighter.

Lenia opened her eyes. "Are you not going to be attracted to me when I get older?"

Kase couldn't tell if Lenia was joking or not. "Of course I will be," he said. "I just thought I'd grow into it with you."

"Please don't kiss each other now," Cali said. "It took longer than I thought to get that mask on. I don't want you ruining it before it settles, Lenia."

"Yes, mother," joked Lenia. Kase laughed, but Cali didn't. Lenia let go of Kase and returned to her seat in front of the mirror. Aura was fluffing up Lenia's wig.

Cali paced back to Aura's bed and sat on the covers. "Do you ever think of our mother, Kase?" Cali asked. She patted the blanket, gesturing for him to take a seat.

When Kase sat on the bed, he had to do everything in his power not to lie down. He didn't want to sleep just yet, even though that's exactly what his body wanted at the moment. "Not really," he said honestly.

"I've been thinking a lot about her and dad lately," Cali continued. "If we have the ability to sneak around the realm, maybe we can try to find where they were buried?"

Cali and Kase had gotten into arguments before about bringing people back from the dead. Although Kase had brought his friends back to life, he was reluctant to save others. Outside of the kingdom, he didn't know what would happen if the Triple Crown discovered the living dead, and the langaras weren't in favour of having more outsiders in the Kingdom of Moiras.

Although everyone missed their family, no one else in the group had immediate family members that were deceased. With Kase's new power from the doorway of life, it was natural for Cali to be curious about bringing back their parents. He could tell by the gleam in her eyes that she was hopeful.

Kase glanced towards the mirror again. Seeing Lenia and Aura happy together gave him more confidence in Cali's plans. He didn't want to turn Cali down, knowing that she could keep him in the dark again and pursue a trip around the realm without him if he did.

"It would be nice to have them back," Kase said. "Is it fair to the others if I save our parents, but they still can't see their families?"

Aura finished braiding Lenia's hair. "We're okay with it, Kase," Aura said in her normal voice.

"But only if you are," Lenia added. She tilted her head and stared at him.

Kase swayed a little bit and fluttered his eyes. "Can we talk about this tomorrow? I think I'm ready for bed."

Cali shrieked, then reached over and hugged Kase. "Thank you, brother. We'll take every precaution, and make sure we have a foolproof plan before taking any steps. Talen is already doing research in the library." She disengaged and helped Kase to his feet. She glanced back at Aura. "I feel like it's my birthday too!"

Kase was glad to be involved with Cali's plan—even if it had already begun without him. He looked at Lenia again. "Stay safe," he said. He tapped his heart twice, kissed his fingers, and lifted his hand to the sky.

"Always," Lenia said. She and Aura returned the gesture.

Kase stumbled out of the room. He kept his hand on the castle wall and continued down the hall. He felt drunk, but he'd only had one glass of wine with dinner.

When he made it to the last door, he almost fell through the entrance. The setting sunlight was creeping in through the window, but he didn't care. He didn't even take his clothes off: he just headed straight for bed. He heard his door close, and had just enough energy to look back.

"Don't go to sleep yet," Talen said. She hustled to the bed and sat beside Kase.

"Come to tuck me in?" Kase joked.

"I wanted to give these to you." Talen presented Kase with a white wig and a couple of containers.

Kase pushed his torso up and rested on his elbow. He combed his fingers through the wig, which was shorter than Aura's. It looked like it suited him more. "Why?" he asked.

"Cali, Lenia, and Aura don't know that I made them for you," Talen said. "They kept a secret from you, so now it is time for us to keep a secret from them. Promise me you won't tell them about this disguise."

Kase placed the wig on the bed, but then dropped from his elbow. He couldn't keep his head up. "I don't understand."

"You need to see what's going on in the world for yourself," Talen said. "Even though the Guardianship is more focused on the Unicorn Knight, you're both wanted criminals, and sometimes the enemy of your enemy is your friend. If you can track down the Unicorn Knight, you might be able to work together on a common goal, rather than running from the same threat."

"You're silly, Tal," Kase said. He finally closed his eyes. "Can we talk about this tomorrow? I'm going to sleep."

"Promise me, Kase," Talen said. "It's important."

Kase opened his eyes. Talen had crouched down beside his bed, and was almost face to face with him.

"I'm not going to lie to Cali, Lenia, or Aura," Kase said.

"It's not lying if they don't ask you about it," Talen said. "All you have to do is take a look for yourself. Report back to me, and if you feel the same way, we can involve the others. If we tell them too soon, it might ruin their mood."

Kase thought about how much fun Aura was having for her birthday, and how happy Cali looked when talking about their parents. He wanted Talen to feel the same way. "Fine, I promise," Kase said.

Talen removed the wig and stood up. "Thank you," she said. "I'll hide these for you."

Kase closed his eyes again. "Goodnight, Tal."

He heard the door open, but didn't receive a response.

# CHAPTER 3

# No Matter How Hard You Try, You Can't Stop Me Now

Lenia rushed at Kase, her sword low. She sliced at his thigh, but Kase blocked it, deflected it away, and backpedalled.

They were sparring in the open grassland south of the castle. There were a few hilly regions, but no real change in landscape until the edge of the forest miles away. Six langaras sunbathed in the distance, but no other animals were around.

Kase took a few, barely noticeable steps to the increased elevation of the nearest hill. "I like the aggression, but what are you trying to do?" Kase asked.

"I'm trying to win," Lenia said. She attacked again, but she was too far away. Kase dodged it easily. Her momentum took her away from her target.

"Take a look at where we are," Kase said. "What do you notice about your surroundings? Can you use anything to your advantage?"

Lenia remained focused. She didn't look away or drop her guard. She took a few paces up the hill past Kase. "We're in the middle of nowhere," she replied. "There's no loose dirt to kick up, no wind to ruffle your hair, and no tripping hazards to falter your footing."

Kase was proud that her first instincts were still wizard-related. She could use her power to manipulate dust particles to blind her enemy, or provide a gust of wind to cause hesitation; something warriors couldn't do. Being aware of tripping hazards was something he had taught her when practicing her own footwork, along with recognizing that it was also a disadvantage for her adversary.

"Anything else?" Kase asked.

"Time out," Lenia said. She lowered her sword, and Kase followed suit. "Is it something I should see, or something I should feel?"

Kase didn't want to be the kind of professor that danced around the answer for too long. He knew that patience was a virtue, but he didn't want his student to lose interest. "You're on higher ground," he said.

"So I have an advantage?" Lenia asked. She wiped her brow, but seemed confused.

"Hard maybe," Kase said. "Some would argue that fighting from the high-ground is most advantageous in battle, but it really depends on the situation, your adversary, and your skills. If you can recognize your position, you can strike or defend yourself appropriately. Let me demonstrate."

Kase took a few steps down the slope. His head was now in line with Lenia's torso. "Attack me at quarter speed," he instructed.

Lenia lifted her sword, but didn't get into a proper stance. She haphazardly swung her weapon horizontally, aiming for Kase's neck. Kase dropped to one knee, ducking Lenia's blade, and swung lightly at Lenia's boots. He stopped when he made soft contact with her left calf; they practiced with real weapons now, and there was no reason to hurt her to make his point.

"Since you're on higher ground, I might not be able to go for a kill shot, but I can focus on your lower extremities," Kase said. "A strike to your feet, legs, or pelvis can slow you down or throw you off balance."

"Understood," Lenia said. She gripped her sword tighter. "What if I tried a different manoeuvre?" She brought her blade back, stepped forwards, and then attacked with a slow overhead strike.

Kase crouched, used his blade to block Lenia's swing, and grabbed her wrist. He twisted his body, forced his hip into Lenia's midsection, and flipped her over his shoulder.

Lenia shrieked and then landed on the grass with a thud. She rocked to her side and rubbed her lower back.

Kase knelt above her head. "I didn't hurt you, did I?" He dropped his sword and brushed her braid away from her face.

Lenia laughed. "I didn't expect that one," she said. "Nice move."

Kase bent forwards, and even though her face was upside down, he found her lips with his easily. She reached back and rested her fingers on the back of his neck.

"Maybe we should practice it so you can add it to your skillset," Kase said.

Kase stood and helped Lenia to her feet. He climbed the hill, and they both got into a ready position. Kase slowly swung his sword from an overhead position, making contact with Lenia's defending blade. Lenia deflected the strike, grabbed Kase's wrist, and thrust her hip into his midsection. Instead of tossing him over her shoulder, she ended up crumbling under his body weight.

Lenia laughed.

"You're dead," Kase joked.

"Get off me!" Lena laughed again.

Kase planted his hands around Lenia's turtled position and pushed himself up. He helped Lenia to her feet, grabbed their weapons, and they both returned to their sparring positions.

"Let's try this at full speed," Kase said. "When attacking from a higher position, my weight will carry down the slope. It gives my strike more power, but it also makes me unbalanced. It should give us the expected results."

"Roar," Lenia said.

Kase brought his sword above his head, and then swung down heavily. Lenia blocked his strike, but didn't grab his wrist. Her hip went into his midsection, and she easily flipped him down the hill. He landed with a hard thud and slid down the grass a little bit. When he came to a stop, Lenia had the point of her sword dangling above his neck.

"You're dead." She smiled, and then sheathed her sword. "I think I'm done for the day." She helped Kase to his feet.

"Since when do you get to decide when class is over?" Kase asked. He grabbed Lenia by the waist and spun her. She laughed, spread her arms out wide, and enjoyed the ride. When Kase stopped, they stared at each other for a hot moment.

"I promised Cali that I'd help mix some makeup potions with her," Lenia said. "Aura and I used more than we thought we would on our trip last night."

"Better too much and successful, than too little and caught," Kase said.

"Cali and I will test it out next week, and then …" Lenia's eyes moved to the left. "I was thinking that you and I could go on a date."

Kase thought about the white wigs and makeup. He was still against risking exposure by leaving the Kingdom of Moiras. But with Lenia's successful trip with Aura, Lenia's continued progress on her own, and Cali's excitement of reuniting with family, Kase was warming up to the benefits.

"As old people?" Kase replied. "What do old people do on a date?"

Lenia tapped her chin with a smile. "Hmm …" She opened her mouth to speak, but then closed it as she thought some more.

Kase didn't want to disappoint Lenia, or hesitate when she was trying to involve him with her trips. "I'd love to," he said. He kissed her, and then held her tight.

"We'll have the best old person date ever," Lenia said. She rubbed Kase's back, and then disengaged. "Are we actually done for the day? I promised Cali we'd meet before dinner."

Although Kase was the warrior professor, he only controlled the content of his lectures; his student controlled the schedule. "Class dismissed," Kase said. "I have some elk to tend to in the forest, so I'll meet you back at the castle."

Lenia kissed Kase, picked up her sword, and ran off. Kase watched her and sighed. He sheathed his sword, checked his pockets for the bone fragments he kept there, and then headed in the opposite direction.

He jogged until he was just inside of the tree line of the nearby forest. He checked around for predators, then knelt on the ground and placed one of the bone fragments in a clear spot, closing his eyes. He went through a few breathing techniques that he'd read about in a book at the castle library.

When he was ready, he gently placed both palms on the bone fragment. He felt his power flow through him as easily as he felt his breath. He felt a tingle in his arms, then a sharp pain in his chest, but he was used to the healing process. What was different was the frantic, remembered fear of the elk. Then he felt the fire.

A burning sensation encompassed his entire body. It was the same pain he'd felt when he first gained his power, and had dropped into the lava pool through the doorway of life. The liquid melted his skin, separated his limbs from his body, and flowed down his throat. He tried to hold his eyes closed for as long as possible, but the fire always found a way to burn through his eye sockets.

After a few more moments of wrestling with the pain, Kase collapsed and came back to reality. He stared up at the trees while the giant elk he'd brought back to life stood up. The elk panicked, took a few awkward steps, and bumped its head on the nearest tree. It raced a few yards away before reorienting itself. In familiar surroundings, it settled and started grazing.

Kase liked the simplicity of the elk. He didn't share conversations, thoughts, or worries with them. He only felt their emotions, which happened to be either calmness or fear most of the time. He was able to use his animal control abilities on them, but more importantly, he'd learned that bringing them back to life was easier than with humans. His time in the fire didn't last as long, and he wasn't forced to relive their death and final moments as he did with people.

Talen had suggested that Kase should avoid meddling with the circle of life. She'd explained the importance of the balance that was needed in their kingdom. He understood the relationship between predator and prey, but he wanted to do his part in serving the wildlife. Helping the elk live a few more days before becoming another meal seemed like the right thing to do, even if there was an impact on the natural order of things.

Kase dug into his pocket for the next bone, and then brought a second elk back to life. The pain he suffered was still the same, but he endured it. After he was finished with a third elk, he took a moment to watch the peaceful animals. He also connected with all of them to ensure that they didn't feel threatened by their environment.

As a normal wizard, it had been challenging for Kase to connect with a single animal. With the power of the doorway amplifying his powers, he was able to connect with multiple animals at the same time. Practicing on the three elk, he was able to recognize their emotions as well as move them through the forest to help them find food.

But, like the grazing elk, Kase was feeling hungry.

He let go of his connection and walked to the edge of the forest so he wouldn't cause the elk any anxiety. Then, he jogged back to the castle. He thought about searching for Maxim in order to catch a ride, but decided he should finish his training. If Lenia was running back, he wanted to match her intensity and work ethic. It was unfair for him to take the easy way out if he expected her to keep up with her physical routine.

When he arrived back at the castle, he went straight to the kitchen. He was welcomed by the delicious aroma of Aura's cooking, and took a seat next to Talen. A jovial Curtis sat across from them. It looked like they had already finished eating and were enjoying after-dinner drinks. Talen always drank tea, like Kase, but Curtis opted for wine. Aura was cleaning some of the dishes.

Kase grabbed a roll, ripped it open, and dropped it on the centre of his plate. He lifted the lid of the cauldron in the middle of the table and eagerly ladled some elk chilli onto his plate. There was a plate of desserts on the other end of the table, but he would wait until his meal was over before diving in.

"Did Lenia eat already?" Kase asked. She had improved her running, both her speed and endurance, but he hadn't expected her to reach the castle *and* eat before he'd arrived.

"She grabbed something quick, and then went for a walk with Cali," Aura said. She'd stopped cleaning dishes and poured Kase some tea. She brought his cup over to him and gently set it next to his water glass.

"I thought she was helping Cali with some potion making," Kase said. The chilli wasn't hot anymore, which made it perfect for him to shovel into his mouth.

"Potion making, right," Aura said. "What did I say?"

"They are going for a walk to get more ingredients for the potions first," Talen corrected. "So you are both right."

"Thanks, Talen." Aura yawned, and then went back to wiping dishes.

"How was your trip last night?" Kase asked. He'd gotten Lenia's notes about their out-of-kingdom excursion, but he wanted to see Aura's excitement for himself.

"It was okay," Aura said. She didn't even smile.

"You missed her stories earlier," Curtis said, his words a little slurred. He poured himself some more wine.

"I understand," Kase said. "Lenia told me that you both had a great time. I was just wondering if she'd missed any details. I'm glad it was a safe and happy trip for you, Aura."

"Thanks, Kase." Aura finally smiled. "It was a great time, but I felt really awkward. It's been so long since I've talked to anyone that I was a little scared to do anything that used to be normal. It was a lot of walking slow and taking it all in. Hopefully next time we can explore a little more."

"It seems like the world is a lot different," Curtis said. He stood up and grabbed his empty plate. "I don't think I'm ready to find out how much it's changed yet."

"We haven't been here that long, have we?" Kase asked.

"Nine months, seventeen days," Talen noted.

"It sure feels longer," Aura said. "What are you—"

There was a crash as a plate hit the floor and shattered. Curtis was still clutching his wine glass in his left hand, but his right was up and empty.

"Whoops," Curtis said.

Aura looked up to the roof and let out an audible sigh. "Just go back to the table," she instructed.

"I'm sorry, Aura," Curtis said. "I didn't mean to …"

Kase stood. "I can help you—"

"It's okay, Kase," Aura said. "It will give me an opportunity to practise my element control. Please just relax and drink your tea."

Kase shrugged and reached for his tea. Instead of being next to his water glass, his cup had moved to the other corner of his plate. He looked to his left. Talen was sipping on her cup. He grabbed his own, and took a few sips.

By the time he had finished his tea, Aura had cleaned up Curtis' accident. Kase and Talen cleared a few things away from the table before Talen nudged him away. She convinced him to help move some things around her room, since Curtis was in a clumsy mood. They left Aura and Curtis and headed back through the castle.

When they arrived at Talen's room, Talen went straight to her bed. She grabbed the corner of the sheet and looked back. "Lock the door," she said.

Kase did as instructed. He was going to ask what she wanted moved, but when she yanked the sheet up, he realized what she was doing. The wig and potion casks she had stashed were now exposed, along with some new clothes.

"Let's hurry," Talen said.

Kase hesitated. "I don't know, Tal. It's been a long day and I—"

"You need to see what's happening in the rest of the realm," Talen said. "Since Aura and Lenia were successful, it will be safe for you to use the same tricks."

Kase thought about how excited Lenia was this afternoon. "I already agreed to go with Lenia in a few weeks for a date," he said. "I'll just test this stuff out then."

Talen yawned. "You're not the only one who likes spending time with Lenia," she said. "I'd ask her to run this errand for me, but it's part of a gift to show my appreciation for all she's done. It would really help her out if you could do this for me, and then we could surprise her together."

Kase sighed. If it was a way for his friends to show their support to each other, he was happy to do it. "Okay, Tal. I'm in. What do I need to do?"

"Sit down," Talen said. "I'll tell you while I apply your makeup."

Kase agreed and got comfortable on the bed. He had been looking forward to an easy night, but when he put on his wig, he felt a bit of an adrenaline rush. Maybe it was the prospect of a challenge, but he seemed to have more energy than a normal night.

Talen started off excited as she explained her plan, but she quickly became drowsy. She still managed to apply his makeup expertly, and even helped him sneak through the castle without anyone noticing.

By the time Kase started his journey, he was excited to help out his friend, and soon surprise his girlfriend.

# CHAPTER 4

# I Can't Believe The Spell I'm In

Kase dismounted from Turanus. "Thanks for the ride," he said. "It was good to see you," Turanus replied. Like the langaras, Turanus' voice appeared in Kase's head. But unlike the langaras, Kase still spoke audibly to the unicorn. "I'll meet you back here after you're finished."

"I hope I don't get lost," Kase admitted. He'd never been to the town of Cordero before, so Talen had made him a map. He didn't know where on it Turanus had landed.

"Head west," Turanus instructed.

Kase reached out to pet the unicorn, but Turanus disappeared without a trace; he didn't even need to flap his wings to teleport away. Kase may have gotten to know the unicorn a little better over the past year, but Turanus still liked to be mysterious.

Kase looked to the moon to orient himself, and then headed in the right direction. Even though Turanus had assured him they'd travelled to a safe spot, Kase wasted no time in putting on his act. He had a cane in hand, so he hunched over and limped slowly to the edge of the next street, just how he imagined an elderly man would move.

After a block and a half, he was at the main strip of town. He hugged the corner of the nearest building and looked for street signs and storefronts. He pulled out his map, and determined he was three blocks away from his target.

He rounded the corner. Flames flickered down the street, and smoke wafted into his face. A building was on fire, close to where he wanted to be. Shadows slithered towards the light.

Kase assumed there would already be some firefighting wizards trying to extinguish the flames, but he couldn't get a good view yet. He needed to move.

He tried not to get too excited, and instead focused on his pace. Slowly and steadily, he limped towards his goal. He kept his gaze on the ground, trying not to draw attention to himself. A few other onlookers rushed down the street, along with a couple of riders on horseback. Although he didn't get a good look at any of them, he knew they were focused on the commotion of the fire.

He remembered when he was working his warrior practicum with Curtis. He'd convinced his superior to check out the source of a billow of smoke, and it turned into a great experience for him to practice his element control. While Curtis was busy saving an old woman trapped inside, Kase had pulled the flames around like a window curtain. He enjoyed using his magic as a warrior back then, when it was a secret that only he and Lenia shared. So much had changed.

When he reached the block of the fire, he surveyed the crowd. A semi-circle had formed in front of the burning business, but the onlookers kept their distance from the flames. Firefighters had two carts of water, and doused the flames with a controlled spray. The business' sign, now dangling from the overhang by only one cord, read 'Jean's Army.' It was the store that Talen had wanted Kase to pick up some leather from.

"Poor girl," an onlooker said.

"Poor family," another added.

The crowd wasn't closely packed, so Kase made his way through pretty easily. When he reached the front, his heart dropped. A man and woman held their young daughter. The daughter's face was black with soot, her eyes were closed, and her head bounced as both parents wept.

Kase couldn't feel if a person was alive or not, but he still knew the daughter was dead. He sensed the emptiness and sorrow of the parents, and was reminded of how he'd felt when those closest to him had died. He wiped a tear from his eye. He wanted to help.

Everything had changed for Kase's crew when he obtained his power from the doorway of life. He brought his sister, friends, and girlfriend back from the dead. Even though the ritual was painful, he didn't know what he would do without them. If they had stayed dead, he would feel sad, angry, and empty.

He took a step forwards, but stopped himself. As much as he wanted to bring the girl back to life, it would expose his power to the world. The parents would be grateful, but word would spread quickly back to the Triple Crown. He wondered if he'd even make it out of town without the crowd hounding him for more. The Guardians standing behind the parents would definitely take the opportunity to capture him.

Kase looked to the burning building. As much as he enjoyed playing with fire, the destruction that it caused when it went out of control was devastating. He made a promise to himself to return in the future to help the family through their struggle, and hopefully bring their daughter back for them. But he needed a better plan. He needed his friends to help make it with him.

He tried to turn away from the scene, but the crowd had become more compact. It felt like the onlookers were bumping into him on all sides. Then he heard a familiar voice.

"Move!" Jax yelled.

Kase looked down immediately. Even if the local Guardians were more concerned with the Unicorn Knight, Jax wouldn't hesitate to hunt Kase down if he was recognized. Jax had been part of the High Guardian task force appointed by High Warrior Mac specifically to obtain the doorway of life. The threat of someone close to his past made Kase regret his decision to leave the safety of the secret Kingdom of Moiras. Why was he even here?

The crowd pushed Kase to the left. He tried to back up, but he was boxed in. He would have to wait until the crowd dispersed a little before slipping out.

"Mamma, Papa!" Josephine shrieked. Kase didn't look up. Was the whole task force present? Jax, Josephine, and Shay? There could even have been more recruits added to the task force since Kase had seen them last, or some of Mardious' Brotherhood members could have been promoted. He decided to take a peek to find out.

Josephine had her arm draped around her mother. She had removed her helmet, but the rest of her uniform shone in the firelight. Flames reflected off her silver armour and offset her bright golden cape. Josephine held her dead sister's head in her silver gauntlet.

"Who's in charge then?" Shay yelled at the two local Guardians that Kase had noticed earlier.

"Over here!" Jax shouted. His back was to Kase, but he stood just beyond the front row of the crowd.

Kase tapped his head to make sure his wig was still on correctly. He also patted his face to check the crusty makeup.

Shay strode over to Jax, along with a wizard dressed in the red robes of the firefighters. Shay had her helmet on, but her eyes darted around. She gripped her golden-handled sword as she surveyed the crowd.

Kase crouched so that just his eyes and forehead were above the shoulder of the man in front of him. Shay's focus soon turned to something Jax was holding.

"Look at this," Jax said.

"What's so special about an arrow?" Shay asked.

"It was lodged in the father's back," the firefighter said.

"Why would an arrow—" Shay started.

"This was no accident," Jax interrupted. "This was a target."

"What did the parents tell you?" Shay asked.

"Nothing," the firefighter said. "They told us about their daughter being trapped on the second floor. Then they asked us to contact their older daughter, Josephine."

All three members of the group looked towards Josephine and her parents. They were all still sobbing, staring at the deceased.

"Did you recover any other evidence?" Jax asked. "Other arrows? Weapons? Surveillance mirrors?"

"We haven't gotten that far yet," the firefighter responded. "Our priority is to douse the flames so the other businesses don't—"

"Useless," Jax scoffed. He marched over to Josephine, while Shay followed closely. The firefighter bowed respectfully before returning to his crew.

The other Guardians were now trying to disperse the crowd, separating them enough for Kase to move. He crept back into the gaps made available, keeping his head down. To the right of the building, a fourth High Guardian was tending to four stallions with shiny headgear. Kase turned the other way and hobbled down the street.

"If anyone captured moving images before or after the fire, please show me!" Jax shouted. "Any evidence found on your sage mirrors could be worth up to one hundred Aileron in reward!"

The crowd murmured, but Kase didn't look back. He turned down the first road off the main strip and hobbled to the next block. The backstreets were darker, but they made Kase more comfortable. He stopped a few times to make sure no one had followed him, and then continued on his journey back to Turanus.

As soon as he got to the meeting point, Turanus reappeared. "Did you find what you were looking for?" he asked.

"Not really," Kase admitted. He mounted his unicorn friend.

"Maybe next time." Without flapping his wings, Turanus teleported Kase back to the secret entrance of the Kingdom of Moiras.

"Everything seems so different," Kase said. He dismounted, but this time Turanus didn't disappear immediately.

"The world is always changing," Turanus said. "Just like us."

"I guess." Kase was reminded of how much he had changed from being a local Guardian, to a High Guardian, and now an outlaw. He had grown from a naïve warrior, to a wizard student, to a uniquely powerful healer. "I felt the need to help others, even though I don't know them."

"How terrible," Turanus said.

Kase chuckled. He'd forgotten how sassy Turanus could be. "In one way, being out there makes me appreciate all of the good things that I share with my friends: our castle, celebrations, and way of life. On the other hand, seeing the pain and suffering of others makes me want to do what I can to make things right. I just don't think I can have it both ways."

"Some changes are more complicated than others," Turanus said. "You'll figure it out." He nodded and disappeared.

Kase looked to the stars. He wished he could talk longer with Turanus, and ask him for advice, but the unicorn always kept his distance. Kase wouldn't have to figure it out on his own, though, because he knew he had the support of his friends.

He searched the brush for a dead branch. He reached into his pocket, grabbed his fire starter, and lit the torch. He strode through the magical barrier in front of the cave, and then the passage in front of him. He walked until he was in the jungle of the Kingdom of Moiras, and then jogged through the rough terrain back to the castle.

He didn't see any light coming from the castle windows, so he assumed everyone was asleep. He removed his white wig and tucked it away while he walked through the halls, because he'd promised Talen to keep their excursion a secret until they could surprise Lenia with her present. He was determined to share his discoveries with the entire group, but didn't want to upset Talen in the process. He headed to her room first to talk to her about it.

He didn't knock on her door, but slipped in as quietly as he could. He tiptoed to her bedside, and found her sound asleep. He rubbed her arm, but she didn't wake. "Talen," he said, but she didn't respond. "Talen," he said a little louder, but she still slept. He hadn't realized she was such a sound sleeper.

He thought about the fire burning down the store she'd sent him to. He knew she'd be more interested in who he'd seen, rather than the leather that he was supposed to pick up. He tried to remember all the details, but watching Talen sleep peacefully was a gift. He was glad that he still had the most important people in his life, and felt lucky for their good fortune.

Talen had set out some water for him to wash his face with, so he cleaned himself up, hid his costume under the pile of clothes that Talen had hid them in before, and then left his friend to sleep. He'd be able to talk to her in the morning.

He headed to his room as stealthily as he could. He'd been successful at not waking Talen, so he wanted to continue that success with Lenia. Unfortunately, she wasn't in their bed yet when he got there. She was likely in the library studying hard, like she did every other night.

He snuck under the covers and fluffed his pillow. Although he wanted to tell Lenia about the excitement, lying in bed made him instantly tired. He wasn't used to staying up this late. Just after his head hit the pillow, he fell asleep.

# CHAPTER 5

# Won't You Come And Stay With Me

Fingertips danced across Kase's chest. He opened his eyes to find the sunshine pouring in from the windows. Lenia's smile was still brighter.

"You're normally up before me," Lenia said. "It's a nice surprise to find you here." She nestled her head into Kase's shoulder and draped her arm across his torso.

"What time is it?" Kase tilted his head away from the sun. It didn't reach him when he normally woke.

"Brunch time." Lenia giggled.

Kase thought about his trip from the night before. He'd promised to keep it a secret from Lenia, but the longer he waited, the more unfair it was to her. He didn't want to bend the truth, even if Talen wanted their plan to be a surprise.

"I didn't mean to sleep in, but I was up later than normal," Kase admitted. "After dinner I ended up—"

"It's okay," Lenia said. She kissed his shoulder. "You don't have to explain yourself. Try not to think about how you got here; enjoy the moment that's arrived. It's a gift."

Kase smiled. He kissed the top of Lenia's head. He didn't want to ruin the mood by explaining his quest. He knew there'd be another opportunity to reveal his truths. "So I shouldn't hunt for food then?"

"Not yet," Lenia said. She squeezed him tight. "Stay with me now, and I'll help you hunt this afternoon."

Kase squeezed Lenia back. "No combat training today? I hope you've been doing your homework then, because your professor might not accept any excuses."

Lenia giggled. "I want to practice my long-range weapons techniques," she said. "I'm pretty good with the bow and arrow, but I haven't used my spear lately. Hunting might be a great way for you to help me with my form."

"I like that plan," Kase said. "As long as Aura isn't expecting anything right away."

"Let me worry about Aura," Lenia said. "You stay focused on me." She tilted her chin up for a kiss.

Kase and Lenia cuddled in bed for a little while longer, until Lenia decided it was ready to embrace the day. The others weren't in the kitchen for brunch, so they grabbed something quick to eat before starting their adventure together.

They each grabbed a throwing axe, spear, and bow from the armoury for their hunt. Instead of joining the langaras for big game, they decided to play it by ear and catch whatever came their way. It was better for training, since different weapons worked better on different animals, and Lenia wanted to get in as much practice as possible. With Kase's ability to bring their kills back to life, it meant they didn't have to settle for animals on Aura's approved grocery list.

Lenia wasn't joking when she claimed she was pretty good with the bow and arrow. She didn't miss a single target, including birds. Although they were Lenia's biggest fear, no matter what size they were, having a weapon in hand helped her remain steady rather than irrationally seeking refuge. Her spear throwing skills, however, needed much more practice.

Rather than hunting with the spear, Kase took Lenia to an open field. They practiced her stance, grip, and follow-through. She was able to judge how much effort she needed depending on the distance, and grew more accurate as the afternoon progressed. They played a few games together, which were filled with competitiveness and laughter. Kase only lost one to Lenia, but her smile was worth it.

As their day finished, they decided on eggs for their supper. Although not as normal as for brunch, breakfast for dinner was still an acceptable feast once in a while. Curtis wasn't feeling up to joining them, and Cali was wrapped up in the library, but they shared dinner and cold tea with Aura and Talen. Lenia decided to help Cali again, and left Kase in their room to relax.

As soon as she left, Talen had found her way to Kase's room.

"How was your trip last night?" Talen yawned. She closed the door before exposing the wig and makeup she hid in her sac.

Talen sat beside Kase on the bed while he told her of his journey. Her head swayed as if she was going to nod off, but she managed to stay awake for the important parts. Kase made sure he described the High Guardians with as much detail as he could remember.

"Sorry I didn't get your supplies for Lenia's gift," Kase said. "Of all the stores that you could have sent me to, that one had more action than I thought possible."

"I'm glad you're safe," Talen said. "But I'm also glad that you saw how different the world is now. I doubt tonight will be as eventful."

"Oh, I'm not going tonight," said Kase.

"Why not?" Talen asked.

"We need to have a discussion with the entire group," Kase said. "It doesn't seem right for us to keep them in the dark. We all need to be aware of the risks if we're going to attempt to visit towns. We can't risk getting captured on these new surveillance mirrors Jax mentioned, or being caught by our enemies."

"But our surprise for Lenia isn't complete yet," Talen said. "I just …" she yawned again.

"We'll still surprise her," Kase said. "It will just take a little more time."

Talen looked to the floor. "There's something else," she said. She pulled a sage mirror from her pocket.

Kase leant back. Sage mirror technology was controlled by the Triple Crown, and with the advancements made over the past few years, the team had decided that the mirrors were a bad idea. Even though there was no proof that the Triple Crown could see information, conversations, or images on personal sage mirrors, the team had decided not to take the risk by having any around.

"Mirror, mirror, show me Article Thirty-Three on the Unicorn Knight,"

Talen said. She angled the mirror towards Kase.

Kase extended his palm, blocking his view. "Why do you have this?" he asked.

"Don't worry, it's an old model," Talen said. "Cali helped with sage mirror development, and she knows that the Triple Crown can't access these ones; she and I both have one to help with research."

"How can you be sure?" Kase said. He didn't want anything to expose them.

"Trust me," Talen said. But she picked up on the worry on Kase's face. "We don't have to look at it if you don't want to. I just wanted to show you proof of how dangerous the Unicorn Knight has become. The fire that you witnessed isn't the only target in the news lately."

Talen tucked the sage mirror back in her pocket.

"Josephine isn't the only High Guardian to lose a family member," Talen said. "All members of your old task force have suffered from tragedy. Jax lost two of his brothers, Shay lost her mother, and High Warrior Mac lost a few new recruits. Even Guardians lower in the hierarchy have been targeted, and their families mourn their losses."

"And you think I should bring them all back?" Kase asked.

"No." Talen yawned again. "I want you to check on Curtis' family. He hasn't been himself lately, but I think knowing that his family is still safe will help lift his spirits. Can you do that for me? Can you do that for him?"

"It will be the first thing I do after I tell the group what we're up to." Kase smiled.

"And you're sure they'll have the same agenda as you?" Talen asked. "What if we delay too much? What if Curtis' family suffers?"

"Curtis understands my power," Kase said. "He knows that if his family members die at the hands of the Unicorn Knight, I can bring them back some day."

"What will happen to the members of Curtis' family that have to live with more grief?" Talen asked. "If they already mourn Curtis, how much more pain are you willing to have them endure?"

Guilt crept in at Talen's words. The reason Curtis had to live in their kingdom was because Kase and Talen had convinced him to help them in their quest for the doorway of life. At the time, none of them knew what they'd need to sacrifice, or the effect that would have on their families, but Kase still felt responsible for the aftermath. He didn't have a valid reason why he couldn't grant Talen's request, and it wouldn't cause anyone harm if he were to travel to the rest of the realm to check in on someone.

"Okay, what do I have to do?" Kase asked.

As Talen affixed Kase's wig and put on his makeup, she explained her plan. Kase was to travel to the port city of Bargebank where Curtis' family worked building luxury ships. There was a local pub that they often frequented after work; it had large exterior windows that Kase could look through without being noticed, unlike their family home. Talen had images of Curtis' brothers on her sage mirror, so Kase studied their features. They looked exactly like Curtis.

After sneaking out of the castle, Kase was joined by Maxim. The langara gave Kase a ride to the entrance to the Kingdom of Moiras, making his trip much faster. Kase jogged through the cave entrance and was greeted by Turanus almost instantly. After a few jokes at Kase's expense, Turanus teleported Kase to the port city.

Since the port was in the far west, the sun hadn't set yet. Kase wandered the streets, his cane at his side, until he found the pub where Curtis' family was supposed to be. A sign with a ship's wheel announced that it was the Broken Galver.

The pub was mostly outdoors, with the bar at the back. Chandeliers hung from the planks of exposed wooden rafters. It looked like an unfinished building, with a covered bar at the back. Picnic tables were set out so patrons could sit and enjoy their food and beverages. There was a band setting up on a stage near the back, but they hadn't started playing any music yet.

Kase thought about how much Curtis would enjoy the festivities at the pub with his family.

Kase could see everyone in their seats without having to go into the bar, which made his stakeout much easier. He found a bench close to the water, but with a great view of the bar scene. Before he took a seat, he purchased some bread from a nearby bakery. He acted the part of the old man, and fed the seabirds while watching the sunset.

Kase sat on the bench for about an hour before getting antsy. Although a lot of people frequented the bar, Kase never saw Curtis' family members. Even those passing by the Broken Galver weren't a match, which made Kase wonder about Talen's information. He had always trusted the facts when Talen laid them out for him, so he hadn't considered they may be wrong. He wondered how she'd mixed them up.

He was about to go for a walk and stretch his legs when he noticed a group of eight local Guardians marching down the street between him and the pub. They didn't seem merry and in the mood to celebrate after a long day at work, and there were too many of them to just be on patrol. They were on a mission.

They marched past the pub to a barn-like structure two buildings down. The leader unlocked the barn door, and slid the massive panel to the side. The others snuck inside, but the leader checked up and down the street before following. The door slid shut.

Normally, patrolling Guardians worked in teams of two, so it was odd to see them in a large group. The caution they were taking was even more suspicious. Their secrecy intrigued Kase, but he needed to focus on his own mission.

He looked up and down the street again, and then returned his gaze to the pub. The same patrons were drinking in the same spots, so he couldn't help but look back to the barn-like structure.

Kase noticed something move on the roof of the structure in the light of the setting sun. The figure was dark, but the unicorn horn on the helmet stood out. The figure moved through an open window at the apex of the barn.

Kase jumped to his feet, then quickly looked around to see if anyone had noticed. He shuffled down the street, barely using his cane. He was a little nervous, but also a little excited. It was good: he hadn't felt nexhilarated in a long time. He wanted to see how the group of trained warriors handled the infamous criminal.

When he got to the building entrance, he stopped himself from opening the barn door. What was he thinking? As much as Talen was talking up the Unicorn Knight, Kase was still one of the most wanted criminals in the realm. If he showed his face, the Guardians might focus on him instead of the vigilante. He needed a better plan.

He hustled to the far side of the building and looked for a way to get up to the roof. The entrance the Unicorn Knight had used was likely more secretive than walking through the front door. It would also serve as a better vantage point, assuming the fight didn't occur in the rafters. Kase didn't find stairs or a ladder, but he was confident he'd find something at the rear of the building.

There was a back door, but that entry was just as obvious as the front. Kase passed a few rain barrels on the back wall, and then peered down the other side of the building. There was no way up, so he checked the adjacent buildings. They were all too far away to make a jump. He must have missed something. How had the Unicorn Knight made it to the roof?

He looked along the back wall again, and noticed that part of the wall was missing behind the rain barrels. The wood was jagged at waist height, but there was a noticeable deterioration of the wood panels behind where the water was collected. He looked around to see if anyone was watching, and then tipped the first rainwater barrel over.

With the barrel out of the way, he had a viable entry. He ducked under the jagged edge and shifted his body as he slipped through. He cut his forearm on the sharp wood, but he quickly healed himself before going forwards.

He was in a back closet, but when he cracked the closet door open, there was an entire room of lockers that housed uniforms of some kind. Before he could check any of them, screams echoed from deeper inside the building.

Kase rushed out of the room, slid cautiously down a dark hall, and passed a couple of other storage rooms on his way. The centre open room held a massive ship sitting on some rolling timber. Kase stayed close to the corner of the hall, where there was a wall rack with some chains and tools hanging from it. He was careful not to bump them, and snuck a peek at the commotion.

Beside the ship, the Unicorn Knight was wielding a flaming sword.

Four of the Guardians were already on the floor; their bodies were limp, their hands empty. The remaining four had circled the Unicorn Knight, but they were all waiting to make a move. Their foe was as steady as a snake, waiting for the right opportunity to strike again.

Kase kept still. The massacre in front of him wasn't as brutal as witnessing a langara tear apart its prey, but the langaras killed for food. This battle was like two predators fighting for territory. Although the Unicorn Knight was outnumbered, he already seemed like the king of the jungle.

Kase studied the movements of his adversaries, not knowing which ones he might have to face in the aftermath. The army of his enemy was a familiar foe, but the murderous vigilante seemed more of a threat than a viable adversary. If Talen had witnessed the bloodshed at the hands of the Unicorn Knight, would she still consider him a friend? Kase thought about proposing a new theory to Talen: that the enemy of his enemy was also his enemy.

The Guardian furthest away from Kase stepped forwards with a strike. The Unicorn Knight blocked it and spun, slicing the Guardian behind the knee where there was no armour. The Guardian screamed and fell to the ground. His comrade stepped forwards with an attack of her own to defend him. The Unicorn Knight spun, his cloak almost covering his entire body, and then stabbed the Guardian in the stomach.

Kase felt disappointment in his gut. As a warrior, he understood the risks that Guardians faced in battle, and the nobility, heart, and valour that they fought with. Each one of them wouldn't hesitate to put their lives on the line, and would fight with everything they had for the safety, protection, and freedom of the realm. This was their duty.

But no matter how pure their intentions, even the greatest warriors failed in battle. Kase's grandparents had fallen to Mardious Hood, and now the army of the Triple Crown was falling to the Unicorn Knight. It was disappointing that both sides seemed to have the same disregard for life, instead of appreciating how valuable it was.

Kase studied the Unicorn Knight's technique. He struck with speed and precision, his footwork was impeccable, and he used his cloak as a viable distraction. It was obvious the knight was classically trained, but he didn't waste any time with unnecessary movements. He was a killer, and showed no mercy during his battle. Kase understood why the Triple Crown wanted to catch the Unicorn Knight: because he wasn't just a threat to the Guardians; he was a threat to everyone.

The injured Guardian that had taken the hit to the back of the knee crawled to safety. One of the remaining Guardians tried to mimic the Unicorn Knight's spin move, but the vigilante didn't engage. Instead, he used the distraction to attack the fourth Guardian, slicing just above the Guardian's gauntlet. With a shout the Guardian dropped his sword, and the Unicorn Knight moved in quickly to slice his throat and finish the job.

The last Guardian standing screamed and raised his sword high. He swung in a barrage of chaotic attacks, seemingly with no real strategy, but the Unicorn Knight casually backed up out of range. The Unicorn Knight then blocked an overhead blow, reached into his belt, and stabbed the Guardian with a dagger. The Guardian fell over in defeat.

Kase wondered what other weapons the Unicorn Knight had as he sheathed his hidden knife. His sword remained on fire as he strode menacingly to the first Guardian that had attacked. The Guardian was leaning against the wall, clutching his hurt knee with one hand and waving a wiggling sword with the other.

With little effort, the Unicorn Knight swatted the Guardian's sword aside, sending it across the floor with a scrape. He grabbed the Guardian by the collar and mumbled something to him. The Guardian unwrapped the sage mirror that was strapped to his forearm and turned it towards himself.

"Mirror, mirror." The Guardian hesitated. "Contact High Warrior Mac."

The Unicorn Knight snatched the sage mirror away. He held it up so that the viewer on the other side of the mirror could see the hurt Guardian and the Unicorn Knight together. He turned the mirror around to show his handiwork with the other Guardians.

Kase ducked away so that he wasn't seen in the background. He rested his back against the wall of tools and felt a few of them rub his back. He froze, hoping that none of them would fall. He took a few deep breaths, counted to three, and then slowly craned his neck back around the corner.

The Unicorn Knight held his flaming sword high, and then drove the tip into the injured Guardian.

"What do you want?" High Warrior Mac screamed through the sage mirror.

Kase felt like asking the same question. Was there a method to the Unicorn Knight's madness? Was High Warrior Mac the real target? What would stop the Unicorn Knight from killing more Guardians, setting shops on fire, or hurting the innocent?

The Unicorn Knight dropped the sage mirror, and then hammered his heel down. The mirror shattered, ending the communication. His flame extinguished as he sheathed his sword. He strode to the other Guardians that were splayed around the room, crushing the sage mirrors on all their wrists.

The Unicorn Knight had shown the High Warrior the room, so there was no doubt that other Guardians were on their way. With little time before being ambushed by a wave of warriors, Kase stepped away from the wall. A few tools crashed to the ground, clanging against the floor.

Instead of running away from the obvious, Kase revealed himself to the alerted Unicorn Knight. "Very impressive," he said in his old man voice. He crept forwards with his cane, keeping an eye on the vigilante.

The Unicorn Knight stared at Kase. He grabbed the handle of his sword, but Kase put his hands out and stood tall.

"Wait," Kase said in his normal voice. He didn't want to get involved, but stopping a formidable foe would help the realm. He had an advantage over the fallen Guardians, since he couldn't be killed, but was there another way to win this battle? "I'm not here to fight you. I just want to talk."

The Unicorn Knight drew his sword. Fire ignited the blade from cross-guard to tip. Kase was intrigued. Was the weapon a magical artefact? Had he applied a potion to the blade? Was there a fire-starter built into his hilt? The knight stood confident in a battle stance, holding his weapon with a two-handed grip.

Apparently, talking was not an option.

Kase hustled to the closest fallen Guardian and picked up his sword.

The Unicorn Knight let him gain a weapon, which was promising, but Kase still didn't want to fight. Maybe if he could disarm the knight, he had a chance of bringing the vigilante to justice without the loss of more lives. He got into a battle stance, and waited for an attack.

The Unicorn Knight sliced through the air, but not close enough for a blow. He spun, his cape swirling with the movement, a move Kase recognized from earlier. Kase blocked the incoming stab, but didn't dance away fast enough. He got caught with a right hook to the jaw.

Kase used his momentum to fall away, but he still remained composed. His healing power took the sting away.

The Unicorn Knight kept slashing, but Kase was in full defensive mode. He blocked every strike fast enough to escape any tough combination, all the while looking for a weak point. The one thing that stood out to Kase was the long unicorn horn protruding from the knight's helmet.

After another spin from the Unicorn Knight, Kase jumped to the side and swung up. He clipped the unicorn horn with his sword, sending the knight's head snapping back. As the Unicorn Knight came forwards, Kase slammed his fist into the centre of the purple glass on his mask, shattering it instantly. The Unicorn Knight fell back, turning his back to Kase and covering his face.

Kase worried about his own disguise. He tugged at his white wig, but it was still in place. He was a little sweaty, but he wasn't as concerned about his makeup falling off. Last night he'd needed a lot of water to wash the residue away.

Instead of facing Kase, the Unicorn Knight reached into his belt and tossed two silver pellets to the ground. They exploded on impact, covering the floor with smoke. If it wasn't for the illuminated sword, Kase wouldn't have been able to see where the Unicorn Knight stood.

It seemed like the Unicorn Knight was unwilling to give up.

Kase searched for a breeze. He could use his element control to gain an advantage, instead of being partially blinded by the smoke. He manipulated the air coming in from the roof window, blowing it down and across the floor.

As the breeze pushed the smoke away, he launched himself forwards, swinging his weapon above the flaming sword. To his surprise, he didn't make contact with anything.

Kase reached up and manipulated the air faster. The entire area in front of him cleared, but the Unicorn Knight was nowhere to be seen: just his flaming sword, jammed point-first into the wooden floor. Then Kase felt a prick in his rib cage as a thin dagger jammed through his left side and into his heart.

Kill shot.

Kase swung to his left, but continued to spin. He fell to the ground as his body went into shock. He stared at the flaming sword stuck in the floor. The Unicorn Knight cautiously picked it up and sheathed it once again.

After erecting the doorway of life, Kase had relived the moments of Lenia's death when he brought her back to life. The wound here felt exactly the same. Kase thought about how long it had taken her to perish after receiving such a blow. He'd watched her take her last breath as High Scholar Sheese stood over her corpse. He'd heard Mardious Hood laugh in the aftermath.

He watched as the Unicorn Knight rushed to the front door and slid the barn door open enough to squeeze through. He didn't look back. Kase had hoped to catch a glimpse of the knight's face through the broken visor, but the Unicorn Knight didn't oblige. The knight escaped into the dimly-lit street.

Like bringing anything back to life, Kase went through the same process. He felt the fire burn through his body to the core of his soul. He felt his skin melt and his eyeballs fall into his skull. The pain was excruciating, but it was soon all over. This time, his essence floated like a ghost up into the air. He couldn't see everything around him, but he could feel it. It was like his body was waiting for the right time to be embraced again.

When he opened his eyes, he was standing tall, but his sword and wig were on the floor. He had never been murdered before, and should have used the opportunity to test out his resurrecting process. But he reminded himself of the Guardians likely on their way.

He picked up his wig and ran to his cane. He thought about leaving through the front door, but heard some horses hooves skid to a stop.

"Be careful!" someone yelled.

Kase didn't waste any more time. He sprinted to the back room, found the closet with the hole in the wall, and squeezed through. He didn't cut his arm this time, but still stopped as soon as he was through. Turanus rested on the ground directly behind the building, waiting for Kase to mount him.

"This is convenient," Kase said.

"Hurry," Turanus responded. "They're coming around the building."

Kase jumped on the unicorn's back and was teleported in a flash.

He took a deep breath of forest air as he dismounted in front of the entrance to the Kingdom of Moiras. He petted his unicorn companion, rustling his mane, but questions started flooding him.

"Why did you show up at the exact moment I needed you?" Kase asked. "Our plan was to meet where you dropped me off, but somehow you knew exactly where I was so I could escape. Are you psychic?"

"No," Turanus said. "I was watching over you."

"But why?" Kase asked. Usually the unicorn disappeared right away, so Kase wanted to get as much from the opportunity as he could.

Turanus didn't answer.

"If you saw what happened, did you see the Unicorn Knight?" Kase asked. "Do you know who he is, or where he's hiding?"

"I'm afraid that is something you will have to discover on your own," Turanus said.

Kase tried not to roll his eyes. He was appreciative of his friend, but a simple 'I do not know' would have sufficed. "Okay," he said. "So why me? Do you help others, or just me?"

"We share a bond older than your memory," Turanus said. "We're family. You might not have noticed, but I'm adopted."

Kase chuckled. "So, you're like my uncle or brother?"

"You should ask your mother," Turanus said.

"You knew my mother?" Kase said. Did Cali know about this story? Why hadn't he heard about this before?

Turanus disappeared without another word.

Kase took a deep breath. He was disappointed in another disappearance, but was grateful for the short conversation he was able to have with Turanus. "Thank you, uncle brother."

Kase thought about his family as he ran the trail back to the castle. It was pitch-black, but he knew the trail well. He wished Maxim could have picked him up, but she was likely sleeping already.

After finally entering the castle, he snuck around until he was back in Talen's room. She was fast asleep again, and couldn't be woken. He removed his makeup, hid his disguise, and then let her be. He would have liked to discuss his adventure with her first, but he knew he had to talk to Lenia about it. Although his initial mission was a failure, he wanted to share everything with her and the rest of his crew.

As he headed to his room to change out of his sweaty clothes, he noticed Aura lounging on a chair across from his door, reading a book.

"Oh, I didn't expect to see you here so late, Kase," Aura said. She poured a cup of tea from the platter sitting on the side table.

"Do you normally read here?" Kase asked. He thought she'd be reading in the more comfortable chairs in the library, or in her bed.

"Sometimes," Aura said. "Routine is important. Would you like some tea before you sleep?"

"I don't—" Kase started.

"It's a new blend." Aura presented the cup to Kase.

Kase shrugged and accepted the drink. Aura had always taken care of him, but he was interested in someone else. "Do you know where Lenia is?" he asked. He took a sip. This batch was much stronger. He blew across the teacup to let some of the flavour out of his mouth.

"How's the tea?" she asked.

"Delicious," Kase said. He took another sip to be kind.

"Lenia's sleeping already," Aura said. "Why?"

Kase thought about what Aura might think of his adventure, seeing as she'd had a similar one on her birthday, but he didn't want to discuss it with her yet. Lenia deserved to know first. He slammed back the rest of his tea.

"Thanks for the nightcap," Kase said, ignoring Aura's question. "See you in the morning."

"Goodnight, Kase," Aura said. She closed her book, placed Kase's cup on her tray, and then took the platter with her down the hall.

Kase took a deep breath, and then entered his bedroom. He removed his clothes and slipped into some clean bedtime attire. He crept to the bed and slid under the covers next to Lenia. Her back was to him, so he gently wrapped his arms around her. He instantly felt tired.

"Another long night?" Lenia said.

"You're awake?" Kase said. He leant on his elbow, but then felt woozy. He let his head fall back to his pillow. "I need to tell you something."

"I'm tired," Lenia said. "Let's wait until morning."

Kase closed his eyes. Before he could respond, he was already asleep.

# CHAPTER 6

# I Forgot To Be Your Lover

Kase rolled over. His draping arm hit nothing but an empty sheet. Lenia was gone.

Kase yawned, covering his eyes from the glare of the window. The sunshine reached his face, which meant that it was close to noon. He rolled over, hoping for a few more minutes of sleep, but Talen's curious expression next to his bed made him jump.

"Good morning," he said. He jerked himself up and leant on his elbow. He pulled the blanket up to cover his bare chest.

"How was your night?" Talen asked. She took a sip of her tea.

Kase searched the room. The door was closed. There was a full breakfast plate on the night table, along with a steaming teacup. "Shouldn't we join the others?"

"They're gone for the day," Talen said. She handed the plate to Kase. "Did anything interesting happen?"

Kase sat up. "I need to talk to Lenia," he said, pushing the plate away. "I'm sorry, Tal, but I'm done sneaking around. The only way for us to make sense of my experience, and figure out what to do next, is to come together."

Talen took another sip of her tea. "I agree," she said. "Unfortunately, we can't involve the others yet, because they went to the capital today."

"What?" Kase shouted. He leapt out of bed and searched for his clothes.

"Please, eat some brunch and tell me what happened last night." Talen stood and presented the plate again to Kase. "I can't help you bring everyone together if we don't talk about it first."

Kase hopped around while he put his boots on. He glanced out the window and took a heavy breath. He couldn't go to the capital without his makeup, especially during the day when the shadows wouldn't help him sneak through the streets. He needed to find Lenia, but Talen would likely help him find her faster.

"Fine," Kase huffed. He sat back down on the bed and accepted his breakfast. He told Talen every detail of his encounter with the Unicorn Knight. Talen didn't ask any questions, but listened intently as Kase talked and ate.

When he finished his story and his breakfast, Talen pulled out his wig and makeup. Her calmness in the face of the situation and gentle touch as she applied Kase's mask helped ease Kase's anxiety.

"What do you think the Triple Crown will do in retaliation?" Talen asked.

"They're already on high alert for the Unicorn Knight," Kase said. "I can only assume that instead of chasing him, the entire Guardianship won't hesitate to take him out without warning. The Triple Crown is likely trying to set a trap."

"And you think the Unicorn Knight will fall for that?" Talen asked as she slathered some paste on Kase's cheek.

"I don't care about his fate," Kase said sternly. "I need to find Cali, Aura, and Lenia so that they don't get caught by mistake. We're safe here in the Kingdom of Moiras, and they need to stay here until the heat dies down. For their safety; for ours."

"You don't think that this is a better time to journey throughout the realm?" Talen asked. "With all the attention on the Unicorn Knight, even the Guardians in the capital will be focused on capturing the vigilante instead of looking for us while we're dressed up as elders."

"Sneaking around in masks is exactly why we should stay home," Kase said. "If someone notices their makeup now, while the Unicorn Knight is in hiding … I need to have their back, because I know they have mine."

"But we can have each other's backs in different ways, right?" Talen asked. She used both hands to shape Kase's fake, elongated nose.

"How do you mean?" Kase asked. He didn't want to guess at Talen's intention, because he knew her words would be wiser than his.

"Lenia, Cali, and Aura might trust you to have their back, but they also trust you to know they're safe," Talen said. "They know the risks too, and aren't going to do anything to get caught. They might want to look to you for support and understanding when they return, rather than your worries or concern."

Kase closed his eyes, partly because Talen was rubbing makeup near his eye, but also because he needed to think about her words. "I understand, Tal, but I need to communicate those ideas to the others. I don't want to just assume they're being safe, or that they appreciate my support. I want to tell them directly, and open up that conversation so we're all in the know."

Talen leant back. "Okay, but if you're going to Kimroad to look for them, would it hurt to also figure out the identity of the Unicorn Knight?"

Kase opened his eyes in shock. "How?"

"What if you brought one of the Unicorn Knight's victims back to life?" Talen asked. "Wouldn't your magic unveil details of their death? That could be useful."

Kase thought about his connection with the deceased. For a brief moment, he relived their experience before they passed. If the Unicorn Knight had made any threats, removed his mask, or left something behind, Kase would be able to see it through the eyes of the victim. Any clues might help Kase end the Unicorn Knight's reign before more lives were lost.

If Kase was already going to the trouble of applying his makeup and venturing to the capital, it didn't seem like a bad idea to do some extra work. His primary concern was on finding Lenia, Cali, and Aura, but it was a big city. If he was unsuccessful, he could make it a worthwhile trip with a side quest.

"How would I find the right person?" Kase asked.

"I've been paying attention to the news," Talen said. "Although most names have been removed from public record, out of respect to the families, there's one victim that slipped through the cracks. I recognized his name because we've met him before."

Talen leant back in her chair, satisfied with her makeup application. She looked underneath her chair, and then grabbed Kase's wig.

"Who is it?" Kase asked.

"J.R. Tamworth," Talen replied.

Kase shook his head. J.R. was the son of Porkchop, the leader of Mardious Hood's gang in the Badlands, the Brotherhood. Kase had met J.R. and Porkchop when he had ventured to the Badlands during the Academy's Quest Series. There, he and Lenia had to fight their way out of a tricky situation. Although not a main player in the grand scheme, J.R. was definitely a worthy adversary.

"Why would the Unicorn Knight target J.R.?" Kase asked.

Talen plopped the wig on Kase's head, and adjusted it accordingly. "We know that J.R.'s associated with the wrong people," she said. "It's likely he's treated the Unicorn Knight with the same amount of discourtesy he's treated us."

Kase nodded. "Wouldn't he be buried in the Badlands, though?"

"Maybe he should have been," Talen said. She combed through Kase's bangs. "But he wasn't. His tombstone looked pretty extravagant in the images I saw. It's about six feet, two inches high, with an eagle clutching a snake on top. The company he runs, Brothers' Inc., has a lot of influence in Kimroad now."

Kase tried to poke holes in Talen's plan, but the more Talen talked about it, the more it seemed like a viable option. Kase would spend the afternoon and early evening searching for their friends. When darkness hit, he'd have an easier time digging a grave without being noticed because the graveyard was closed to the public.

Kase would bring J.R. back to see details of his death, but was he prepared to send him back to an eternal slumber? J.R. had played a role in Lenia's death, but he didn't deserve to die; no one did. He may be associated with bad people like the Brotherhood, but he also had good people who loved him—like his little sister, Robyn. Who was he to take J.R. away from her?

The only justification that Kase could think of was that J.R. was a liability to the secret Kingdom of Moiras. If J.R. escaped after Kase brought him back to life, he'd tell his father, Mardious Hood, and the rest of the Triple Crown about the experience, which could ultimately lead to Kase and his friends being captured.

So no, he couldn't let J.R. live now.

Talen gave Kase a few Aileron that she had saved from Lenia's excursions; the jewellery from their castle usually sold for more Aileron than Lenia could spend.

Kase armed himself with two small daggers that were easily concealable, since an old man carrying a sword might draw too much attention. He'd also look suspicious if he carried a shovel everywhere, so he'd be on his own for finding the right tools for grave digging later.

Kase left the castle in the early afternoon, and was quickly met by his favourite langara. Maxim flew him to the cave entrance of the Kingdom of Moiras. As usual, Turanus appeared on the other side and teleported Kase to the capital city. Being helped by his animal friends gave Kase hope that he'd be successful on his journey.

Although unable to give Kase any information on Lenia, Cali, and Aura's whereabouts, Turanus assured Kase he'd keep a watchful eye. Kase was under the impression that Turanus always looked after Lenia when she went on her excursions, but he'd never received an explanation from the unicorn. Turanus' silence on the matter wasn't surprising, but it was disappointing, especially when Turanus could cover more ground by teleporting.

Kase might have been alone in his quest, but he reminded himself of the positive opportunities in front of him. He played the part of the old man, strolling through the streets with his cane in hand. He rested on park benches, fed some birds with breadcrumbs from his afternoon snack, and read a few pages from a book that was left on a park bench. It was a story of how a hero manipulated mice to save the world. It forced him to consider his own magical limits; even these fantastical stories hardly seemed beyond him now.

The capital city was different from what he remembered. It had never been the friendliest of cities, but there seemed to be added hostility in the air. More Guardians patrolled the streets, adapted magic mirrors—surveillance mirrors, presumably—were mounted high on almost every street corner, and wanted posters were hung in every storefront window. The public was certainly aware of the Unicorn Knight, but also of the Liberati and some wanted criminals from the Badlands.

Ironically, the added security and awareness within the city walls made Kase feel less worried. While the risk of getting caught was amplified, he trusted that Cali, Aura, and Lenia were taking every precaution to stay safe. They wouldn't let their guard down by accident, because the heightened security forced them to be diligent.

The darkness of night arrived faster than Kase had hoped. He hadn't found what he was looking for in the city, so he decided to move on to Plan B. More information on the Unicorn Knight would be useful for the group, when they eventually got a chance to speak all together.

Talen had drawn Kase a map, but Kase didn't need it. He had taken some time during the afternoon to scout the graveyard that J.R. was buried in. The surrounding fence was easily scalable, and the gravestone couldn't be seen from the nearby street. Kase remembered the city's changes and made sure there weren't any surveillance mirrors pointing in the direction of the graveyard either.

Kase had found a secluded spot near a tree to sneak onto the grounds. He kept low as he strolled past each row of gravestones, playing the part of his costume. That way, even if he was caught in the graveyard, he could pretend to be a confused old man.

When he reached J.R.'s tombstone, he surveyed the landscape again. The darkness made it difficult to see beyond twenty yards, as the graveyard was only illuminated by starlight. A few trees swayed in the breeze, but since there wasn't anyone roaming about, Kase felt safe and alone.

Kase didn't have a shovel with him, but he had other plans. He knelt down in the grass, and carved a grave-sized rectangle in the sod with his dagger. He remembered the hole he'd dug for Lenia's grave before bringing her back to life, and assumed that J.R.'s coffin would be about the same size. He peeled back the grass, using his magic to help him tear the grass away from the soil. Because of his influence over the grass stalks, it was like flipping the page of a massive book.

Kase brushed the loose dirt off his hands. He leant on his cane and thought about the book he'd read. The hero in the story used a special sceptre to control a large mischief of mice. Controlling one mouse wasn't that useful, but controlling a whole horde played to the hero's advantage. Together, the mice were able to carry him across busy streets, connect to create a short ladder, and create a burrow into a nearby basement.

Like the hero, Kase had experience controlling small animals, but he didn't need a sceptre to do it. As a warrior-wizard, he'd been able to feel a bird's presence, calm a cat to crawl out of a tree, or help herd animals on his uncle's old farm. But now, with the power of the doorway of life at his fingertips, he wondered if he could amplify that control. He couldn't think of a better time to try it out.

Kase focused his energy on his surroundings. He could already feel a few ground squirrels resting in the earth beneath his feet. He felt a few birds cuddled in their nests, but they wouldn't be of use for the task at hand. He connected with a few roaming cats in the streets, but he needed to expand further.

His power went beyond the graveyard, reaching throughout the city and well below the ground. He gathered as many squirrels, gophers, dogs, and badgers as he could, and helped them all crawl through the shadows to reach his location. It would have been peculiar to see so many animals travelling at once, so Kase took his time to gather his new friends.

Each animal had their own duty, and their efforts worked wonders. The digging started from underground, with some animals burrowing beside, above, and below J.R.'s coffin. Inch by inch, earth was transferred from above the coffin to below, with some of the badgers pushing up on the casket to move the box along. When the coffin was near the surface, the dogs and cats helped shovel dirt away with their paws.

While the animals worked, Kase kept a watchful eye on the graveyard. No shadows moved around him, and the only sounds were his animals working.

When the coffin lid was finally exposed, Kase led the animals around the perimeter of the grave. Predators and prey stood proud together while Kase moved to the next phase of his plan.

Kase was proud of himself and the development of his power. It had been a struggle for him to control one animal before, but with the doorway of life at his fingertips, he was able to break through those barriers. He'd gained confidence in his ability, and was proud of his innovative technique to control multiple animals. He couldn't wait to tell Lenia about his accomplishment.

Kase slammed the edge of his dagger into the side of the coffin and propped the lid open. J.R. lay gently on a bed of silk. His blue robes were clean, and reflected some of the starlight. He had gold chains draped around his neck, and silver rings on each finger. His body had yet to fully decompose, but he smelled awful.

Kase took out a handkerchief and covered his mouth. He then removed some rope from his pocket and used the short pieces to tie J.R.'s legs together, as per his and Talen's plan. He moved J.R.'s stiff arms behind his back, and then bound them as well. A handkerchief got stuffed into J.R.'s mouth and secured around his jawline. Kase's last handkerchief was used to cover J.R.'s eyes, which he tied around J.R.'s head.

Kase peeked above the wall of animals that protected him. He was still alone in the graveyard. He took a deep breath, made sure he still had control of his new friends so that they wouldn't flee or attack each other, and then touched J.R.'s hand. He felt a slight tingle in his chest before his connection strengthened and his viewpoint changed to J.R.'s.

J.R. crawled towards the portal keystone. His leg was limp and bleeding. But if he could escape, he'd be able to get reinforcements. He just needed to make it a few more feet.

A scream echoed through the courtyard. He didn't want to look back, but he couldn't help it. In the corner of the broken fence line, the Unicorn Knight was pulling his flaming sword from Ian's chest. A few yards away, Sarah lay motionless.

J.R. shuffled forwards, then used the pedestal to lift himself up. He searched his pockets frantically for Aileron.

A sharp pain flared in his good leg. He screamed. He fell to the ground hopelessly, the Unicorn Knight towering above him.

"You'll pay for this!" J.R. shouted. "Do you even know who I am?"

The Unicorn Knight steadied the point of his burning blade near J.R.'s feet.

He nodded.

"My father will hunt you down," J.R. threatened. "The Brotherhood will make you suffer. You'll be begging them for a quick death, but they'll—"

"I'm not afraid of death." The Unicorn Knight's voice was low, steady—and feminine.

J.R. swallowed hard. No wonder the Unicorn Knight hadn't been found by the Triple Crown; they were looking for a man.

"Death is easy. It's what's left behind that suffers," she continued.

If she wasn't afraid of him, was his fate sealed? Would she accept a bribe instead?

"I can pay you," he offered. "I have gold; I have jewellery; I have land. I can give you anything you want."

"I want justice," the Unicorn Knight said. She swiped her fiery sword above J.R.'s face.

He brought his hands up to shield his eyes, turning away from the heat. Then he felt the blade thrust through his chest. He tried to scream. He wasn't ready to die. All he could do was cough, twice. Then he closed his eyes.

Kase was brought back to the lava of fire that gave him his power. He fell into the pit, the liquid fire splashing around him. He felt his arms and legs burn before his skin started to melt. The fire reached down into his soul. He wanted to scream like J.R., but he was still conscious of the world around him. He tried to focus on his animal control instead.

After a few moments, he opened his eyes. All of his animal friends were in the same position, guarding the grave like a fortress wall. Not one of them made a sound. Not one of them felt fear, anger, or pain. Not like him.

Kase sat down hard in the dirt. He thought about the voice of the Unicorn Knight, and how angry she was.

He didn't understand how Lenia could be so cold.

J.R. wiggled around and shouted, but his gag muffled the sound. J.R. screamed a little louder, so Kase used his magic to manipulate one of the dog's into growling. J.R. quickly fell silent, and then started to sob. With the blindfold on, and his feet and wrists tied, he likely felt trapped.

Kase drew his dagger, and decided to put J.R. out of his misery. There was no way that he could let J.R. live, especially now that he knew Lenia was the Unicorn Knight. If J.R. gave details of her identity to the Triple Crown, they'd be able to focus their search a little more.

But Kase didn't feel any worry or fear; it was anger and betrayal that stirred inside him. The Triple Crown wasn't what Lenia had to worry about.

Kase sliced J.R.'s neck, letting the portly Brotherhood member bleed out for a second time. Kase didn't wish death upon his enemy, but he needed a better plan before he could let him live. No one deserved to be treated with such disregard; not Lenia when she had been killed by the Brotherhood and the Triple Crown, and not the Brotherhood dying for justice—or rather, revenge.

Kase didn't bother untying J.R.'s corpse; he didn't even wipe the dagger clean. He just left the weapon in the coffin, closed the lid, and stood tall. He looked around to make sure the graveyard was still clear, and then used his power over the animals to return the coffin underground. When the coffin was at the right depth, Kase helped the animals return to their homes. He even re-rooted the lawn once again. But through it all he felt stiff.

As he stumbled through the graveyard, he thought about everything that had happened over the last few months. Lenia had been so jovial around him. How could she have been so angry on her own without him knowing? For that matter, how did she even have time to be a masked vigilante? She was—had been—so loyal. How could she lie to him?

He wondered if he even knew her at all.

Was she Lenia by day, and the Unicorn Knight at dusk? Or maybe she was really a killer, and just pretending to be the woman he loved. Which mask was her true face?

He needed to talk to her, but wondered if he wanted to. How would he bring up that he knew her secret? Did Cali and Aura know of her double life? Would Talen and Curtis be safe with a killer in their castle? Would the paradise they built in the Kingdom of Moiras still exist, or would it be changed forever?

Kase rested on a bench inside the cemetery. He stared at the stars for a few moments, hoping that he'd gain the strength he needed to make the right decision.

He knew he was about to have the biggest fight of his life.

## CHAPTER 7

# I Was In The Dark But Now I See

Kase sat in the armoury, going over his plan step by step. Although Lenia and Curtis had set up a sharpening wheel, Kase preferred to finish his blade with a handheld whetstone. He methodically stroked the edge of his blade with the stone, getting it ready for his battle against the Unicorn Knight.

He'd spent the night with Maxim and the other langaras, since they were the only ones in the Kingdom of Moiras that he could trust. He'd wrestled with all of his thoughts and emotions since discovering Lenia's alter ego, and came to the conclusion that he'd have to face her head-on. There was no way around the inevitable; they needed to get the truth out in the open. But he was struggling with how exactly he was going to do it.

He thought of his hunts with the langaras. They didn't always rush in. They were able to surround their target, carefully and quietly, before going in for the kill. Any sudden movements or loud sounds could scare their prey, resulting in escape if every angle wasn't covered. And so they practised patience to succeed, even if they were instinctively savage and brutal killers.

In the same way, Kase had to be patient when luring Lenia into conversation. Because of their short swordfight at the docks, she knew he had a costume of his own, and travelled to the realm. She didn't know how frequent his trips were, or what he'd learned, but one of his secrets was exposed.

Lenia didn't know that Kase had discovered her secret identity. He wanted to give her the benefit of the doubt, and listen to her confession that she was the Unicorn Knight. If she were to openly tell him of her plans, he felt like their bond would remain strong. But if she kept lying, he knew she could be a danger to him, the rest of their friends, and the entire realm.

Kase didn't want to, but he had to prepare for the worst.

He'd found an old, golden chest plate that fit around his torso. It had a langara etched into it, and he liked the symbolism. More importantly, it would protect him from any surprise attack—like a dagger into his ribcage and through his heart.

Kase's rhythmic motions faltered. She'd killed him, just as she'd been killed. Was that intentional? Was she warning him to stay away, because she knew his heart might break if he pursued the truth? Or was she simply buying herself some time to escape?

Kase sharpened his sword some more. He didn't want to get into a physical fight with the woman he loved, but sometimes warriors only knew one way to solve problems. He wondered if Lenia was more warrior than wizard now.

The door creaked open. "Kase?" Lenia asked.

Kase took a deep breath. "Over here," he said. He continued to sharpen his sword; he wanted to appear intimidating.

Lenia strode over to the sharpening area confidently. Her hair was braided, falling to her left. She had a new outfit on, complete with strikingly-sleek brown boots. She pulled her sword out of her sheath and grabbed a whetstone. "Good idea," she said.

Kase gripped his whetstone tighter. They both sharpened their blades with the same rhythm. He didn't want to speak first, so he concentrated on the noise of stone hitting blade. He didn't need to press very hard, because he was already satisfied with its sharpness. He reminded himself to be patient; he didn't want to rush the conversation.

"How was your night?" Lenia asked after an eternity.

Kase exhaled. How long had he been holding his breath? "I spent some time with Maxim," he said truthfully. "I was so tired, I ended up just sleeping on her back."

"Her hair is really soft," Lenia said. "Did you clip any for a wig?" She didn't look up from sharpening her weapon.

Kase thought about his disguise when he'd faced the Unicorn Knight. She knew he already had a wig, so he tried to change the subject. "I'll need one for our date," he said calmly. "Do you have any more ideas of what we're going to do? Or are you bored of leaving the kingdom since you, Cali, and Aura seem to do it so often now?"

Lenia flipped her sword to sharpen the opposite edge and sighed. "I don't really like going with Cali and Aura," she admitted. "They have their own agendas, which makes it feel too much like work. I want to have some fun. But it doesn't really matter where we go, as long as you're with me."

Kase felt his heart drop. He wanted, more than anything, to escape with Lenia. His favourite dates with her were wandering the cities, eating sugary snacks as they went along, laughing and skipping and dancing together.

"That sounds lovely," Kase said. He reminded himself of how different things had become. "Can we go shopping? I wouldn't mind some new clothes, or boots like yours."

"Definitely," Lenia said with a smile. "We shouldn't try anything on though, to prevent shopkeepers from accidently seeing our uncovered skin."

"So we just buy things without seeing if they fit?" Kase asked.

"If they don't fit, we can just give them away," Lenia said. "I usually give Talen the boots that are too small for me. Are you looking for anything specific? More armour maybe?"

Kase checked his chest plate. He thought about telling Lenia the new name he'd thought of for himself, but it might seem too passive-aggressive. "I found this a while ago in one of the treasure rooms," he said. "It needs something more, though. Maybe a cool mask, or a cape."

Lenia hesitated, but continued sharpening her blade. "I don't think you could pull off the cape look," she said.

Kase felt the mood change. He decided to push a little harder. "I think it would make me look cooler," he said. "Plus, it might help me with some advanced battle moves."

Lenia stopped sharpening her sword. Her eyes darted left and right as she hunched over. "What kind of advanced battle moves?" she asked.

Kase stood up. "I think I would work in a few spin moves," he said. He twirled a few times, aiming for the door. After his second twirl, he had successfully obstructed Lenia's path to the armoury entrance. "I could use it to block an enemy's view, making my sword harder to track. Maybe I could even get one thick enough to block arrows."

Lenia didn't turn around, but her posture straightened. "So you're going to work that into our classes, professor? Or are you thinking of fighting someone else with your armour and arrow-blocking cape?" Her sharpening strokes had become longer and more forceful.

"Our enemies are still out there, hunting us down," Kase said. "We need to be ready if they find us. Isn't that why we're training so hard?"

Lenia stopped sharpening her sword. She swivelled in her seat, locking eyes with Kase. "We're not training to protect ourselves, we're training to protect the innocent," Lenia said. "Isn't that the duty of a warrior? To serve?"

"We serve to protect everyone," Kase said. "But we are not above the law. We don't manipulate the rules to make them fit our actions. We're not—"

"Like the Triple Crown?" Lenia said. She tossed her whetstone and stood. The anger in her voice made it sharp. "They claim to serve everyone, but they only serve themselves."

Kase felt like he was getting to know Lenia on a deeper level. They hadn't talked about the Triple Crown like this before, even though they both shared the same loathing for those responsible for their situation. Maybe the Unicorn Knight wasn't so misguided after all: just misunderstood. He decided to push harder.

"For them, death is easy," Kase said. "But they don't realize that it is what's left behind that suffers most."

Lenia furrowed her brow and tilted her head. "Where did you hear that from?"

Kase softened. "From the lips of the Unicorn Knight herself."

Lenia covered her mouth. Her eyes widened, like she'd seen a ghost. She stumbled back a few steps. "You know," she mumbled.

"How could you?" Kase struggled to ask.

Lenia turned away. "I wish I'd never have to see you look at me that way."

Kase felt his shoulders droop towards the floor. He could sense the turmoil in her voice. But was she frustrated by her actions, or by the fact that she'd been caught?

Lenia disappeared.

"Lenia?" Kase looked around the room, but she was gone. She'd teleported, just like she used to with her trident. But her trident had been lost when she'd died. They hadn't really had a chance to search for it before they returned to the Kingdom of Moiras. Had she found it in her excursions across the realm? She wasn't holding it, so had she found a piece of it, or did she now have a new magic relic as a focus?

It seemed like Lenia had even more secrets.

Kase rushed to the armoury entrance, but paused to grab some supplies. He slipped a couple of daggers into his beltline; he found his fire starter, in case he had to cross fire swords with the Unicorn Knight; he also grabbed his shield, so that this time he could mount a proper defense.

Kase wasn't sure if Lenia was going to become a terror, or escape to the realm at large. He hoped it was neither. He sprinted out of the armoury, crossing the grassy terrain that led to the castle. The route felt longer than normal.

"Lenia!" he shouted. "Lenia!"

He tried to communicate with the langaras too. "Maxim!" He thought she might be able to search the kingdom for any trace of Lenia. He didn't know what his range of communication was with the langaras, though.

"Kase!" Cali yelled from behind him.

Kase stopped running. He turned slowly, sword in one hand, shield in the other.

Cali stood with a book in her hand. Lenia was to Cali's left, and Aura to her right. Lenia was wearing her black Unicorn Knight armour, but she didn't have her helmet. Her trident was nowhere to be seen.

"What's going on, Cali?" Kase asked. Cali and Aura didn't seem surprised by Lenia's attire; the three of them stood strong and united.

"It's … complicated, brother," Cali said. "Please don't judge us. We're trying to do the right thing."

"By murdering the innocent?" Kase yelled. He stalked towards the group. "Don't we all understand the value of life? It was taken from every one of us, and now we're taking it from others? Are we no better than the evil leaders of the Triple Crown?"

"That's what we're trying to correct," Cali said. "Please stop, so we can explain."

Cali and Lenia hadn't wavered, but Aura looked scared. Kase checked his grip, and noticed his sword was shaking. His anger and frustration were influencing him physically. He threw his weapon and shield to the ground. "Enlighten me." He crossed his arms.

"We live in a prison, brother," Cali said. "It's a beautiful prison, with everything we could ever ask for to survive, but it still separates us from the rest of the realm. We aren't free to travel as we please; we can't make friends or share experiences with new people; we can't even see our families."

"Tell me something I don't know," Kase scoffed.

"My sister is getting married next month," Aura said. "I won't be able to stand by her at the ceremony. I can't help make it special, and I won't be able to celebrate with the rest of my family as we officially accept her husband into our lives."

Kase tapped his foot. At least Aura's family was safe. If the Triple Crown knew where she was, there might not be a wedding at all.

"We already missed Lenia's brother's wedding," Aura added. "Now we're going to miss the birth of her niece or nephew."

Kase stared at Lenia. "What?"

"The Triple Crown has stolen these moments from us," Lenia said. "They did it with such ease, ignoring the suffering that comes along with their actions. We're not the only ones missing out on these milestones of life; our family members are, too."

Kase thought about the anger in Lenia's voice when she'd struck down J.R. "So you're showing them what it's like? Revenge isn't the answer."

"The Unicorn Knight is a necessary evil," Cali said. "He's depleting the Triple Crown's Shadow Army, creating fear among the commoners, and forcing the leaders to focus elsewhere so that we can sneak in and eliminate them."

"I understand why you want to," Kase said, "but how does eliminating them help?"

"It's like cutting the head off a snake," Cali said. "But in the aftermath, we help the people appoint a new head. Since we created a villain in the Unicorn Knight, we create a hero to conquer him and take the mantle of ruler of the realm. Someone who is pure of heart, understands the value of life, and can change the world so the corrupt can never rule again."

"Like you?" Kase asked. "You sound power hungry, Cali."

"No, brother," Cali said. "Like you."

Kase shook his head. He understood how powerful he was, but being strong with magic didn't necessarily make him a worthy leader of the realm. "What if I don't want to rule?" he asked. "What if I don't support your plan?"

"You're the most powerful person in the realm," Cali said. "You have the same abilities as King Michael, but without his fierce nature. You'd be a perfect leader, as long as you maintain that calm, noble, and honourable temperament. If you had to do what the Unicorn Knight does …" Cali looked to Lenia.

Kase didn't like being compared to the ancient ruler of the Kingdom of Moiras. "Are you saying I couldn't handle it? I'm unable to understand those dark emotions? That I can't grow the way that you've grown?"

"I'm saying that I can take on this burden, so that you don't have to," Lenia said. "I can attack the Shadow Army, expose the Triple Crown's true nature, and ensure that what they've done to us never happens to anyone else. And then together, we can make the world a better place."

Although Kase appreciated what Lenia was trying to do, he still didn't agree with the way that she was doing it. "We should have worked on this plan *together*. We could have avoided all this misunderstanding, and we could have prevented the innocent from getting caught in the war. Is killing a little girl something you really had to do?"

"Which girl?" Lenia asked.

Kase went cold. 'Which girl'? Was there more than one? "The daughter of the leather store owners in Cordero," Kase said. "I think she was Josephine's sister."

"How did you know about that?" Cali asked. "It wasn't in the news."

"I was there," Kase said. "I was running an errand for Talen, but saw the aftermath of your destruction."

"Talen, of course," Aura said, rolling her eyes.

"See if you can find her," Cali said to Lenia. "Might as well grab Curtis, too."

Lenia nodded, then disappeared.

"Wait, what's going on now?" Kase asked.

"We didn't know how you figured things out," Cali said. "Talen was in on our plan, but it seems like she has different motives after all." She crossed her arms over her stomach, as if she were cold. "Looks like we'll get it all out in the open now."

Kase glared at Cali. "Feeling betrayed?" he asked. "Doesn't feel good, does it?"

Cali glared back at Kase. "It's not betrayal, it's just disappointing," she said.

"And Curtis?" Kase asked.

"He's been too busy drinking to get involved in our plans," Cali mocked.

Kase crossed his arms again. His sister was stubborn, but maybe it ran in the family. He wasn't willing to change his feelings towards their dark goal, but he wished he had a better solution to propose. If Talen and Curtis were on his side, maybe they could come up with something together.

He looked up to the sky, his eyes focusing on his winged companion. She had heard his call after all. "Hey," he said to Maxim. "Can you stop by the field outside the armoury? I need some help."

"Of course," Maxim replied.

The winged beast darted towards Kase. Cali and Aura both looked to the sky, and then huddled together. When Maxim landed, Cali and Aura were noticeably concerned.

"Can you ask your friend to leave?" Cali asked. Both she and Aura had been killed by a langara before, and were traumatized by the experience. Even though they knew that the langaras were friendly with Kase, they didn't want to be around the deadly beasts.

"Maxim has never lied to me," Kase barked. Cali and Aura went silent.

"Is everything okay?" Maxim asked. She growled low, sensing anger.

"I think so," Kase told her. "But I want to intimidate them a little bit, just in case."

"Understood." Maxim crouched into an attack position. Her glare was menacing.

A few moments later, Lenia returned with Talen and Curtis. She wasn't holding her trident. Kase still wondered how she was able to teleport.

"How did we …?" Curtis started. He swayed a bit, and then leant over to vomit. Luckily, nothing came up.

"The ruse is up, Talen," Cali said. "Kase knows of our plans, no thanks to you."

Talen looked at Kase, then back at Cali. "I didn't tell him anything directly," Talen said. "I guess he finally figured it out on his own."

"Figured out what?" Curtis asked.

"Lenia is the Unicorn Knight," Kase said. "Cali, Aura, and Talen have been helping her, and they've been lying to us the whole time."

"What?" Curtis gave his head a shake, blinking blearily. "Why?"

"They have a master plan," Kase said. "They seem to know what's best for all of us."

"That's not what we're doing, Kase," Cali said. "We've been tactful. We've been careful. We've come so far over the last few months, and we can't turn back now. You need to trust us."

"How can I trust you when all you've done is lied?" Kase said. "The only reason you kept us in the dark is because you knew what you were doing was wrong. How does doing wrong help us trust you to do the right thing?"

"I agree with Kase," Talen said. "We need to stop travelling the path we are on and find our direction again. I'm glad he figured out what was happening. Now we can get his input, and work on something else—together."

Cali shook her head. "Curtis, do you agree?"

"I'm not really sure what's going on," Curtis admitted. "But whatever it is, I'm with Talen and Kase. They're the reason I'm here. They're the reason that we're all here, together."

"So we're divided, three to three," Aura noted.

"Maxim is with us," Kase said. "So four to three."

"She doesn't count," Cali said.

"Do you want to tell her that?" Kase asked. Cali couldn't even look at Maxim.

"Your vote doesn't count," Lenia yelled at Maxim. "If you have a problem with that, come at me." She drew her sword.

"Don't threaten her," Kase said. He picked up his sword and shield.

Lenia looked to the side, then smiled. Her smile was more wicked than playful; something Kase hadn't seen before. "Maybe you and I should fight for the final vote."

"Fight how?" Kase asked. Their last encounter hadn't ended well for him, but he was ready for another round with the Unicorn Knight. "You have an advantage if you can teleport."

"You have the advantage of healing yourself," Lenia responded. "Plus, you can talk to giant, killer beasts. So maybe we should just duel as warriors. No magic. No element or animal control. No teleporting."

"Wait," Cali said. "What are we fighting for?"

"If Kase wins, we'll stop our plans and make a new one," Lenia said. "Something that everyone agrees on."

"And if you win?" Kase asked.

"When I win … again"—Lenia smiled—"Cali, Aura, and I get to call the shots around here. No more sneaking around. We'll spend all of our time strategizing and implementing our plan, and you, Talen, and Curtis will obey."

Kase stared at Lenia's green eyes. Her emotions were getting the better of her, and her confidence was outweighing her skills. After spending months teaching her his techniques, he knew she still had some things to learn. At the same time, her willingness to throw caution to the wind and put everything on the line was admirable.

"Warrior to warrior," Kase said. "No tricks. First one to yield?"

"You can yield," Lenia said. "But you're going to have to kill me to win."

Kase looked at his friends. Curtis was confused. Talen was statuesque.

Cali was confident, but Aura was scared. Maxim was licking her paws.

"Deal," Kase said. "When do we begin?"

"Now," Lenia said. She took a few steps forwards, and swung her sword from overhead.

Kase easily dodged it. He backpedalled away, trying to get away from the group and let his muscles warm up. His blood was already piping hot. "Professor versus student," he said. "I hope you've been doing your homework."

Kase lunged forwards, but Lenia danced away. Kase swung a few more times, but Lenia easily blocked his sideswipes. Her footwork was precise, she defended from a strong position, and she remained perfectly balanced throughout his onslaught of attacks.

"Way to go, Lenia!" Aura cheered.

"Let's go, Two Lions!" Curtis yelled louder.

"Two Lions?" Lenia snickered. "That's kind of a lame warrior name." She returned Kase's strikes with a few of her own: one from the left, the other from the right. Kase easily blocked both.

"I was hoping for the Langara Knight!" Kase shouted. He held his shield in front of himself while he edged further away from the group; they were providing too much of a distraction.

"How about Lame Lion?" Cali teased.

"Nah," Curtis yelled. "What about Lionheart?"

"Those are definitely worse," Lenia said. She pivoted, swirling her cape to block Kase from seeing her oncoming attack. She ducked and sliced sideways again.

Kase didn't even try to block it, or to counterattack: he jumped back completely instead. The edge of her blade missed his shield by a few feet. "Don't you have any new moves?" he teased.

"What about the Dandy Lion?" Talen shouted.

Lenia hunched over, her sword tip hitting the ground. "Time out," she said. She covered her gut and laughed. "The Dandy Lion," she repeated. "I love it."

Kase stood tall and threw his hands up in the air. "Why?" he asked Talen.

"Dandy means excellent," Talen said. "Plus, the dandelion is Lenia's favourite flower. You were supposed to take advantage of it throwing her off."

Lenia laughed some more. "Okay, nice try, Talen. I do love dandelions, but I love the Dandy Lion nickname even more. I might just be more motivated now, so I can call you the Dandy Lion forever."

"Nope." Kase got into his battle stance again. "When I win, you're not allowed to call me that ever again."

"Okay, Dandy Lion," Lenia said. She got ready to fight again, gripping the handle of her sword with both hands. "Time in."

Kase and Lenia traded more blows. Even though Kase was stronger physically, Lenia's form took away from his power. He thought about losing his shield, but he knew there would be a time to use it to his advantage. He just needed to wait for an opening.

He studied Lenia's Unicorn Knight uniform. She had black gloves that covered most of her forearm. Underneath her black garments and cloak, she was wearing some kind of chainmail. It looked expensive, and didn't seem like it was something left over by King Michael. She'd spent some time and Aileron picking out her modern armour.

But modern and fancy didn't protect against everything.

Her neck and face were exposed without her helmet. It was doubtful that her chainmail extended beyond her hips, so anything below the waist was likely exposed. Her boots only went halfway up her calf, and judging by the way she was moving, her knees weren't protected. A teleporting warrior wouldn't need much protection. But she wasn't teleporting now.

Kase blocked another overhead strike with his shield. The blow wasn't as forceful as her first ones had been. The more time that went by, the more the battle favoured Kase. He simply had more physical endurance than Lenia, and would soon be able to take advantage of her weakened state. He danced around a bit more, throwing in a few strikes of his own to make it interesting, but ultimately let her keep swinging away.

Curtis, Aura, and Cali kept cheering. Maxim and Talen stayed relatively silent. It was a serious fight, but Kase found he was enjoying it. He was proud to see the results of Lenia's hard work over the past few months. Her dedication to the craft was inspiring. A warrior's skills were admirable ones to have, and it was relieving to know that he had been a successful professor. He had one more lesson to teach her, though.

Instead of blocking Lenia's next overhead strike with his shield, Kase slipped to the side. Lenia went falling past, hitting the ground with the tip of her sword. Instead of swinging with his own sword, Kase slammed his shield on top of Lenia's wrists, trapping her weapon. He used the blunt pommel of his sword to knock her in the jaw, sending her sprawling to the ground.

Before she had a chance to slip away, Kase dropped his shield and pounced on her. He pinned her shoulder to the ground with his free hand, straddled her hips, and pinched his knees to stop her from squirming. He slammed the tip of his sword into the ground, as close to Lenia's cheek as possible.

Lenia froze.

"Kill shot," he said.

Lenia moved her eyes to the blade, then up to Kase, assessing the situation as she tried to catch her breath. She licked her bloody lips. "Nice move," she whispered. Her right hand moved up the back of his arm gently, but then dipped to his chest plate. She rested her palm there. "Is your heart beating as fast as mine right now?"

Kase leant closer. All of the anger and frustration had melted away during their fight. Now that it was over, he felt elated. He felt like they'd grown closer.

Lenia's fingers crawled up Kase's armour to his neckline. She pulled on his collar as she closed her eyes and puckered her lips. Even though they had just fought to the death, Kase couldn't help but kiss the woman that he still loved more than anything in the world.

Kase shifted his palm from Lenia's shoulder to the ground. Her lips were as soft as ever. He leant on his sword, imbedding it further in the ground so he could kiss her deeper. Lenia's hand combed through his hair as their tongues danced together. For a moment, he forgot where he was.

A blade jabbed into his neck.

Kase lunged back, but Lenia kept her grip strong. She rolled him onto his left side as the blood flowed down his throat and into his lungs. He tried to cough, but couldn't even do that. His body was already in shock.

Kill shot.

"I win," Lenia said. She rolled Kase onto his back, and then pushed herself up off his chest. She stood tall, stretched her arms out wide, and looked to the sky. "Kiss of death!" she yelled.

Cali and Aura cheered, but Kase wasn't focused on the noise. He was embarrassed, yet proud. He was in love, yet completely disgusted. He was upset that he'd lost, but there was no shame in losing to another warrior—even if her methods were different from his.

He closed his eyes, and waited for the oncoming fire.

# CHAPTER 8

# Your Wish Is My Command

Lenia squealed. She pulled herself as close to the rock wall as possible, turning her head towards Kase. She closed her eyes for a second, but then peeked one eyelid open.

Kase stretched to look around her. There was an empty nest, but no birds. Kase searched the sky, and used his power to see if he could feel any birds flying about. There weren't any around.

"So you've battled the realm's most elite Guardians, but the thought of a bird still scares you?" Kase asked.

"Some things will never change," Lenia said.

Kase almost lost his grip. So much *had* changed. He felt exhausted, not because of the extra-long training session today, but from trying to figure it all out. It seemed like his body was now feeling the same effects as his mind and his heart. He took a deep breath to focus.

Lenia tilted her head, straining her neck to look at the ledge above. "I'm going to skip the rest. Would you like to come with me, or are you going to finish your climb?"

As tired as he felt, Kase wasn't about to quit. "I'll meet you there," he said.

Lenia nodded, then disappeared.

Kase wiped his brow before securing his next hold. He was able to make it up two more before his mind wandered again. Was he selfish for questioning his fate? He shook his head, and pulled himself a little higher. Was he moving closer to Lenia, or were they drifting apart? He climbed a little higher still. When he reached her, would she stay with him, or move further away?

He'd replayed the battle in his mind many times. His strategy was sound, but he'd let his guard down. He appreciated Lenia's resourcefulness, and her determination to do whatever it took to do what she thought was right. And yet, he should have predicted it. Was it just his adversary that made him blind to unorthodox tricks?

He focused again on his holds. A power shift had occurred within the group as well. Lenia called it 'Election by Combat.' Curtis tried to argue vehemently that Kase had Lenia in a mercy position first, but Cali pointed out that Lenia had said she wouldn't yield, and even Talen couldn't argue with her logic. So the Unicorn Knight prevailed.

Kase didn't argue with the results. He'd known the risks when he'd agreed to the fight, but he couldn't shake the feeling of failure since the battle. He'd let Curtis and Talen down, but they hadn't spoken to him or complained about his performance. They seemed supportive to him still, but were they just masking their resentment?

Despite the tension, in the end it was Cali who took on more of a leadership role. Cali continued to plan the schedule of the Unicorn Knight with Lenia; Talen helped them with some of the research and prep work.

However, not everything had changed. Aura still planned and prepared all the meals for everyone, because she liked to cook and host. Kase and Curtis had a bigger role in clean-up and gardening, but it wasn't too much of a stretch from their normal routine.

Kase had nearly reached the summit. Lenia's legs were dangling from the ledge. How different would things have actually been if he had won? Would Cali, Aura, and Lenia be content with the rules of the Election by Combat, and obey Kase's orders? Could he be happy if they were miserable?

Aura had admitted to putting a sleeping potion in his tea every night, so Lenia would have more time to travel the realm after dinner. It was difficult for Kase to swallow that truth, but they were both relieved to be done with that routine. Since she didn't have to do that anymore, Kase had more time to help out with chores, among other things.

Cali had enforced the greatest change to Curtis' routine. He wasn't allowed to drink any wine or ale for three months. He also needed to be available for any weapon or armour building with Lenia, and he was required to join their warrior training in the afternoon. Cali wanted Curtis to get back into shape, so he'd be battle-ready when needed. As much of a shock as it was to his system physically, Curtis had a pretty good attitude about everything. Despite his protests following the duel, he seemed happy to change things around.

Kase looked down to the ground, but Curtis hadn't made it to the rock wall yet. The trail run wasn't too difficult, but Curtis was an admittedly slow runner, even before his wine- and ale- making days. Kase resumed his climb to the ledge, and noticed the end of Lenia's trident butted to the short grass at the top of the rock wall.

Lenia had explained to Kase that Turanus had guarded her trident while she was in her grave. He'd taken it to a remote unicorn grove, to remain safe until Lenia could wield it again. After Kase had brought Lenia back to life, Turanus had taken her to the location of her trident, but didn't let her take it away just yet. Without words, she knew that Turanus was trying to give her guidance, but she needed some time to figure things out.

She admitted that something dark had stirred inside her from the day when Kase had brought her back. It wasn't anger, frustration, or distress, but more of an empty void. It was a different kind of brokenness: she felt a loss of purpose.

She needed to figure out how to recover what the Triple Crown had taken away from her, but she knew she couldn't do it on her own. With Kase having done so much to bring her back, she hadn't wanted to disappoint him with her burdens. She understood the dangerous path, and wanted to keep him safe for as long as possible.

Lenia had turned to Cali for advice, and that's when the Unicorn Knight idea was born. Since Cali also wanted to get back at the leaders of the Triple Crown for using her, the thought of creating an entity that could do their dirty work for them was compelling.

As the Unicorn Knight, Lenia could do the things that were necessary and keep the dark emptiness she felt within the confines of the Unicorn

Knight's character, sealing herself off from guilt and remorse. It also allowed her to enjoy her days with Kase, and still be the woman that he'd fallen for.

"Nice work, Curtis!" Lenia yelled. "Keep it up!"

"Thank you, Your Highness!" Curtis yelled back.

Kase pulled himself over the edge and sat next to Lenia. Down below, Curtis leant against the rock wall, not attempting a climb yet.

"You're right," Lenia said. "It's getting a little annoying now."

"He'll likely get more creative with it," Kase said. "Just like his 'Twos' nicknames for me, he'll probably keep things fresh with yours. If only there were other variations of the Dandy Lion …"

Lenia chuckled. "That nickname is perfection." She hugged Kase's arm, and gently leant her head on his shoulder. "But it's reserved for me. I'm not ready to let anyone else call you that yet."

Kase leant his head on Lenia's. Although he was the self-appointed Langara Knight, Lenia shared more characteristics with the langaras than he did. She was beautiful, graceful, passionate, and fierce when she needed to be. She was loyal to her pack, but feared by everyone else. She killed out of survival, but did so with precision, confidence, and skill. She was a natural assassin.

Kase reflected on his own stature, and decided he needed to be more like a unicorn. Just as Turanus was a patient protector, Kase needed to be more of an observer, rather than an instrumental player in Cali and Lenia's dangerous game. He needed to understand their intentions without judging them too quickly. They needed his support now more than ever, and he couldn't let his own emotions cloud the bonds he shared with both of them.

He couldn't risk losing them again.

Lenia had shown him that she could handle herself well; he wasn't worried about her failing to reach her goals, or falling in combat. He was worried about the storm swirling inside of her. As much as he wanted to save her from her struggle, he didn't need to fight her battle *for* her; he needed to remain by her side and fight *with* her instead.

He reminded himself to be patient.

"Are we going to stay here to watch the sunset?" Kase asked. There were still a few hours before sundown, but the view they had over the trees was perfect.

"I'd love to, but we should head back soon," Lenia said. "I need to prep for Cali's next mission."

"Maybe tomorrow then?" Kase asked.

"Absolutely." Lenia squeezed Kase's arm, but Kase moved it around her shoulders instead. She adjusted her arms so they wrapped around his torso. "I don't think Curtis is going to make it up here anytime soon."

Kase peered over the edge. Curtis had sat on the ground, but he didn't seem hurt. "Should we do him a favour and end our training for the day?"

"Let's give him a few more minutes," Lenia said. She nestled her head into Kase's chest.

Lenia soon teleported Kase and Curtis back to the castle. They all cleaned themselves up, and then grabbed dinner with the rest of their crew. Aura had ventured in costume with Lenia to a market for groceries, so she prepared a few new cheesy dishes. It was nice to have more options, rather than being limited to what they could grow or hunt in the Kingdom of Moiras.

After dinner, Curtis went straight to bed. He was tired from a day of training, but it was the tea Aura made that helped put him to sleep. Aura and Cali had raised their concerns about Curtis' addiction to drinking, and he thought going to bed early would help with his cravings. It wasn't a permanent solution, but it was a nice crutch to help Curtis take the edge off.

Since there wasn't a need for Kase to drink Aura's sleep potion tea anymore, he had some free time until Cali's plan would involve his skillset. She had requested that he and Talen study in the castle library, to help familiarize Kase with the history of their kingdom.

Kase called the study time 'King Class.' Talen wasn't keen on the name, but she was excited to discuss the politics, decision-making, and power of King Michael. She focused on the similarities between their time and King Michael's, even though there were thousands of years in between.

"Did you complete your assigned reading?" Talen asked. She sat at an old, onyx-stained table across from Kase.

"Yes, Professor Sparwood," Kase said. He sat straight, hands clasped on the table in front of him. Talen stressed the importance of good posture, since keeping a proud chest and making oneself look larger was associated with dominance and power.

"Which competition did you find the most intriguing?" Talen asked.

King Michael had many journals, but the one Kase had finished reading was about the king's approach to unifying the realm after he'd obtained absolute power. With no one left to conquer, King Michael struggled to keep his loyal subjects from turning on one another. One way to keep their spirit alive was with a schedule of competitions that challenged their skills.

"I thought the World Warrior Federation was the most elaborate," Kase said. "It was pretty gruesome to read about the combat that occurred in front of fans, but with the king's ability to bring the fallen back to life, it made for some interesting storylines."

The World Warrior Federation was King Michael's favourite form of entertainment. It kept his warriors' killer instinct alive by forcing them to fight, but the crowds that it drew in added to the intensity of it all. He allowed warriors to insult each other, play to the crowd, and compete for a golden crown.

Some warriors played the part of the hero, winning over the crowd. Others played the part of the villain, and drew ire from the masses. According to his journal, seeing the crowd's reaction to bringing a villain back from the dead was one of King Michael's favourite twists.

"It was also the most lucrative competition," Talen said. "Warriors were paid very well; not just for winning in battle, but winning over the crowd. I thought it was interesting that he would schedule "Royal Wars" when there were too many favourites. With up to fifty warriors fighting each other in one battle, rather than the usual one-on-one style, it eliminated old favourites so that newcomers could rise. It's similar to how nature balances ecosystems between predators and prey."

Kase nodded, agreeing with Talen, but not really seeing the correlation. "What did you think about the Jester Joust?" He knew Talen was afraid of jesters, but was curious if she appreciated other components of the comedy competition. It wasn't just about clowns dressing up, but about telling jokes, acting out short stories, and singing parodies.

"Not my favourite, but it was also very popular," Talen said. "It sometimes drew stadium crowds like the World Warrior Federation."

"I tried thinking of a few jokes of my own," Kase admitted. "Would you like to hear one?"

Talen raised an eyebrow in intrigue. "Yes," she said.

Kase cleared his throat. "Why do they call it the Kingdom of Moiras? They should call it the Kingdom of More-Ahhs! Like, Ahh … a langara! Ahh … a black mamba! Ahh … a bird!"

Talen smirked, but didn't laugh. "I like how it plays to a particular audience," she said.

"I still need to work on my routine," Kase said. "That was my best joke. I hope one day I can write one so good that it actually makes you laugh."

"I tend to enjoy physical comedy more," Talen said.

"Noted," Kase said. "I think you'd be an excellent judge of the Jester Joust."

"It's important for leaders to keep a sense of humour," Talen noted. "Too often, their daily tasks are so serious, they can lose track of the lighter side of things. King Michael appreciated the arts, but I'm glad you also want to join in on the entertainment."

"I'll be a king for the people," Kase said. "The People's King."

Talen nodded. She made a note in her book. "What did you think about the Discovery Innovation Challenge?"

"I thought it was interesting in theory, but there weren't any good examples," Kase said.

The Discovery Innovation Challenge was to encourage new applications of magic. Competitors didn't necessarily need to prove their application would work, just argue theories and processes that could lead to success. It sounded like a lot of debating and report writing to Kase.

"King Michael's wizard abilities were extremely advanced due to the power of the doorway of life; therefore, it was difficult for applicants to be granted recognition in the Discovery Innovation Challenge," Talen said. "But

I found an interesting report about one of the winning entries that's consistent with his philosophy about adapting or dying." She wandered to a bookcase behind her and removed a thin notebook.

Talen flipped past the first few pages, then presented a diagram to Kase. It looked like a map with clouds and arrows on it. Kase waited for an explanation, rather than risk voicing any unintelligent questions. In one of their previous King Classes, Talen had taught him to use silence as a tool, rather than giving away his position on particular matters.

"This submission outlines the theory behind controlling weather patterns," Talen said. "Basically, it involves using wind control to move storm clouds to different areas, depending on what the wizard wants to use them for."

Kase nodded. A few confident ideas had already sparked. "Like if there was a drought, King Michael could have brought water to dry farmland," he said.

"Exactly," Talen said. "But since King Michael was a bit of a tyrant, he used weather magic for immoral reasons. Like bringing lightning to a region, and manipulating the bolts so that they struck structures he wanted to destroy, or people he wanted to kill."

"Weaponized storms?" Kase asked.

"He called it 'Dry Lightning,'" Talen said. "He didn't have to move an entire thunderstorm to an area: just a piece of it. The clouds were still electrically charged, but from the ground, the sky looked clear. He'd move these tiny lightning clouds over his target, and then direct the lightning using his magic. Like anything, it just took practice to master his precision."

Kase nodded. "It would take a lot of focus and power to be successful."

"But do you think you could do it too?" Talen asked. "In the event there was ever a teleporting wizard that you had to face in combat?"

The tightness in Kase's stomach returned. "She's not going to beat me again," he said defensively.

"Well, she's undefeated against you." Talen's words were true, but surprisingly painful. "I'm sure you don't want to hurt her, and I don't either, but mastering dry lightning could be a useful skill for any king. Would you like to try it?"

Kase smiled. "I guess adding a new skill couldn't hurt," he said. Talen's concerns forced Kase to think back over his battle with the Unicorn Knight.

He took a deep breath and stared at Talen. "I didn't have a chance to say this earlier, but thanks for having my back during our impromptu election. Cali, Aura, and Lenia made me feel alone in our kingdom, but you and Curtis give me confidence that we can all live in harmony someday."

"You're welcome." Talen smiled at Kase, which was a nice surprise. "I like it here, and even if things change a little bit, I want to ensure that we all stay together through it all. Should we take a break from studying, and go try some weather control?"

Kase and Talen left the library and exited the castle. Since the source of King Michael's power, and Kase's power, was the doorway of life, Talen thought it best to start their new journey there. Just like how Lenia could teleport all over the realm while holding her trident, but only had a small radius of teleportation when away from it, Talen thought Kase would have a seventy-two percent better chance of controlling the wind and thunderclouds while at the doorway of life.

By the time they made it to the giant stone pentagram embedded in the earth, the sun had completely set. Talen returned to the castle to grab some candles, but Kase sprawled himself out in the middle of the pentagram to begin his manipulation attempt. He closed his eyes, cleared his mind, and focused on his emotions to access his power.

It was easy for him to connect with the wind right away, since he had practice manipulating air currents from when Lenia was teaching him to be a wizard. With the power of the doorway of life, he was able to feel a more abundant wave of airflow; it was like the difference between feeling the flow of water from one bowl to another, and feeling the flow of an entire river. His power maximized his connection, and he felt like he was a part of the breeze. Even though he couldn't see well in the darkness, he picked a direction and was able to let his emotions take a ride on the flowing air.

When Talen returned, she read some notes from King Michael on the Discover Innovation Challenge submission. She mentioned tricks he'd had to find the right weather pattern, with the most important one being a focus on wind speed. Kase needed to feel the difference between wind speeds in order to locate the areas of low pressure and high pressure that facilitated storms. It was like tracking a wild animal through the wilderness, with each clue leading Kase closer to his desired target.

Kase spent almost an hour feeling the different air currents and patterns. Some winds swirled in a clockwise pattern, which were consistent with high-pressure areas in the region. The counter-clockwise patterns were consistent with low-pressure areas, which were a little more challenging to feel. But when he felt droplets in the air of some swirling winds, he knew he'd found a storm.

He didn't try to manipulate the speed of the wind around the rain clouds; instead, he tried to nudge its direction. King Michael had made some notes that the storm could be lost if there were drastic pressure changes, so Kase thought it best to focus on only one aspect for the night: bringing rain to the castle.

It took another hour, but Talen kept Kase company and helped to pass the time. She even left to grab a couple of umbrellas, which gave Kase encouragement that his weather control would be a success.

When a few drops landed on her arm, Talen jolted to her feet, opened the umbrellas, and gave one to Kase. "You did it!" she exclaimed. "Can you feel any lightning?"

Kase smiled proudly. "I don't think this is a thundercloud, but it is nice and refreshing," he said. The raindrops fell hard, but it was rewarding to hear the pitter-patter on his umbrella.

It was even more rewarding when he dropped his umbrella to the side, looked to the sky, and felt the cool water hit his cheeks. "Wooo!" Kase yelled.

"Wooo!" Talen joined. She, too, had dropped her umbrella, and was basking in the night rain.

"What are you two doing?" Lenia asked. Her trident was already ablaze when she appeared beside them, lighting their little party. She had her hood up to protect her from the rain.

"Weather control!" Talen yelled in triumph. She looked at Lenia, then at Kase. "Sorry, I got a little excited there."

"That's okay, Tal. I'm excited too." Kase turned to Lenia. "I moved this rain cloud using guidance from King Michael's notes. Care to celebrate with us?" He grabbed Lenia's hands and started to dance.

"Absolutely." Lenia dropped her hood and let the rainwater wash over her. "I have some exciting news too."

"Your mission was a success?" Talen asked.

"Yes!" Lenia continued to jump around in rhythmic excitement. "Which means that we can move on to the next phase." She hugged Kase and slowed the pace of their dance. "The Dandy Lion and the Unicorn Knight are about to make their debut together."

Kase suddenly felt a bigger storm brewing.

## CHAPTER 9

# Through The Fire, Through Whatever

"I thought it would be heavier," Kase said. He shook his head, but the helmet remained snug. He was also surprised how much he could see through the visor, even if it was purple.

"It's made of a magnesium alloy, which is a lot lighter than steel," Cali said. "It's not really designed to protect you against impact; it's meant to be a disguise." She dipped her fingertips back into her makeup container, and then applied it to Lenia's nose.

"The only time I've been hit is when you punched me in the face," Lenia added.

"Did you want to get me back?" Kase asked. He danced around a bit and shadow-boxed, but he didn't get the laughter he was looking for.

"It took me a couple of days to fix," Lenia said, referring to the broken glass that Kase had caused. "Maybe after I make your helmet, Dandy, we'll test it out."

"I'm getting my own helmet?" Kase asked. He could barely handle the nickname; he didn't want to wear a costume to match. It would be too embarrassing.

"Of course," Cali said. "But we need to decide on the right colour scheme. I prefer a silver helmet with a white mane, but Talen likes gold and red. Lenia wants you to complement the Unicorn Knight with a purple mask and black mane. Aura has the swing vote, but she hasn't decided yet."

"I'm sure she'll choose the dandiest option," Kase joked. He got a chuckle out of Lenia, but Cali only seemed upset at her movement. Cali quickly fixed her smudge.

"I think I'm done," Cali said. She turned to Kase. "Your turn."

Kase grabbed his wig and sat on the bed. He lifted his chest, practicing his good posture. Cali adjusted the wig first, and then slathered on Kase's makeup. She was less gentle than Talen, but just as efficient. Lenia went over the plan for their date one last time.

Spending time with Lenia was going to be the best part of the night, but the Unicorn Knight and the Dandy Lion were obligated to go on their first official mission together after that. Kase was relieved that there wasn't any murder in the plans, but the alternative reason wasn't much better: the mission involved the first steps to bring his father back to life.

Cali had reasoned that if their father had been involved in gathering the pieces of the doorway of life, he had likely met his demise searching for one of them. Since the group had recovered two of the pieces, and brought them to the Kingdom of Moiras, there were only two other pieces that their dad could have been involved in obtaining: the piece guarded by the Eidola, or the one on Jenim Island.

While studying her notes from Dom's journal, Cali had recognized that the excursion to Jenim Island was quite detailed compared to the rest. With many of the specific dangers identified, mostly in regards to the giants, the feeling Cali got was that their father had been making the necessary adjustments to finalize his trip. She had found a way to support her intuition with hard evidence.

The only known affiliates of the doorway of life were the leaders of the Triple Crown, along with a handful of their carefully-chosen task force. Thankfully Cali, Lenia, and Aura had decided that sneaking into the castle of the Triple Crown was too risky, even for a teleporting vigilante. With the new advances in surveillance sage mirrors, Lenia getting taken in a moving image was just as bad as getting captured. Although the cities held a similar risk, being inside the castle of the Triple Crown felt like they were pushing their luck.

Cali felt they would have an easier time on Jenim Island itself. There was only one portal gate available to access the island. The door opened in the office of an administrator, who would only let registered tourists enter and exit the island of the giants. Since all resources on the island were much larger than in the rest of the realm, the giants needed to keep the entrance secure so that their island wouldn't get pillaged. In response, the giants would not venture to the rest of the realm, where they could equally harm any natural resources that local ecosystems depended on.

But things worked differently for a teleporting vigilante.

Since Lenia had been on Jenim Island before, she could use her trident to teleport to the same locations. Cali noted that the administrator's office would have a record of admission for travellers from the realm to the island. All Lenia needed to do was teleport to the office after it closed, search the logbooks for the correct date, and see who had travelled during that time. It took a few trips for Lenia to find the right entry. Their father had travelled to Jenim Island with four others, but only three of them had returned.

"All done," Cali said. "I have to admit, I feel like I'm getting better at this."

"You look quite handsome, my dear," Lenia said in an old woman's voice.

"Am I as beautiful as the day we met?" Kase returned in an old voice of his own.

"Beautiful? No. Dorky? Yes!" Lenia chuckled.

Cali smiled. "You're both still cute," she said. "Stay safe, and don't get caught." She tapped her heart twice, kissed her lips, and pointed to the sky. Kase was proud that they all still had their team salute, even if they operated under a leadership structure now.

Lenia grabbed her trident, and then teleported Kase to Kimroad. Like Turanus, Lenia found secluded places to arrive, but she didn't like dark alleys. Since surveillance sage mirrors always pointed down, she liked to teleport to rooftops. She had a few favourites, knowing that they could start their trip undetected.

The building she chose this time was close to the popular Domini Promenade. Although not on the main strip, the business of this building boasted premium modern furniture creations. Kase was interested in shopping there, but there was no need for them to purchase items when their castle was already furnished.

Lenia peeked over the parapet, and then gave a reassuring nod. She tucked her trident against the short wall, which was well-covered because of the darkness, and then teleported Kase down to some brush behind the building. They both crouched down and hobbled to the street, making their way to their first destination.

They shuffled down a few busy streets before finding the bakery they were looking for. A bell above the shop door rang upon entry, and a young maiden perked up to see some late-night customers. Kase and Lenia both toddled towards the display and picked out a couple of treats.

"I'll take the blue one," Lenia said. Her shaking finger, in line with her costume, pointed to a plump cupcake with unicorn icing.

"I'll take the pink," Kase mimicked. He brought his arms up slowly, patting his shirt pockets, then his pants. "Now where is my wallet?" He played the part of a forgetful old man perfectly, but knew exactly where his change was kept.

"It's my turn to pay, dear," Lenia said. "We get to spoil each other on our anniversary."

"Oh, how sweet," the shopkeeper said. "How many years have you two been married?"

Lenia pinched her lips and smiled, which made Kase almost start to laugh. He hadn't practiced his old man laugh, so he didn't want to do anything to blow their cover.

"Fifty-five years," Lenia croaked.

"Fives," Kase said. "I'm her dandelion, and she's my little fireball."

Lenia turned away, and Kase noticed her shoulders hitch. He smiled proudly, knowing he'd made her laugh.

"You two are adorable," the maiden said. "Allow me to treat you both tonight. I've got these for you." She handed the treats to Lenia without accepting payment.

Kase noticed Lenia's shoulders still shrugging. "Bless your little heart," he said, accepting the gift from the shopkeeper instead. He stuck his elbow out for Lenia to grab. She leant into him as they made their way out of the shop. The bell chimed on their way out.

After a few more steps, Lenia burst into laughter. "That was too good," she said. She wrapped her arms around Kase's torso.

There was no one in earshot of the couple. "We should pretend it's our fifty-fifth anniversary more often," Kase said in his normal voice. "People are so nice!"

Lenia led Kase to a coffee shop, where they picked up some hot cocoa. The opportunity for them to do their anniversary routine didn't come up again, but everyone still presumed they were an old couple. They hobbled through the main street, blending in with the crowd, before they found a clean park bench to sit on. The bench overlooked a pond and flower garden, but they still had a view of the main street, in case someone tried to sneak up on them.

Kase found it difficult to eat his cupcake. He didn't want any icing to mix with his makeup, and the elongated nose Cali had given him kept getting in the way. Lenia didn't seem to care, and just went for it. She took big bites, but ended up with icing all over her lips, cheeks, and nose.

"You have a little something on your …" Kase pointed to his own face, and outlined a giant circle.

Lenia batted her eyelashes. "Can you get it for me?"

Kase brushed Lenia's hair to the side, curling the edge around her ear. She usually wore her hair in a braid, but it needed to be tucked under her white wig. The white hair was pinned up, but there were still a few wisps that escaped. Kase used his thumb to clear some of the icing from Lenia's cheek.

Lenia closed her eyes. "Use your lips," she said.

Kase hesitated. "Last time we did this, I got caught with the kiss of death," he said. "You're not going to pull that out again, are you?"

Lenia smiled. "That's for special occasions," she said. "But that doesn't mean we can't have other named kisses." She placed her arms around Kase's shoulders and pulled him closer.

Kase didn't have time to clear any icing away. Lenia kissed him hard, their noses scraping each other's makeup. Kase closed his eyes, wrapping his arms around her waist.

A loud bang interrupted them.

Lenia broke the kiss and looked down main street. In the distance, a cloud of smoke rose above a blaze of fire. Bricks had launched into the air by the force of the blast. Everyone in town seemed to stop what they were doing, watching the chaos cautiously.

Lenia's lips curled up. "Explosion kiss."

"It looks like a dragonmite explosion," Kase said. The flames seemed too big to be a single building fire, and the billow of smoke looked like a tiny mushroom. He was reminded of the time he'd watched Mardious Hood use dragonmite to get past the dragon's den on Skyland. Golden dragon parts had flown all over the place.

"Considering the source, it seems kind of odd," Lenia said. "That part of town is a rich residential area; made up of mansions and gated communities. I doubt anyone there is experimenting with enough dragonmite to cause that kind of destruction."

"Should the Unicorn Knight and her trusty sidekick go investigate?" Kase suggested.

Lenia giggled. "Trusty sidekick?"

Kase didn't want to say it, but she had baited him into it. "Her Dandy Lion." He kept his tone overly-sarcastic.

Lenia brought her nose to touch Kase's. "Not tonight," she said. "They have more important things to do." They kissed again, but this one didn't have a name.

Kase and Lenia enjoyed their time together on the bench. They sipped their hot chocolate and watched the main street crowd. Some of them pointed to the site of the explosion, took images with their sage mirrors, and scrolled through content on their reflective devices. Other members of the crowd quickly shifted back to their normal business, not caring about the explosion in another part of the city.

They enjoyed their date for as long as possible before starting on the business portion of their trip. Once in range of her trident again, Lenia teleported it and Kase to the royal cemetery near the castle of the Triple Crown. Buried in one of the plots was their target. But even on such an important mission,

Kase couldn't help but look around at other tombstones.

"I think my grandparents are buried here," Kase said.

"Where?" Lenia asked. She looked around the dark cemetery, but it was difficult to see beyond the plot they were on.

"I don't know exactly, but it would make sense for them to be here," Kase said. "My dad never took me and Cali to visit the gravesite. I wanted to visit it when I became a High Guardian. It just … never happened."

"Well, my sweet Dandy Lion, we should get this over quick so we can look around," Lenia said.

Kase nodded, and then closed his eyes. He searched the graveyard for a connection with a ground-dweller. He easily felt a family of rats nearby in an underground den, and used his powers of animal control to force them to burrow to his location.

When Lenia, Cali, and Kase made the plan, Cali had suggested getting just a piece of a corpse, rather than bringing the whole coffin to the surface. If a rodent could get into the coffin underground, remove a finger bone from the dead body, and bring it to the surface, it would be a lot easier, quieter, and safer to transport.

Since Kase had brought animals back to life from small bones, it seemed plausible for him to do the same with a warrior. He also liked the idea, because then he wouldn't have to kill anyone at the gravesite. He'd take the fragment of their target's body, teleport back to their kingdom, and set the stage for their interrogation as a team.

Kase manipulated one of the rats to nibble through the wooden casket, and then crawl into the coffin. He liked the rat's forefeet, because he could feel different shapes through their long appendages. He located the curled fingers of their target, and sawed off one of the bones using the rat's sharp teeth. The rat climbed back into its tunnel, and then burrowed to the surface. It presented Kase with the treasure.

"Well done," Lenia said. She took a few cautious steps back from the rat.

"That was the easiest recovery I've made yet," Kase said. He studied the old bone before putting it into his pocket. He thought about his grandparents.

"Do you think it would be okay if I brought my grandparents back to life?"

Lenia tilted her head to the side. "Would it make you happy?"

"I've never met them, but they're both an inspiration to me," Kase admitted. "Since they're both warriors, they'd really add another level to our training sessions. Learning from the notes my father made is one thing, but in-person sparring lessons from both of them would be amazing."

Lenia smiled. "You don't have to sell me," she said. "If it makes you happy, then we should definitely try it. Cali might need some convincing, since she has precise plans for who we should be bringing back, but I believe in you." She grabbed Kase's hand and squeezed it tight.

Kase liked the support, even if disagreements had led to this moment. "Thank you." He squeezed her hand back. "Sugar crawl, explosion kiss, and bringing my grandparents back from the dead; this is a classic Lenia and Kase date."

Lenia chuckled. "You have been on absolute fire tonight!" She fell into his arms and laughed again.

Kase laughed too. He was happy that this audience liked his jokes.

With her trident in hand, Lenia was able to scan tombstones faster than Kase. They split up and took different rows, but Kase felt safe in the darkness. He knew they were alone, and there were no surveillance mirrors to capture images of them. It was getting late though, and he wanted to find his grandparents soon so that he and Lenia could go home.

While studying a clean tombstone with fresh flowers at its base, he was suddenly teleported to a mossy tombstone. A hand had swiped through the name on the front, revealing Helena Garrick's name. Beside her grave was a matching tombstone, with Roman Garrick's name cleared away.

Lenia moved a few steps away, and Kase brought his new rat friends to the graves. He split the group in two, and quickly manipulated them so they dug down at the same rate. The rats chewed through the coffins, gathered a finger bone from each, and then returned. Kase was sure to get an index finger from his grandfather and a pinkie finger from his grandmother, in order to distinguish between the two.

After returning the rats to their den, Lenia teleported Kase back to their kingdom. When they arrived, they were shocked to see Cali resting on their bed, glued to her sage mirror.

Cali's eyes widened when she noticed them, but she quickly pivoted and sat on the edge of the bed. Her hand rested over her heart. "I'm glad you two are okay."

"Everything went according to plan," Lenia said. "We—"

"There was news of a terrible explosion in Kimroad," Cali said. "Everyone is blaming the Unicorn Knight." She turned her sage mirror to Kase and Lenia, pointing to the article she was reading.

"'No one is safe from the Unicorn Knight,'" Lenia read. She turned to Kase. "But that wasn't me."

"No, but it could be a copycat," Cali said. "I've been trying to find out who the victims of the blast were, but no names have been released yet. I have a feeling that someone is using your celebrity in order to get away with their own wrongdoing. The Triple Crown comes to mind."

"You think the Triple Crown is behind this?" Kase asked.

"They're behind everything," Lenia said. "They play with people's lives as if they don't have value. They get what they want while the realm suffers. This time, the wealthy must have done something to challenge their power."

Cali rubbed her forehead. "This is starting to get way more complicated than I could have imagined. We need help to pivot and adapt a new strategy. You said everything went to plan?"

Kase reached into his pocket and displayed the bone of their target. "Do we want to interrogate her tonight?" he asked.

"We can wait until morning." Cali stood from the bed and tucked her sage mirror away. "I'm tired, and I need to clear my mind a little bit before we head to the next stage. Good work, though." She patted Kase on the shoulder as she moved past him to the door.

Kase turned towards his sister. "I also recovered these," Kase said. He reached into his other pocket and pulled out the other two bones.

Cali turned, her eyebrow raised. She didn't have to ask. King Michael would have been proud of her power move.

"Roman and Helena Garrick," Kase said. "Do you think they could help?"

Cali softened.  "I hadn't considered them before, but they both fought against Mardious Hood." She tapped her chin again. "We don't really know them, though, do we?"

"They're family," Kase said.

"Exactly," Cali said. "It makes them harder to eliminate if they go rogue. If they're a threat to our security, are you willing to get rid of them?"

Kase scratched his head. He hadn't even brought them back to life yet, and Cali was already talking about killing them. He'd been so focused on Lenia; he wondered how he missed his sister becoming so ruthless too.

"Of course," Lenia said. She wrapped her arm around Kase. "If it turns out that now is not the right time to bring them back, we'll just try again in the future. But it's important to see what they're like, especially if they're half the warriors that you both have claimed them to be."

Kase nodded, and then shrugged at his sister. Lenia was right. He could bring his grandparents back at any time. It didn't matter when, or how many times they died between now and the perfect time, but at least he had control over the situation. Although he was more optimistic about what they would be like, he was trying to adapt to the new way of thinking that Cali and Lenia displayed.

Cali kept tilting her head back and forth, as if she was weighing the options in her mind.

"Let's decide tomorrow," Lenia said. She disengaged from Kase. "I need to get cleaned up. Would you like to join me?" She tossed her wig to the floor and peeled off the old woman's garb she was wearing.

Cali covered her eyes. "Yes, tomorrow," she said. "Have a good night." She crept out of the room and closed the door.

Kase watched Lenia as she walked away. Her bare back was soft and smooth, unlike the wrinkly makeup that covered her neck and chin. Lenia reached up and pulled the pins out of her hair, letting it fall across her shoulders.

She shook it out and combed through it with her hands.

Kase shoved the bones he was holding back into his pockets, and then removed his wig and clothes. The past could wait until tomorrow. He wanted to focus on how wonderful tonight was.

# CHAPTER 10

# Leader Of The Pack

Curtis twisted the key a few more times, ensuring the grease inside the shackles properly lubricated the lock. The steel chains were rusted, but they'd hold strong. At least there weren't any skeletons down in the dungeons anymore; they had made Curtis nervous.

"Do you know what this warrior looks like?" Curtis asked.

"Why, are you looking for a date?" Kase replied. He swung the steel gate of the cell open and closed, to work the same lubricant into the hinges.

Curtis chuckled. "I'm not ready for that yet, Too Funny. I'm concerned with her size. Do you think we can both take her?"

The only thing Kase knew about their prisoner-to-be was that she had worked on a Triple Crown task force. "You've been training hard the last few days, so I bet you can take her all on your own," he said.

"Thanks for the vote of confidence, but I'd rather not face her one-on-one," Curtis said. "Maybe we should bring your grandparents back first. I have a feeling they'll be on our side, anyway."

Kase stopped swinging the door. The hinges barely made a sound anymore. "Our side?" he asked.

"If your grandparents join you, me, and Talen, maybe we can have a little more influence on the others' plans," Curtis said. "Maybe get things back to the way they used to be."

Kase realized he hadn't had any alone time with Curtis since the trial by combat. He'd been so focused on abiding by Cali's rules, trying to learn more about Lenia's burden, and spending time reflecting on his King Lessons that he hadn't considered how Curtis felt about the whole ordeal. "Are you still struggling with your sobriety?"

Curtis shook his head. "No ... well, yes, but not like that," he said. "The addiction is real; I didn't realize how strong the impulse was until I stopped. I'm not sure I could stick to it on my own, so I'm thankful for the support from everyone. It was depressing to look in the mirror and see what I'd become, so I'm glad that's changed. Plus, I don't mind helping out more. One of the reasons I drank so much is because I felt removed from everyone else's schedule. I like being needed."

"I'm sorry you felt that way," Kase said.

Curtis dropped the shackles. "Don't be," he said. "It's not your fault. With Aura's help, I've learned to take responsibility for my addiction, and I can work hard to get past it. But I hope the change in leadership here isn't going to ruin the good things that we have. Cali, Aura, and Lenia might want to get back to the rest of the realm, but I don't. I like it here in our kingdom."

Kase nodded. "I like it here too, but I want us all to be happy."

"That's a nice sentiment," Curtis said. "The others have talked about this kingdom being a prison, but it's the rest of the realm that feels confining to me. I spent too long living out the dreams of the Triple Crown, when I should have taken more time figuring out my own. I also think Cali is poking the beast, and it's only a matter of time before it bites back. If we can't help her see that, maybe your grandparents can?"

Kase stared at the ground. They were about to bring someone back to help them find the man Cali had looked up to. Cali had admitted she needed help, but would Dom help her see what Curtis wanted her to see? How could they guarantee that they were making the safest, smartest decisions?

"It couldn't hurt," Kase admitted. "For now, let's focus on our task at hand. We can't underestimate this warrior. The only way to succeed is together." He tapped his heart twice, kissed his fingers, and pointed to the sky.

Curtis followed suit.

Since the cell was ready, they decided to track down Cali and Lenia. The small prison was a circle of cells, with a wide staircase in the centre.

Light shone down the stairs, but that was the only glimpse of the outside world.

After searching the kitchen and grabbing a snack, Kase and Curtis found Cali and Lenia in the library. Talen and Aura were there too, reading some fiction books for fun; they didn't need to be part of the interrogation. After finishing her own reading, Lenia teleported Kase, Curtis, and Cali back to the prison.

Curtis and Kase entered the cell they had cleaned while Cali locked the gate behind them. She remained on the outside with Lenia, and had taken a step back from the bars. Other than that, she didn't let her nervousness show. She nodded for Kase to begin.

Kase pulled the bone fragment of their target from his pocket. He knelt on the ground, placed the bone gently on the soft dirt, and closed his eyes. He quickly found the connection he was looking for.

Jem patted the handkerchief that Zuke—no, Mardious— laid across her lap.

"Wine?" Mardious asked.

"Please." Jem placed her fingers around the stem of the glass while Mardious poured. She took a quick sip once he finished.

"Do you like it?" Mardious asked. "It's from my hometown." He placed the cork back in the bottle.

"It's delicious," Jem said. "I've never had wine from the Badlands before. Are you not having any?"

"No, I'm afraid this wine isn't something I want in my system," Mardious said. He wiggled his gloved fingers. An illusion of his former lover, Amelia, appeared beside him at the head of the table. Her black hair touched her bare shoulders, and a medal around her neck dangled over her red dress.

Jem felt her chest get heavy. She tried to move her hand to her heart, but she couldn't lift it up. It was like her body was melting away, pulling her deeper into the seat of her chair. She thought she might slide off, but she didn't move.

"It's too bad that you saw me." Amelia's blue eyes sparkled. "You were a real asset to our cause."

Mardious sat down. He lifted his handkerchief above his mouth, holding it up like a mask, and then placed it gently on his lap. "I'm sorry for misleading you," he said. His dark eyes glared at Jem. "One woman already has my heart, and I am doing everything it takes to bring her back. I cannot risk having my real identity revealed."

Jem couldn't breathe. She felt like she was going to sleep, but she couldn't shut her eyes.

"We're halfway there, babe," Amelia said. She placed her hand on Mardious' shoulder.

Mardious looked back at her lovingly. His glove touched the diamond protruding from Amelia's finger. The illusion disappeared.

Kase entered the pool of magma. He felt the liquid melt his skin, crawl down his throat, and seep into his veins. He felt like screaming, but his throat burned too much. He expected the pain to subside soon, but the magma lingered longer than normal. It was the most excruciating feeling he'd ever experienced, but it wouldn't stop. He wished for it to end.

Finally, he felt the dirt of the prison cell beneath his knees. He collapsed and rolled around on the ground. The pain didn't seem to want to escape his memory.

"Oh, my," Curtis said.

Jem shrieked. She sat up and covered her naked body. "What is this?" she asked.

Kase crawled to the side of the cell. He wanted to stand, but he needed to take a few breaths. He felt exhausted.

"Go grab a robe," Cali said to Lenia, who disappeared right away.

"What happened?" Jem started to shake. "Is this some kind of sick joke?"

"It's okay," Curtis said. He had stretched his arms out, but remained a few steps away. "We brought you back from the dead. I understand what you're going through, but please try to remain calm."

"What do you mean? I didn't die," Jem said.

"Mardious Hood poisoned you," Kase said. "He implied that you had figured out his identity. He didn't need you messing up his grand scheme, so he treated your life as if it was worthless." He looked at Cali, but it didn't seem like his sister understood what he was trying to show her.

"You've been dead for over a decade," Cali said. Her arms were crossed and she glared at Jem. "If you don't answer our questions, you'll return to the grave."

Jem stared back at Cali, then looked at Kase. Her attention was only diverted by Lenia when she returned. Lenia held a green robe by its collar. She passed it to Curtis through the bars of the cell.

"Allow me," Curtis said. He draped the robe over Jem's shoulders. She tried to cover herself while she slipped her arms in, and then quickly tied the robe around her waist. Curtis and Kase respected her privacy.

"What would you like to know?" Jem asked. She seemed calm and collected, now that she had something to wear. Curtis and Kase looked to Cali for instructions, but she didn't give any indication that they should restrain their prisoner.

"We understand that you travelled to Jenim Island to recover an artefact," Cali said. "We're looking for a member of that team."

Jem shrugged. "Which time? I was a Triple Crown ambassador. I travelled to Jenim Island often to discuss relations with the giants and give them gifts. I also received many artefacts as tokens of peace."

Lenia covered her mouth and whispered something to Cali.

Cali nodded. "The trip I'm referring to wasn't envoy related," Cali said. "It was off the books, organized by Sheese Lenon."

"Who?" Jem asked.

"Sheese Lenon," Cali repeated.

"Hmm … I don't think I know who you're referring to," Jem said. She looked at Curtis and Kase with a smile. "Maybe if I had something to eat, my memory might come back to me."

"Lock her in," Cali huffed.

Curtis nodded. Kase stood up to help, but hoped Curtis would take the lead; he was still weak. Instead of wrestling Jem, Curtis gently grabbed her wrist. He walked her to the back wall, without any fuss from his prisoner, and locked Jem into place. Jem didn't seem to mind, and smiled at Curtis again.

"I'm only going to ask you one more time," Cali said. "Where is—"

"I don't think I'm going to answer any of your questions until I get something to eat," Jem said. "I'd like a prime rib, medium rare, with mashed potatoes and asparagus. Red wine to drink, but hold the poison." She winked at Kase.

"If you don't talk, we're going to—" Cali started.

"I don't think you're going to do anything," Jem said. "It looks like your wizard went to a lot of trouble to bring me here. Plus, this gentle giant doesn't seem like he's willing to cause any harm. They don't even have any weapons with them."

Lenia teleported into the cell, and slammed the base of her trident into the ground. Flames sparked around the prongs. "I have a weapon," she sneered. "Would you like to see what it could do?"

"Now we're talking." Jem smiled. "But pain doesn't equal torture. If you're trying to intimidate me, you should have started with the Baroness Technique. From how this is going, I can tell none of you have any experience with interrogation."

"Fine, you win," Cali said. "Let's see how hungry and thirsty you get while left alone here. Regroup."

Lenia teleported Kase, Curtis, and Cali back to the library. Cali started pacing instantly.

"She's such a liar!" Cali shouted towards the ground. She squeezed her fists as she kept pacing.

"What was she lying about?" Curtis asked. "I actually found her quite pleasant."

"We could tell," Lenia snapped. She looked at Kase, and he could tell she wasn't as mad as Cali. She softened and shrugged, then tilted her head towards Cali. Kase nodded back.

"She's smarter than we thought, but we'll get to her, Cali." Kase smiled at his sister, but she wasn't looking.

"We shouldn't have given her the robe," Cali said. She hit her forehead with her closed fist. "Ugh, I'm so stupid. Now she's testing us with dinner and wine. I think she's trying to figure out where we're holding her."

"What's the Baroness Technique?" Curtis asked. "I've never heard of interrogation methods having names like that."

"She might have made that up too," Cali said. She stopped pacing and looked at Talen, who was sitting in the corner, book in her lap. "Talen, have you heard of that interrogation method?"

"No," Talen said. "But the only examples I've read about are from this library. It's possible that the Triple Crown has different methods, names, and training."

"Is there any other place we can go to find those methods?" Lenia asked. "Or should we actually try to torture her? King Michael did have some crazy contraptions in his books."

"She's not afraid of us right now," Cali said. "We need to get that fear back; then we can use those methods to convince her to talk."

"What if we feed her to Maxim?" Curtis suggested. "That would be torture to me."

Cali took a deep breath, and then tapped her chin. She seemed to be thinking about more possibilities.

Kase felt the bones in his pocket.

"What if we bring back our grandparents?" Kase asked. "Jem would likely know of Roman and Helena Garrick. Plus, they might be familiar with the interrogation techniques that are used by the Triple Crown. Maybe they could help?"

Cali looked back towards Talen and Aura. She tilted her head again, and then nodded at Kase. "I like that idea, brother," she said. "Our grandfather was feared by many criminals in the realm, and Jem would likely know of his notoriety. If interrogating Jem leads to recovering the body of our father, I think Roman would be of great value to us."

Kase felt his energy return. Knowing that he could finally bring his grandparents back gave him hope that he could help his sister adapt to a new ideology; one that would involve less murder. Maybe he had a voice in this new hierarchy after all.

The group quickly adapted a new plan. Since bringing people back from the dead using a bone fragment led to nudity, Kase and Lenia gathered some warrior uniforms to make his grandparents comfortable. The rest of the group focused on a plan to make them feel welcome.

Instead of starting in a dungeon, they moved outside to the grassy fields. Maxim even joined in on the event, since Kase was proud of his connection with her. He was excited to show his grandfather how great he'd become in his own right. He also wanted Lenia to show off her warrior skills to them.

When everything was laid out, Lenia, Curtis, and Cali gathered around Kase. The sunshine was warm on Kase's skin as he closed his eyes and searched for his connection. He was a little nervous about feeling the pain of bringing someone back to life for the second time that day, but his excitement gave him energy.

He already knew how his grandfather had died, so the location he was taken to was familiar.

Roman charged at the Badlands army. He swung his sword as hard as he could, aiming at the head of the closest thug. As soon as his blade touched the black helmet, the warrior disappeared.

With nothing to stop his swing, Roman almost fell over, but he regained his balance. He sliced at the next fighter, but that warrior disappeared as well. Roman stood tall and stared out over the masked army. He noticed that none of them had eyes, or any distinguishing features. There was only darkness through the visors of black masks.

He looked beyond the rows of poised soldiers ready to fight. Mardious Hood was at the back of the crowd, overlooking the mayhem from his perch on the short hill. His fingers fluttered in the air, but no one else moved. Not even Roman's slain wife, who lay at the feet of the madman.

Roman reached out and poked one of the warriors, instead of swinging his sword. The soldier disappeared.

The army was an illusion, but what else wasn't real? Was his wife really dead? He felt the hope rise in his chest, but he quickly pushed it down. It seemed too good to be true.

He stared at his wife as he climbed the grassy hill. He felt the breeze that flowed across the Pink Lakes, over the short beach, and around the surrounding hills. It smelled like rotten fish, but that didn't bother Roman. He had only one concern.

He was nearly to the top of the hill. He saw his wife's necklace dangling outside of her uniform. It dripped with blood from her slashed throat. Her skin was dirty, her hair was ruffled, and her eyes were wide open. There were too many intricate details for her to be an illusion.

Roman felt his chest tighten.

He'd sworn an oath to Helena, beyond their marriage vows, to fight to the death with her. They had protected the realm for years, and she had led a noble life. But it was all over now. He didn't blame her for her bravery, and he couldn't blame himself for eventually falling at the hands of a notorious madman.

But part of him still felt like recent events could have been avoided.

When Roman reached the top of the hill, Mardious appeared ready for a fight. He blew a potion into the air and quickly fluttered his fingers. For Roman, there was no battle left. He knelt down to hold his wife in his arms one last time. He felt tears run down his cheeks.

"Together, forever," Roman whispered to her. He took a deep breath, and then looked up at her killer.

Mardious' eyes were filled with hate. Roman knew of Mardious' background, and some of the things that had led to their encounter on this hill. Roman regretted some of the consequences of his actions, and wondered if his ignorance had led to this fateful day. He hoped that future generations wouldn't have to suffer because of his mistakes with Mardious Hood.

"I'm sorry," he said.

Suddenly, everything became amplified. The sunshine was brighter, the lakes were pinker, and the sky was bluer. An aura hung around Mardious' body, radiating a powerful energy that seemed to transfer to the sword he was wielding.

Mardious drove the sword into Roman's chest.

The pool of magma appeared. Kase went through the physical and emotional toll that came with bringing something back to life. He thought

Jem had been the most excruciating return he'd ever experienced, but this time seemed ten times worse. It seemed like it wouldn't ever stop.

When Kase felt the ground underneath him again, he collapsed and rolled onto his back. He closed his eyes, trying to forget about the pain. He heard something move near his feet. He was so exhausted that he couldn't even roll over.

"Good afternoon, Roman Garrick," Cali said. "I'm sure you have a lot of questions right now, but we're here to answer them for you. There's a warrior uniform beside you. Please make yourself comfortable."

Kase focused on his breathing. He was trying to slow his heartbeat, so that he could gain the energy he needed to meet his grandfather. It was important for him to make a good first impression on the warrior that he had looked up to for so long.

He wondered why bringing Roman back to life had taken such a toll on his body. Why was it getting harder? Were his emotions getting the best of him? Was there a price to pay for bringing too many people back? He opened his eyes. Roman's shoulders were so broad, his arms were so large, and his legs were so powerful, that it seemed like his muscles somehow had muscles.

"Where am I?" Roman asked. He stood in only his undergarments. He held up his uniform, but tossed it back to the ground. It was too small.

"This is the Kingdom of Moiras," Cali said. She opened her arms wide. "It's a part of the realm that's protected by magic, because it holds an artefact that grants the power of life. Your grandson, Kase, used this power to bring you back from the dead." Cali gestured towards Kase.

Kase stood, using every ounce of strength he had to stand tall. He covered his heart, and felt the rush of energy he needed. "Welcome back, grandfather," he said.

Roman picked up the sword they had provided along with the uniform. The golden handle looked small in Roman's bear-like hands. "I don't have a grandson," he said. "Especially one who's a wizard." He unsheathed the sword and swung it towards Kase's neck. He stopped when the point was inches from Kase's skin.

Kase didn't move. He wanted to show strength, honour, and poise. He also wanted to remain calm, since most people he brought back to life were often confused.

"You also have a granddaughter," Cali said. "My name is Cali Garrick. Kase and I are the children of your son, Dominic."

Roman turned his attention back to Cali, but kept his sword near Kase's neck. "Where is Dominic?" he asked.

"He died almost ten years after you did," Cali said. "We want to bring him back too, but in order to do that, we need to find where he was buried. That's how Kase's power works."

Roman looked back to Kase. "You don't look like Dominic," he said. "You can't fool me, wizard."

Not looking like his father felt like a compliment to Kase. "What if we duelled?" Kase asked. "A warrior can tell a lot about another warrior during battle. Wouldn't a swordfight prove to you that I am your descendant?"

Roman lowered his sword and looked Kase up and down. "*You're* challenging me?"

Kase stared back, trying to match the confidence of his grandfather. He nodded slightly.

"Grab your sword." Roman smirked.

Kase looked to Lenia, who couldn't hide her smile. She disappeared, but teleported back a few seconds later. She held Kase's shield and sword from her battle with him.

Kase accepted his sword. "I don't need that," he said, pushing the shield away.

"Interesting choice," Roman said. "Not worried about protection? Especially without armour?"

Kase gripped his sword with both hands. He'd need all the leverage he could get, especially when working from a defensive position. He was worried about not being able to block a strike from such a stronger warrior. "Would you like it?" he asked.

"I don't need it either," Roman said. He also gripped his sword with both hands. "Even my uniform would be too restrictive." He smiled as he got into his battle stance.

Kase took a few steps away from his grandfather, to give him a wider berth. Roman didn't move, so Kase circled his adversary like a shark in the water. He needed to stay fast, both when on the defensive and the offensive. His grandfather had too much of an advantage if the space between them were to be cut too close, because of the leverage he could apply as the physically bigger warrior.

Roman pivoted, but did not strike. He kept his sword steady, angled towards Kase. It felt to Kase like his grandfather was waiting for him to make the first move. According to the journal that Kase had read as a young man, patience was necessary in battle. The lessons that Dom had transcribed from Roman Garrick started flooding Kase's mind.

Kase took note of his surroundings. They were in an open, level field with no glaring obstacles or advantages within the terrain. Cali, Lenia, and Curtis were clear of the battle, and Maxim was taking a nap well behind them. The sunshine felt warm, but the gentle breeze carried away any scorching heat. It was a great afternoon for sparring.

"Let's go, Kase!" Lenia cheered on.

Kase stepped forwards and swung his sword at Roman's. He didn't try to strike Roman, but aimed for his blade instead. Roman easily deflected the blow, forcing Kase's sword in the opposite direction. Kase turned quickly to circle his target the other way, staying light on his feet in the process.

Roman stayed patient. He continued to track Kase with his blade, showing no urgency to attack. Kase swung his sword again, using his hips to gain more power and speed. Roman deflected it, but Kase had anticipated another easy defensive slide. Kase swung two more times, changing his angle on each slice, but Roman's defense seemed effortless. Kase backed off again.

"You generate considerable power for your size," Roman said. "But is that all you've got?"

Kase raised an eyebrow, but he didn't lose his focus and he didn't stop moving. He wondered if his grandfather was baiting him into making an emotional mistake. Since Roman had a physical advantage, Kase wondered if his strategy was similar to when he'd fought Lenia. Was Roman trying to tire Kase out, waiting for fatigue to set in before going on the offensive?

"Just trying to not get too dizzy," Kase quipped, seeing as he was moving around in circles.

"Good strategy," Roman said. He took a few steps in Kase's direction, angling for an intercept.

Kase pivoted the other way, but Roman was already committed to an attack. Roman swung his sword, missing Kase completely. Even with Kase moving backwards, Roman was able to close the gap between them. Roman swung his sword again, forcing Kase to deflect it. Roman's strength was considerable, but blocking the first blow made Kase feel like he could manage it.

Kase tried to get away, but Roman kept pushing forwards. Strike after strike was blocked and parried, until Roman slammed the edge of his blade into the hilt of Kase's sword. Roman twisted his weapon so that it forced Kase's sword flat to the ground, and then stepped on the thickest part of the blade. Kase's arms were exposed, so Roman lifted his sword higher, and swung at Kase's wrists.

From pure instinct, Kase let go of his sword so his hands wouldn't get chopped off. He fell to the side, but placed his palm on the grass. As Roman's sword missed, Kase shifted his weight into his supporting arm, and kicked Roman in the stomach with both feet.

Roman was forced back, freeing Kase's sword. As Roman stumbled, his blade caught Kase's exposed shoulder, slicing through the uniform. It was just a scratch, but the blow stung nonetheless. Kase quickly grabbed his sword, and jumped back so that he could regain his composure.

"Nice work, Two Kicks!" Cutis yelled.

Kase tapped his shoulder, just to make sure the cut wasn't deep. He thought about healing himself, but didn't want to gain an unfair advantage. He had too much respect for his grandfather to use any magic during the fight.

"Thought I had you." Roman smirked.

"I'm not that easy," Kase said. He didn't waste any time, and stepped up his aggression. He knew the only way to beat power was with speed and precision, so he worked fast this time. With a few different combinations, Kase was able to keep away from Roman, but still inflict a slash on his grandfather's shoulder. Now they both had matching stingers.

"Yes!" Lenia cheered, but Roman didn't even flinch.

Kase and Roman continued to spar, but the intensity had ramped up considerably. Roman continued to swing his sword powerfully, but failed to deal any blows. Kase, on the other hand, was so quick on his feet that he was able to dodge Roman's attacks and still land a few more stingers. With Roman not wearing a uniform, it was easy to see where he'd been hit. His body was dripping with blood after Kase had carved him up.

After spinning away from an uppercut swing, Kase delivered a deep slash to Roman's back. Roman crumbled from the blow, dropping his sword and falling to his knees. He bent over and breathed heavily. "I yield," he said. He rolled onto his side, then lay on his back and stared at the sky.

Lenia and Curtis cheered again. Cali clasped her hands over her mouth.

Kase rushed to his grandfather's side. "Just relax and I'll heal you," he said. He dropped his sword and placed both of his hands on Roman's shoulder.

"No need," Roman said. "I'll recover in a couple days."

Kase's palms were already glowing. Healing someone was much easier than bringing them back to life. Before the doorway of life, he'd had to focus on every cut, absorbing the pain of his victim and transferring it to his body. This time, there was just a tingle throughout his limbs. All of Roman's cuts were healed in a matter of seconds.

"All done," Kase said. He leant back, and smiled at his grandfather.

Roman sat up, opening and closing his fists. "You fought well, Kase," Roman said. "You're right, I learned a lot from our battle. I only know of one fighter that moves like you."

Kase nodded. He felt like he'd won the respect of his childhood hero. He looked away, in case he was blushing. Lenia and Curtis were both beaming, and skipped towards Kase and his grandfather. Cali followed less enthusiastically.

"His name was Dominic Garrick," Roman said.

Kase felt his elation escape. "Dominic wasn't a warrior, like me and you," Kase said. "He was a scholar, like Cali."

"You have tremendous skill, but are you a warrior?" Roman asked. "How often do you train?"

"Every day," Kase said. "I actually coach and train with Lenia and Curtis." Kase gestured to the both of them.

"It's nice to meet you, sir," Curtis said.

"It's an honour," Lenia added. She crouched beside Kase, and put her arm around him.

Roman looked at Curtis, but seemed more intrigued with Lenia. "May I ask you a question about strategy, Lenia?" he asked.

Lenia puffed her chest out. "Of course," she said.

"How would you best someone stronger than you?" Roman asked.

Lenia looked at Kase and smiled. "Speed and precision beats power," she said. "At least, that's what my professor tells me."

Roman looked at Kase and smiled. "Interesting answer," he said. "I've always believed that power beats power. It's something that I learned as a warrior, and it pushed me to always be stronger than my opponent. My son tried to prove me wrong, though, and came up with the mantra that you just used."

Kase looked to the ground. He thought that Dom had written a guide for him to train like Roman Garrick, but it had been misleading. It seemed like Dom had given Kase his own lessons, masking them as Roman's to fool Kase. Even though the skills Kase had mastered had helped him at the Academy, in his brief role working for the Triple Crown, and now in winning a battle against his grandfather, he felt cheated.

"Dominic challenged you?" Cali asked.

"He was relentless," Roman said. "It put a strain on our relationship at times, but I tried to do the best I could as a parent. I hope I can help you all and bring him back, if that's still your plan."

"It is," Cali said. "There's a lot we need to do first, though."

"I understand," Roman answered. "But can I get some pants first?"

Curtis and Cali laughed, but Kase kept staring at the ground. He tried to balance the emotional highs and lows that he was feeling. Lenia rubbed his shoulder.

He felt a little better.

# CHAPTER 11

# Can You See What I See

Roman forced some air through the side of his cheek, creating a perfect duck sound.

Helena laughed. "You think that's going to help us hunt?" she asked. "No duck is going to be attracted to that."

"It's not meant to attract the ducks," Roman said. "It's bait for a response. If we hear a duck return the call, then we'll know we're close."

"I'm not convinced," Helena said. She placed a blanket into her wheelbarrow. She and Roman each had their own wooden wheelbarrows to store their items for the weekend. They were planning to find the best fishing and hunting grounds in the Kingdom of Moiras.

"Kase's is better," Talen said. She inspected another hook from Roman's tackle box, and returned it to the right section.

"Of course it is," Curtis said. He was gathering arrows for Helena's quiver.

"Is that so, potential grandson?" Roman elbowed Helena. His eyes twinkled as he looked at Kase.

Kase blushed. He was enjoying spending time with his grandparents, even if things over the last few days hadn't gone quite as expected. He puffed up his cheek, forced some air above his gum line, and pursed his lips. He returned Roman's duck call.

Roman smiled. "Beautiful," he said proudly. "We'll have to go on our own hunt when you return."

"Count me in, grandson," Helena said.

Kase smiled politely. He continued to load a few food items into his grandparents' wheelbarrows, but he couldn't quite relax and joke around like they were. He couldn't shake the feeling he'd gotten when they had interrogated Jem. Both Helena and Roman had seemed barbaric, instead of the heroes of legend that he assumed they would be.

Since bringing back their son from the dead was important to them, Helena and Roman led the interrogation. Jem recognized who they were, and was much more afraid of them than she'd been of Cali, Lenia, Curtis, and Kase. Because Jem was locked up, she had nowhere to hide, but it didn't stop her from holding out for as long as possible.

Helena started the violence, beating Jem down every time Jem lied or withheld information. Helena's hands became bloody from all the blows, but the damage was mild compared to Jem's face and belly. Jem's eyes had both swelled, and blood dripped from the many cuts on her head and cheeks. Still, it wasn't enough to make Jem talk.

When Helena tired, Roman followed with his sword. He took away pieces of Jem, little trophies that she couldn't get back. He started by cutting off all the toes on her left foot, and then moved up to a couple of fingers. When he sliced off Jem's ear, her screams rang off the cold, brick walls of the cell. It was the most hair-raising scream Kase had ever heard, worse than a few of the screams he'd experienced bringing his friends back to life.

Roman's tactics had worked though, because Jem told them exactly what they needed in order to find Dominic Garrick. Unfortunately for Jem, once she'd given up, Roman and Helena left her for dead. They instructed Cali that she should let Jem bleed out slowly—to which Cali agreed. Luckily for Jem, Lenia went back later to put her out of her misery.

Kase didn't think it was possible that his notoriously humble grandparents would make the Unicorn Knight look like an angel, but they had. He continued to question everything he'd grown up knowing.

"Are we all ready?" Cali asked, walking out of the castle with blankets in her arms. Lenia followed with a few pillows. They both tossed the items into Kase's wheelbarrow.

"We are, potential granddaughter," Roman said. "Retirement had seemed like a dream, but here we are: day one." He put his arm around Helena and pulled her close.

Kase took a deep breath. His grandparents embracing retirement rather than helping to find their son was a little bothersome. He didn't want to say anything, because he was happy to have them both in his life, but it was disappointing nonetheless.

He felt strange assuming that they'd be more understanding and supportive of his ideas, and had hoped that they'd help him convince his friends of a more righteous plan. But it seemed like his grandparents favoured Cali, and would help her reach her goals instead, no matter what the immoral costs were.

"Are you ready, Dandy?" Lenia said. She wrapped her arms around Kase's waist.

"I'm as ready as I'll ever be," Kase said. With his current opinion of his grandparents, he was reluctant to go on a trip to bring back the father that had abandoned them. He thought he might be able to put a positive spin to the trip, but he didn't feel like forcing it.

"You've done so much to get to this point, there's no way you'll fail," Helena said. "We're grateful for everything you've done, and we'll have a glorious celebration when you and Dominic return."

"Should we start planning the party now?" Curtis asked Cali. He was still dutiful, even though things hadn't gone as he'd expected either.

"Work with Aura for the next few days," Cali instructed. "If she doesn't have too much for you to do, maybe you and Talen could take a holiday too."

"We thought that we might try swimming lessons again," Talen said. "Provided Aura is up for them too." She tapped her heart twice, kissed her lips, and pointed to the air, signalling her good-bye.

Kase and Lenia returned the gesture.

"Good luck." Roman smiled. Kase hadn't explained their sign, but he felt like his grandfather recognized the group's pride, respect, and cohesiveness.

Curtis and Talen returned to the castle, while Roman and Helena hauled their wheelbarrows away. Before teleporting to Jenim Island, Lenia presented Kase with a bracelet. It was a slim gold chain, with seven tiny golden cylinders on it. Each cylinder had its own initials.

"It's beautiful," Kase said. He didn't think it looked special, but his comment made Lenia smile.

"Hopefully we won't have to use any of those," Cali said. She checked the dagger she had sheathed in her belt.

The journey through Jenim Island to Dom's burial place would be filled with giant creatures that could easily kill Kase, Lenia, and Cali. Cali thought that if she or Lenia were to get eaten by an animal on Jenim Island, their body might be lost forever. Since Kase needed a piece of them in order to bring them back, there was a concern that he might not be able to find them.

Cali hypothesized that since Kase was able to bring someone back to life with a finger, he'd be able to do the same with a different body part. Since none of them wanted to give up anything valuable, the best they could think of parting with was a piece of hair. Kase practiced bringing back mice with a tuft of fur, and was successful, so Cali's hypothesis was supported.

Lenia made a bracelet to capture a hair from everyone, not just those on the current mission. They also had backups in the castle, but it might be too costly for Kase to make his way back to the castle if Cali and Lenia were lost. They wanted to keep their focus on making it to Dominic, and bringing him back so they could figure out their next move.

When Lenia teleported the group to Jenim Island, Cali took a few moments to take in their surroundings. She looked up to the sun, through the giant trees, and let out a sigh of relief. "It's so nice to be somewhere new," she said. She glanced at her map, and then started down the trail.

The forest they were in was like the forests in the Kingdom of Moiras and the rest of the realm—just bigger. The rocks on the trail were like boulders, the grass was as tall as trees, and the trees were so tall and wide that they didn't seem real. It took a few moments for Kase to orient himself.

"Aren't we going to find some better transportation?" Lenia asked. "It's a long way to walk."

"Still tired from our training this morning?" Kase quipped. He pushed the wheelbarrow along, but his legs also felt weak. Roman and Helena had sparred with Lenia and Kase for a couple of hours just after dawn, and even though he enjoyed it, Kase felt fatigued.

"I am, to be honest." Lenia giggled. "I'm not complaining though. I'll march as far as we need to."

"Me too," Kase said.

"You both will still probably outlast me," Cali said. "I hope we run into a creature soon, but Kase will need to determine which one works best. Hopefully it's a friendly animal, and not one that has us on the menu."

Kase felt his surroundings with his wizard senses. He didn't detect any candidates. "There are a few birds nesting in the trees above, if we want to change our plans and consider them," he lied. He wanted to see Lenia's reaction.

"No, no, no." Lenia cuddled up to Kase, wrapping her arms around his left bicep. "Don't even joke about that." She squeezed tight.

Cali stepped towards Kase's right, but didn't hold him. "It's a little funny, but I hope we don't get surprised by one."

Kase, Lenia, and Cali crept forwards. Their journey started on a path that giants used for transport. Grooves large enough for Kase to lie across were likely made by the wheels of giant carts. It didn't take long before the trio felt their first rumbling, and hid in the rough grass on the edge of the path to remain undetected.

A single, horse-drawn cart galloped down the road. The hooves of the great horse would have easily crushed Kase. It kicked up so much dust that Kase had difficulty keeping his eyes open. The ground shook, the wheels rumbled, and the breeze surged past the group. The giant and her horse-cart sped away without incident.

"Do you think you could control a horse that big?" Lenia asked.

"I don't think it would be much different than a normal horse," Kase replied. "Could you teleport us on its back, if we see a wild one?"

"I could, but it might be hard to stay on," Lenia said.

"And balance a wheelbarrow full of supplies," Cali noted.

"It's too bad Turanus isn't here," Kase said. "Do you have a special way of calling him?"

Lenia looked confused. "I've never called him," she said. "He just sort of shows up when he wants. I like to think it's to help me out, but I have no idea."

Kase nodded. He thought of all the times Turanus had presented himself, and the vague explanations that came along with the surprise visits. He was a little disappointed that he had never pushed further. He again thought about the lessons of patience that he'd learned from his king studies, and from Turanus himself.

The trio continued on their journey, but they quickly got bored. Instead of a fun stroll through the strange woods, their trek felt extra-long. It took so much time to move past just one of the giant tree trunks alongside their path, that it felt like they weren't making much progress. All of the greenery seemed to blend together too. Luckily for them, they stumbled across a suitable animal that was lazing in the forest.

"I feel a wolverine," Kase said. "I think she's big enough to carry all of us, plus our loot. Should I bring her over?"

"A wolverine?" Cali asked. She looked up instead of around. "They're nocturnal hunters. Will she be mad if we wake her?"

"She's not sleeping," Kase said. "She's also not moving very fast. She doesn't seem injured or anything, so maybe she's just lounging around?"

"Is she friendly?" Lenia asked. "Maybe you could talk to her, and see if she'd be willing to help us."

Kase had only talked to unicorns and langaras thus far, but he'd never met a wolverine before. It would be nice to discover a new animal to talk to. "I could try," he said. "How do I address her? Miss Wolverine? Mrs. Wolverine? She's alone, but maybe her family went hunting without her."

"Are you implying something?" Cali crossed her arms. "Do you wish you were hunting with Grandpa Roman and Grandma Helena?"

Kase sighed. He didn't want to fight with his sister; he honestly enjoyed the time he was spending with her. "I'll have lots of time to spend with them in the future," he said. "But I'm still adjusting to … they're a lot to handle."

Cali dropped her arms and smiled. "I'm glad you said that, brother," she said. "I feel the same. I love them, and I'm glad you brought them back, but they can be a bit much. Especially around the dinner table."

Lenia laughed. "Still upset about the glasses?"

Cali chuckled. "I guess we should have had bigger ones right from the beginning, but Grandpa didn't have to break his."

On their first night, Cali had wanted to have a special dinner for their grandparents, so she'd set the table with fancy dinnerware they had found in the castle. The glasses were pristine, but they were a little smaller than normal. Roman and Helena had made some jokes, and then Roman snapped the stem on his. Cali had looked terribly embarrassed at the time, but at least she was having fun with it now.

The trio moved off the path and stumbled into the woods. The grass reached well above their heads, but it was soft enough to easily push through. They scuttled under a few bushes, crawled over a few branches, rounded some large trunks before they made it to the wolverine's den. When they arrived, the wolverine was chewing on a rabbit carcass.

"Yikes," Lenia said. "She looks like she just rolled out of bed."

Kase laughed. The wolverine wasn't a majestic animal, and this one did look a little messy. Her short, reddish hair was splattered with mud. Her eyes were black, and one eyelid looked a little puffy. Her teeth were jagged, with some longer than others; it seemed like a few were missing. She also had a tuft of hair that stuck up from her right ear, as if she had pillow hair.

"She looks exactly how I feel," Cali said.

Kase looked at his sister, then at Lenia, then back at his sister. "What?"

Cali smiled. "She's rough around the edges, but she's ferocious. She's a survivor. Maybe she could be my animal identity."

Kase was still confused to hear Cali associate herself with such a hideous beast. She'd always made time for personal care, and had a reputation for having a beautiful appearance. "Animal identity?"

"We've talked about it before," Lenia said. "I have the unicorn, and you're the Dandy Lion, so what would the others be? Something else from the animal kingdom, to match the theme. Aura and Cali were undecided, but Talen has already claimed the Shark Knight."

"Predictable." Kase knew how much Talen loved sharks. "So you want to be the Wolverine Knight, Cali?"

"Maybe just The Wolverine," Cali said. "But we can figure that out later. Definitely not the Dandy Wolverine."

Lenia laughed, which made Kase smile. "I'm okay with that," he said.

"Me too." Lenia moved her eyes left, then smiled at Kase.

"Perfect!" Cali clasped her hands together, and then hopped up and down. "Can I pet her, or will she eat me? She's really tearing through that rabbit."

Kase focused on his connection with Cali's animal. "Hello," he thought, trying to communicate with the wolverine the way he did with Maxim. Unfortunately, the wolverine did not respond, or even seem to register his greeting. He gained control over the giant beast, keeping her heartbeat steady as she stopped devouring her meal. She lay obediently, her forepaws on the ground, and her head steady above the bloody carcass.

"Let's go," Kase said. He led Cali and Lenia in front of the claws of the wolverine, which were each as long as they were tall.

"So fierce," Cali said. "I wonder what else she uses these sharp claws for, besides hunting. Are they good for digging? Climbing?"

"They'd probably be good for scratching our backs," Kase said. He pretended to have an itch on his back shoulder that he couldn't reach.

"Tridents are good for that too." Lenia poked hers softly into the area Kase couldn't reach with a giggle.

"I can't wait to learn more about her," Cali said. "Should we go for a ride?"

Lenia teleported the team to the wolverine's back. Kase used his power to direct the wolverine where they wanted to go, but the ride was a bumpy one. The wolverine didn't have the smooth gait of a horse, or the powerful strides of a lion; instead, it bounded through the forest like a bull. Its rolling shoulder movements made it challenging for Kase to keep the wheelbarrow straight, and for Lenia and Cali to hang on, but they all managed.

They returned to the giant cart trail, with Cali guiding them along. They were still able to avoid giants, birds, and other dangerous predators. Based on the notes and map that Cali had, the journey was expected to take more than a week. But with the wolverine covering a lot more ground, they were able to cut that time in half.

For their first night of camping, they found an old chipmunk burrow. Kase felt exposed because the entrance was at ground level, but they hauled some old twigs to build a barrier. They didn't want anything digging for them while they slept, or munching on them in the morning.

On the second day, they woke to find the wolverine had disappeared into the wilderness and back to her normal routine. Instead, they rode a white wolf through the forest. Although the wolverine wasn't with them, it didn't stop Cali from talking about how great she had been. It was a little annoying for Kase, but seeing his sister happy was worth it.

They camped that night in what appeared to be a hollowed-out log, but to giants it would have been more of a branch. They ate some snacks and told stories before bed, and then got up extra early the next day to finish their journey.

When they made it to their destination, they all stared up at the tall tree. Lenia teleported up the branches to find the correct hollow, and then gathered the rest of the group. They all entered the hollow and climbed down the ladder that had been carved into the tree centuries ago.

At the bottom of the inside of the tree was the gateway created by King Michael to guard the green piece of the doorway of life.

"I don't see any bones here," Kase said. "Do you think Jem told us the truth?"

"She mentioned she was on the ground, but Mac, Dad, and another warrior named Buck were the ones that found the green piece," Cali said. "With Mac being the only one left in the tree, he tossed the bodies back down here so that they didn't have to waste time burying them. Maybe the doorway was still open when he did?"

Kase stared at the silver stone beneath his feet. The circular doorway had a giant's handprint embedded into it. It wasn't just the size that gave it away: giants had five fingers and a thumb. But that wasn't the most interesting part. Jem had mentioned that the team had hauled dirt up the tree, then poured it down onto this doorway. Since the stone was clean, he wondered where it had gone.

"So how do we get in?" Kase asked. "The doorway we opened in Skyland needed dragon fire. The doorway in the Leviathan Triangle couldn't be opened underwater. Are we supposed to cover this one with dirt?"

Cali bent down. Lenia and Kase did too. Cali ran her finger along the inside edge of the handprint, and then rubbed her finger with her thumb. "I think just the handprint," she said. "If we were to fill the impression with a hand, then the door would open. Since we don't have a giant with us … well, I don't know how we'd get that hand down here anyway, but it seems like Dad used dirt as a substitute. It's brilliant."

Kase didn't think of his father as a brilliant man, but he liked Cali's deduction about the imprint. He looked back up from where they'd come from. "I guess they used the pulley system we saw to haul the dirt up and down," he said. "If they had a wizard, they could have just used the elements to their advantage. I can do it much faster."

"That's a brilliant idea too," Lenia said. "But can I try? I haven't practiced my element control in a while. Plus, you might be better than me at defending us from birds."

Kase thought about how he would battle a giant bird. It might be too big for his sword to have any effect. Then he thought about his lightning control exercise that King Michael had used. "I've got your back," he said.

Lenia teleported the group back to the top of the tree hollow. Cali stayed covered, but Kase and Lenia ventured a few feet away. While Lenia concentrated on the swirling winds, and gathering the dust from the ground below, Kase focused on any storms in the area. He felt some rainclouds in the distance, and tried mimicking the feeling he'd captured before.

"How much do we need?" Lenia asked. She'd already brought some swirling dirt up to the hollow, letting it fall through the opening and down towards the doorway.

"I'll climb back down and check," Cali shouted. "This wind isn't as bad as I thought. I'll yell when it's time to stop."

As Lenia brought bits of dirt up and into the tree, Kase relaxed and let his emotions balance with his surroundings. He was still searching for storm clouds, but he also concentrated on things closer to him. He felt the breeze that Lenia was manipulating, he sensed a few moose in the distance, some rodents underground, and a multitude of insects. He didn't feel any birds, so he knew that he and Lenia were safe on the branch.

After a few minutes, Kase felt some rain in the distance. He tried bringing a few clouds closer, to see if he could generate some lightning if he needed to. He didn't really know what to search for, but he felt a disturbance that intrigued him.

"That's enough!" Cali yelled.

Kase opened his eyes, and noticed Lenia do the same. The wind stopped swirling, Kase stopped focusing on the storm clouds, and Lenia quickly grabbed his hand. They returned to the wheelbarrow to grab some supplies, including a blanket, and then returned to inside the tree.

Cali was on her knees spreading the dirt around, trying to evenly fill the handprint.

Without warning, the doorway panels in the ground slowly started to separate. The dirt pile flowed into the expanding gap, but there was nothing to see beyond the blackness. It was consistent with the other doorways that King Michael had created, and Kase was excited to see what treasure might be in this cache.

The trio stepped into the darkness together, but they didn't fall. They instantly stood overlooking the cache. The surrounding walls were made of tree trunks, although light shone through the gaps. The air smelled like a carpenter's workshop, but there wasn't any furniture in the room. Instead, it was littered with gold, artefacts, and books, just like the other caches they had seen. At the far end was an empty stand that the piece of the doorway of life would have sat on.

"Oh no." Lenia quickly jumped back. "I think I stepped on someone."

Kase glanced down and noticed the two skeletons that were sprawled on the platform. One of them was wearing armour, while the other had torn, ragged clothing. He knew which one was Dom.

"Should we do this now, or take a look around first?" he asked.

"He's what we came for," Cali said. She knelt beside the skeleton with the ragged clothing. "Are you able to bring him back, or do you need a minute?"

Cali's expression had softened. Kase was glad that he was with her on this trip, because she'd shown a lot of vulnerability. The comments about the wolverine, the laughs they'd shared while camping in the giant wilderness, and now the hope in her eyes of their goal being fulfilled helped Kase feel more connected to her. It almost outweighed the disgust he felt looking at Dom's bones.

"We should come back here again though," Lenia said. She was looking out at the room. "I wonder if there are any secrets in here that aren't in our castle."

"Are you suggesting that you'll bring me with you this time?" Kase asked. He felt like he'd missed out on her adventures when she had teleported back to the dragon cache without him in the past.

"Of course, Dandy," Lenia said. "As long as you're my sidekick, you'll be with me everywhere."

Kase sighed and rolled his eyes. Lenia was poking fun, but he was glad to be with her everywhere. He smiled at Lenia and received a classic Lenia look in return. So bolstered, he then knelt down at Dom's legs. He placed his hands on the bones, closed his eyes, and searched for his power. The connection was successful.

Dom stood on the branch, sword drawn. The giant bird was crushing Buck like a ragdoll, even though the warrior had plenty of weight in his belly. The bird's talons were soaked in Buck's blood, but there was still hope for the warrior to be saved. There was hope for the team to be saved.

The bird bobbed towards Dom, but he was too quick. He easily dodged the bird's beak, and lunged towards its talon with speed and precision, since it was the most exposed part of its body. He sliced just above the claw, causing the bird to screech, flap its wings, and lift its foot. Unfortunately, it didn't fly away just yet.

The talon came back down quickly, and even with his speed, Dom didn't have time to get away. He was caught under it as the bird used both feet to launch itself from the branch. Its weight crushed his ribcage. He instantly felt blood fill his lungs.

He coughed. Mac had recovered from the bird's initial attack, and came to Dom's aid. The warrior rolled Dom over so that he could breathe, but Dom knew it didn't matter. Seeing Buck's dead eyes in his line of sight confirmed Dom's realization that he was also doomed.

"I'm going to get you out of here," Mac said. "We'll find a healer and—"

"It's too late." Dom coughed up more blood. "Just promise me you'll get the relic to Sheese. He's the only one who can fix everything." He tried to blink away the black spots that clouded his vision. He thought about his wife: he'd failed her. "Ashlyn," he whispered.

"I'll do right by you, Dominic Garrick," Mac aid. "You saved my life, and are a true hero. I'll make sure your children know of your bravery today."

Dom thought about his children. He'd miss reading to Cali every night. He wanted to see Kase swing his new sword.

He'd done all he could for them.

Kase fell into the lava, and the painful process began. It seemed to linger longer than Jem, but thankfully shorter than his grandparents.

When it was over, he didn't collapse over in exhaustion, but quickly stood and walked away. Kase didn't want to look at Dom after learning the final details of his death.

"Dad?" Cali's voice quivered.

Dom's last thought was confidence in knowing that he'd done everything he could for Kase and Cali? By abandoning them? Dom could have stayed and cared for his children. That would have been worth more than chasing a magical relic.

"Cali?" Dom asked. "You're … grown!"

Kase turned back towards the group. Cali was bent over, hugging their father, who had sat up. Cali had already wrapped a blanket around his shredded clothes. Cali's eyes were closed, and tears ran down her face. Lenia was staring at the two of them, her hand over her mouth.

"I missed you so much." Cali sobbed and hugged Dom tighter.

"Thank you for saving me," Dom said. "I'm glad Sheese was eventually successful, but it appears we have a lot of catching up to do. Hopefully we can make up for lost time."

Cali disengaged, stood straight, wiped her eyes and laughed. "We'd like that, wouldn't we, brother?"

Dom looked to Lenia, and then turned to Kase. His mouth dropped open. "Kase?" he asked.

"Dom," Kase said, holding back his anger.

"My boy!" Dom pushed himself up and stood, but he wasn't as tall as Kase. He held his blanket and hugged Kase awkwardly. Kase didn't return the gesture, and just let his arms dangle at his sides.

Dom leant back and held Kase's bicep. "Look at you! You've really grown into the warrior that I knew you'd become." He slapped Kase's arms, but it wasn't that forceful. He turned to Lenia. "And who are you? I think I'd remember having a second daughter."

Lenia looked at Kase with raised eyebrows and a soft expression. She smiled politely at Dominic. "I'm Kase's girlfriend, Lenia," she replied. "It's nice to meet you, Mr. Garrick." She stuck her hand out. Her gesture helped ease Kase's anger for the moment, because he recognized that even now, she still didn't like hugging strangers.

"What a nice trident you have," Dominic said. He held Lenia's hand and bowed over it. "Thank you for returning my life, Chosen One."

Lenia chuckled and looked back to Kase. "It wasn't me," she said.

"It was all of us," Kase said. Dominic's jumping to conclusions fuelled Kase's fire a little more. Of course he'd assume that a chosen wizard would be the only one that could harness the power of the doorway of life, and it wouldn't be his warrior son. "But we brought you back for a reason." He nodded at Cali.

"Kase is right," Cali said. "We need to catch you up on what's happened since you've been gone. We're not working for Sheese: we're on the run from the Triple Crown, and need to formulate a plan to strike back against them. We should really get back to the castle, to a more comfortable setting. Plus, I'm hungry."

Lenia and Kase nodded to Cali.

Dominic looked dumbfounded. "Hungry?" he asked. "I thought I named you Cali."

Kase closed his eyes, looked down, and shook his head. He knew what Dominic was trying to do, but the joke was just not funny. Kase heard Lenia chuckle.

"Hey, at least Lenia got it," Dominic said with a smile.

Kase peeked his eye open in Lenia's direction. She was covering her mouth, staring right at him.

"Good one, Dad," Cali said. "I think you and I should teleport out of here first, then Lenia, you can come back for Kase and our supplies?"

"That works for me," Lenia said. She reached out to touch Dominic and Cali.

"Teleport?" Dominic asked. The three of them disappeared.

Kase turned back towards the cache. He looked at all the treasure, and wondered if it would be enough to survive on. He didn't want to be in the castle with Dom, but he could live on Jenim Island on his own. Then he thought about Lenia, and how the cache would never feel like home without her.

He felt her arms around his waist as she hugged him from behind.

"Do you think we could live here?" Kase asked. He rubbed her hands gently.

"It's definitely in my top three tree houses," Lenia replied. "Could we get a waterfall in here? Maybe a hot spring?"

"Anything for you, Chosen One," Kase teased.

"Please don't call me that," Lenia said. "I know he meant well, but it's worse than your highness, or princess. He's … how do you feel now that he's back?"

Kase didn't want to think about Dom any more. The few minutes they spent together were already more stressful than he'd predicted. He was glad that Lenia wasn't impressed by Dom, and that he had her to talk to before bringing Dom back, but he might need to rely on her more.

"We can talk about that later," Kase said. He turned and held Lenia in his arms. "Thank you for being with me through this."

Lenia stared back at Kase, moved her eyes to the left, tugged his collar, and then kissed him deeply. As much as he was supposed to enjoy the moment, something tugged at his insides. Somehow, the top three tree house kiss felt worse than the kiss of death.

CHAPTER 12

# Wherever He Laid His Hat Was His Home

Lenia stared at Kase. She brushed the hair away from his eyes, and then placed both her palms on his chest. She traced her fingers along the claw marks that Maxim had carved into the thin, metal vest. "I think you should go shirtless."

Kase thought the golden vest was a little bright for his costume, but Talen assured him that it would complement his helmet. "I'd be more susceptible to a fatal strike if I take it off," he said.

"It would hurt, but you'd survive," Lenia said. Her fingers brushed Kase's bare shoulders.

"So if I go topless, you will too?" Kase asked. He wrapped his arms around her waist.

Lenia giggled. "Maybe just in private?" She stood on her tip-toes to rub her nose against Kase's.

"Dad alert!" Dom shouted.

Mood ruined.

Lenia rested her cheek against Kase's chest. "Good afternoon, Mr. Garrick," she said.

"Kase, my boy!" Dom said, ignoring Lenia's greeting. "I finished your bow. I have to say, it's some of my finest work yet!"

Kase didn't want to let go of Lenia, but she leant away. Dom had hustled in faster than Talen, who was carrying a wooden box. Lenia accepted Kase's bow on his behalf, inspecting the craftsmanship. "It's perfect!" she said, handing the bow to Kase.

The upper and lower limbs of the bow were curved, and appeared symmetrical. The grip and arrow rest were smooth, and the string was taut. It wasn't the best bow Kase had held, but it served the purpose of the mission: it matched Kase's costume, it was disposable, and it was untraceable.

"Your grandparents used to take me camping when I was younger," Dom said. "I used to sit around the fire and carve weapons out of tree branches. I enjoyed designing bows the best, because I could test them right away. The entire process was soothing, methodical, and exciting at the same time."

"Can you make me a bow like this?" Lenia asked.

"Absolutely!" Dom said. He waved his hands in the air. "Abracadabra … poof! You're a bow like this!" He lifted his arms in the air and smiled like a jester.

Kase rolled his eyes and looked away. He noticed Talen shake her head. Lenia giggled.

"Let's see if it works." Kase grabbed the leather quiver that Lenia had made and slung it across his back.

"Of course it works," Dom said. "I can't wait to see Lenia practice. She's the only wizard warrior I know."

"Well …" Lenia picked up her black bow and matching quiver. She looked at Kase and shrugged. She'd promised Kase that she wasn't going to break the news to Dom that his son was a wizard warrior too.

Kase'd had plenty of chances over the last few days to tell Dom that he held the power of the doorway of life. But Dom had been so quick to jump to conclusions that Kase didn't feel like sharing the news. Lenia thought he was being a bit stubborn, but Kase had promised her that he'd tell Dom on his own terms. He decided to remain quiet so far: through all their planning, when showing Dom the doorway of life platform, and even when introducing the langaras.

Protecting his identity from Dom made Kase feel like he was in control of his past. He hadn't needed Dom to help him grow up, and he didn't need Dom to understand him now. Kase was his own person, no thanks to a bow-making, conclusion-jumping, and bad-joke-telling buffoon.

"Wait," Talen said. "You might as well practise with your new helmet on." She placed her box on the ground, lifted the lid, and pulled out a golden helmet. The front was similar to the Unicorn Knight's helmet, but with a red visor instead of purple. It also had ears shaped on the top to resemble a lion's, and a flowing red mane. The hair had been donated by Talen's favourite langara.

"It's beautiful," Kase said. He set his bow down gently, so he wouldn't break it, and then lifted the helmet out of the box. He tilted the helmet, and noticed the leather padding on the inside. He tossed his hair back and then slipped the helmet on. It was a perfect fit.

"How do I look?" Kase's words echoed. The red tint of the helmet made the storm clouds in the distance look darker.

"Dandy," Lenia said with a wide smile.

"Definitely a member of the A.K.," Talen said, using her own nickname for their new band of vigilantes.

"Have you thought of a design for your helmet yet?" Kase asked.

"No, I haven't found the perfect shark yet." Talen sighed, a sign the conundrum was really bothering her. "I love the hammerhead shark, but as a helmet, it's too awkward. I want to stay away from the great white shark, because it's the most popular, but there are too many other options: blacktip, nurse, whale? I just can't choose."

"I've been thinking about my addition to your Animal Kingdom," Dom said. "What do you think of The Goat?"

Of course Dom would selfishly turn the moment around to him, instead of complimenting his son on his new identity, or helping Talen with her design challenge. Kase liked how his helmet hid his scowl.

"Why the goat?" Lenia asked. "Is that your favourite animal?"

Dom chuckled. "No, no, no," he said. "I like how it doubles as an acronym: Greatest of All Time. In fact, I used to remind myself of that name when I was younger, and competing against The Bull."

"How did you compete against Roman when you weren't a warrior?" Kase asked.

"Well, my boy," Dom started. Kase cringed. "Being the son of two profound

Guardians gave me all the training I needed. I practised good nutritional habits, stayed fit, and worked on all my weapons techniques. But I chose to be a scholar because I wanted to be different from them—that, and I enjoyed learning about everything more than becoming a warrior servant."

It wasn't raining in their area yet, but Kase felt the storm in the distance. Dom's choice of words was interesting: implying that warriors who served the realm with honour were servants to a higher power. Dom made it seem like warriors were so much less than scholars.

"So you fought against Roman in your training?" Lenia asked. "I assume that, as The Goat, you beat him?"

"Well, yes and no," Dom said. "We both had our strengths. He's not a very good shot, so I'd usually dominate in any type of archery lesson. On the other end, as much as I tried beating him in combat with speed and precision, he always overpowered me. Then again, no one beats him in one-on-one combat."

Kase noticed Lenia spin to his direction. She rolled her finger forwards, as if encouraging him to say something.

"Kase defeated Roman in combat," Talen said. "Does that make him the greatest of all time?"

Kase smiled under his helmet. He was proud that Talen had his back, and that she'd voiced what Lenia and Kase had thought. Kase stared at Dom though, who seemed dumbfounded.

"Really?" Dom said. "By yourself? Straight up?"

Kase nodded. He didn't need to defend what he'd already done, even though Dom seemed like he was searching for an explanation.

Dom looked to the ground and smiled. "I wish I could have seen the look on his face." He raised an eyebrow at Kase. "Okay, Greatest of All Time, let's see what you can do with your new bow."

Even though Kase was triumphant, it seemed Dom was only concerned with Roman's loss. But it didn't matter. Kase didn't care about Dom's approval.

Kase turned his attention to what was important: practising for his next mission. He was anxious about the details of their plan, but he was happy to prepare for it alongside the Unicorn Knight. Training with Lenia had always been the best part of his day, and he needed to spend time with her to get away from certain new members of their group.

Lenia had already placed targets in the grassy field. Instead of the targets facing towards them, the rings of the targets were angled towards the sky. There were three rings per target: blue was the outermost, white the middle, and red marked the bulls-eye in the centre. Two targets were fifty yards away, two were seventy-five yards away, and two were a hundred yards away.

Kase tugged at the bowstring. It was braided on both ends, and the tension was consistent with the bows he normally used. Kase pulled an arrow from his quiver, drew the bowstring back, and steadied the arrow on the rest above his grip. A substantial sight window was carved above the arrow rest, giving Kase a perfect view of his target.

Instead of firing directly at the first of the three targets, Kase angled his bow towards the sky. He estimated what kind of arc he'd need based on the strength of his pull on the bowstring, judged the mark based on the direction of the wind, and then focused on his delivery. He took a quick breath, engaged his core, and let the arrow fly.

The arrow soared through the air, arcing like a rainbow to the colourful target. It wasn't a long shot, so the flight was short-lived. The arrowhead pierced the outside edge of the bulls-eye on the target fifty yards away.

"You make it look so easy." Lenia chuckled. "First shot, and you've already got a bulls-eye."

Lenia gawking at him made Kase smile. He had been a little worried that his helmet would hurt his vision, or disrupt his delivery, but his form felt solid.

"Well … barely," Dom said. "He left you lots of room to hit the centre."

Kase glared at Dom. "It's probably the bow." He didn't mean to speak with such a harsh tone, but the words were out before he had a chance to hold back.

"A true craftsman doesn't blame their tools." Dom reached for Kase's bow, but stopped. "May I?"

Kase handed the bow to Dom, and pulled an arrow from his quiver. Dom accepted the arrow, and loaded it quickly. It didn't even seem like he prepared himself for the shot, his motion was so fast. Dom tilted back with the arrow drawn, and released it with barely a pause.

The arrow soared high in the air, with greater speed than Kase's. It soared past the first target, beyond the second, and struck one of the furthest targets from them. Dom's arrow landed in the very centre of the bulls-eye.

"Don't think it's the bow," Dom said. He handed the bow back to Kase, biting his lip to hide his smirk.

Kase felt thunder in the distance.

"Maybe you'd like to use your old one instead?" This time Dom's goofy smile shone through.

"We don't need to be that accurate for this mission," Lenia said. "Let's just get some work in so that we're comfortable."

Kase liked Lenia having his back, and chose to ignore Dom and focus on the training they had planned. He nodded in her direction.

Lenia put her helmet on, and then pulled an arrow from her quiver. She loaded her black, steel bow, aimed at the targets, and fired. Her arrow flew with the same trajectory as Dom's, but it had a little too much speed. She overshot the furthest target by a few yards.

"Nice adjustment to the wind," Kase said. "It was right on line. Keep practising."

"Well …" Dom approached Lenia and extended his hand. "May I see your bow?"

"You're not going to use it to hit the target I missed, are you?" Lenia asked.

Dom laughed. To Kase, it seemed like Dom was forcing it. "No, no, nothing like that. I want to see what you're using. It's important to practise, but if you keep practising bad habits, poor techniques, or with the wrong tools, your development will falter." He accepted Lenia's bow, and pulled on the string.

Kase didn't think there was anything wrong with the way Lenia practised. Since he was Lenia's professor, he felt insulted by Dom's remarks. "She practises good habits. Her technique is perfect. Her bow is top of the line." He nodded to Lenia, showing her he had her back too.

"I agree," Dom said. "This is way nicer than the one I made. May I try it out? I'll shoot at the second target, if that's alright with you."

Lenia nodded and gave Dom one of her arrows. He pulled the arrow back, but took a little more time with his shot. He faced his target, took a noticeable breath, and then let the arrow fly. The trajectory was just as perfect as his first one, and he hit the centre of the bulls-eye on the target seventy-five yards away.

"Did you know that Lenia made that bow herself?" Talen asked. "In fact, she's made all the weapons that the Unicorn Knight uses."

"Is that so?" Dom said. "I can't say it doesn't surprise me. Anyone that bears the burden of the doorway of life is officially the Greatest of All Time in my books. But since you already have an Animal Kingdom nickname, hopefully you'd let me have The Goat."

Lenia crossed her arms and turned. "Kase, what do you think?"

Even though Lenia was wearing her helmet now, Kase could tell by her tone that she'd had enough of his stubbornness. But it still didn't feel like the right time to share his power with Dom. "Sure. Who cares?" he said.

Lenia stared at Kase, but didn't respond. Dom plucked an arrow from her quiver and took aim at the targets again. "Maybe you'd like to choose my name instead, son. Can you think of a better one?" He fired the arrow, hitting the same target that Kase had, but in the centre.

Kase tried to think of an animal that abandoned its young. Something that was obnoxiously loud, ignorant to those around them, but which puffed out their chest like they were the biggest beast in the realm. "How about a rooster?"

Lenia shook her head. Dom raised his eyebrow. Kase smiled under his helmet.

"I like it," Talen said.

Dom chuckled. "Okay, let's make it interesting." He pointed to the targets. "I've hit all three bulls-eyes. If you hit the remaining two in succession, you can call me the Rooster Knight. If you miss one, you'll have to call me The Goat."

"Just The Rooster," Kase said. He felt confident with this bet, even holding Dom's carved bow. Lenia still had her arms crossed, but Kase finally felt like he had something to be happy about with Dom.

Kase pulled an arrow from his quiver, and ignored those around him. He focused on his target at the hundred-yard mark, drew the arrow back confidently, set his angle, took a quick breath, and then fired.

Kase hadn't aimed at the target that Dom hit, but the empty one in line with his first shot. The arrow hit the bulls-eye directly in the centre, just as he'd anticipated. He smiled again under his helmet, and quickly drew the next arrow from his quiver.

"Not bad," Dom said.

"Thanks, Rooster," Kase quipped. He smiled again, turned towards his target, and focused. He let the joy creep in as he thought about his shot. He didn't need to suppress his excitement; instead, he wanted to use it as motivation to hit the bulls-eye. He pulled his arrow back confidently, set his angle, took a quick breath, and fired.

He turned to Dom so he could see the look on The Rooster's face when he was defeated, but Dom wasn't waiting for the shot to succeed. Still holding Lenia's bow, Dom reached into her quiver and plucked an arrow. He quickly drew his bow, focused on the same target as Kase, waited a few moments, and then fired.

The trajectory of Dom's arrow was straight, unlike Kase's. As Kase's arrow arced down towards the bulls-eye, Dom's arrow sped towards the target on a line. Before Kase realized what was going on, the two arrows collided. Both projectiles bounced away, leaving an empty bulls-eye.

Kase was glad his helmet was on. His mouth was wide open. He looked at Lenia, who was staring at the target.

"How is that possible?" Lenia asked.

"It's simple physics," Talen said.

Dom chuckled. "Talen is right, it is simple physics," he said. "But it's also a lot of practising good habits; maybe a few boring camping trips too."

It was an incredible shot, but Kase felt defeated. He'd never tried hitting an arrow with another arrow. It seemed impossible, and yet Dom did it so casually. Kase felt a little rain on his shoulder. He also thought about how two things could be true: Dom was The Goat of archery, but still a rooster.

"Seems like that storm is coming in," Dom said. "Lenia, would you mind teleporting us back to the castle?"

"Not at all," she said. She walked towards Kase first, and grabbed his wrist. It was as if she could feel his remorse.

"I'm going to stay and practise a little longer," he told her.

"I'll come back too," she replied. She turned towards Dom, who handed back her bow. "Do you ever miss, Mr. Garrick?"

"Once," he said. He looked down at the ground. "Everybody misses." He took a breath and then looked to the sky. "Ready when you are." Lenia grabbed his wrist, along with Talen's, and they all disappeared.

Kase removed his helmet and looked up at the clouds. He liked the rain on his face, but it didn't wash away what he was feeling. He was embarrassed to be bested by Dom, jealous that he hadn't shown Lenia any superior archery skills, and got angry every time Dom spoke. He also felt guilty for recognizing this turmoil, and wondered if it meant he was changing for the worse.

If he were destined to be a king someday, would these feelings seep through? Would they cause him to make poor decisions? Would he lash out and hurt others?

The raindrops came down faster. Kase could feel his negative energy flow into his core like a drain. He wanted to scream. He wanted to grab his sword and start swinging away at his emotions. He focused on the ground in front of him, visualizing an enemy in range. He imagined striking his foe down with all his might, and felt the energy surge through him.

A lightning bolt crashed, landing directly at the point Kase had focused on.

"Yes!" Kase shouted. The thunder roared in applause. Kase searched for the feeling again.

He wondered how long the lightning would take to charge. Talen had tried to explain weather systems to him during their training, but he couldn't remember the specifics at the moment. He was going to rely on what he felt. He recognized the stirring feelings inside; he was connected to the storm.

He looked at the targets. He focused on the empty one that Dom had bested him on. He imagined striking it with an arrow again, and felt the energy pool on that target. In a flash, lightning destroyed the target completely, sending wood fragments in all directions.

Kase looked on in satisfaction. The thunder applauded again.

"Random," Lenia said. "Did the weather want to get in some training too?"

Kase chuckled. It felt good to laugh at a timely and well-crafted joke. "No, that was me."

"You?" Lenia asked. "Since when can you control lightning?"

"Since today," Kase said. "Well, sort of. It's something that King Michael wrote about, but I haven't been able to really do it yet. The opportunity just kind of came along."

"That is so cool!" Lenia shouted. "How does it work? Can you show me?"

"It feels like water control, but with a sharper end," Kase said. He searched for the feeling, and felt the energy above him. "It's like the lightning pools together, and then comes to a point. I think about what I want to strike, and then follow through like I would a weapon."

Kase raised his hands for effect, waited a few moments, and then pointed to the target that Dom had hit first. The lightning struck the bulls-eye with more force than its predecessor, but with the same effect. Wood shattered and flew everywhere. Thunder applauded again.

"That is so … ferocious," Lenia asked. "I tried to feel it too, but I couldn't. It's such a spectacle. Should I bring Dom back so you can show off your power?"

Kase couldn't handle more Dom in this moment. "I promise I'll show him soon, but we have training to do." Instead of bringing another lightning strike, he cleared the rain from their training area, like drawing a set of curtains. It still rained around them, but not on the field with the targets.

"The Rooster wanted to prepare dinner with Cali and Aura anyway," Lenia said. She grabbed an arrow from her quiver, and shot at the closest target. She was too far to the right, but it had the right distance.

Kase and Lenia practised for another hour before returning to the castle for dinner. The storm didn't pass, but they had their small field of clarity. They each worked on their arced shots, and even tried a few to mimic Dom's incredible arrow-to-arrow shot. Neither one of them was successful at hitting another arrow at any distance, but it was fun to try without The Rooster around.

# CHAPTER 13

# When You're In Love, You're Happy

Kase and Lenia peeked over the parapet. The red tint of Kase's visor lit up from the street light, but he could barely make out the shadows walking about. "How do you see out of your helmet during a fight?" he asked.

Lenia rested her back against the parapet and slid down. "It's easier when you have a flaming weapon," she said.

Even though Kase couldn't see clearly, he could tell the street they looked down on was more crowded than they desired. He slid down next to Lenia, and thought about the first battle of hers that he'd witnessed. "Will arrows work as well as a sword?"

Lenia nestled up against Kase and held his hand. "I haven't used arrows as much, but the hay wagon will help," she said. "I've tried using flaming battle axes, spears, and daggers, and they all give off some good light, but they aren't as intimidating as a flaming sword."

"As intimidating?" Kase asked. He was intrigued by Lenia's strategy, even though he still didn't agree with her goals.

Lenia stroked the back of Kase's hand. "Cali found a book in King Michael's library about using fear as a war tactic. He'd explained that even though all warriors were taught to stand tall, to never waver, and to remain focused in battle, most were still afraid. The anticipation of what was coming, combined with violence and death, was too much for some to handle."

Lenia leant her head on Kase's shoulder as best she could with her helmet. The silhouette of her unicorn horn took up most of his view.

"King Michael also explained how he tried to use that fear to his advantage,"

Lenia continued. "He tried different ways to shock and confuse his enemy, in order to amplify their many emotions during battle. When Cali read these strategies, she used them in the design of the Unicorn Knight's outfit: the mask, the black clothes, and the potions. The flaming weapon was my touch, but the flaming sword seems to scare Guardians the most."

Kase squeezed Lenia's hand, but he disagreed. "When I saw you at the docks, I didn't think the fire sword was intimidating. If anything, it gave me an advantage because I could see your strikes better."

Lenia giggled. "You're different, Dandy." She squeezed his hand back. "I didn't mean that everyone is afraid of the flaming weapons; some are more confident than others. I've found there are different types of warrior that make up the Guardianship. We might face all three tonight."

Kase wondered why Lenia hadn't brought this up during their planning session with Cali and Dom. "Are you sure there's only three?"

"You'll see," Lenia said. "If we face a group of Guardians, most of them will look scared. One of them, though, will be the self-proclaimed alpha. If we take out the aggressive alpha, the others will barely put up a fight."

She tapped the back of his hand. "High Guardians are the opposite, though. Most High Guardians are aggressive, and will attack at the same time. Too many of them, and we'll have to abort."

When he was a Guardian, Kase hadn't noticed the tendencies of his cohorts—likely because he'd never faced them in battle. He was proud and impressed that Lenia was able to size up her enemies, since they'd only talked about it during their training sessions. He'd tried giving her examples, but her experience seemed to be all the schooling she needed.

"What's the third?" Kase asked, since Lenia had gone silent.

"The Triple Crown task force," Lenia said. "I haven't fought any of them, but I've studied them in the aftermath. The way they command the other Guardians, how they stand, and how they control the crowd is how I expect them to fight. They're focused, calculated, and angry."

Kase thought about Jax, Josephine, and Shay. When he was with them, they were supportive, but that had all been a ruse. They'd all had a hand in deceiving him, killing Lenia, and forcing Kase to find the pieces of the doorway of life. The task force didn't call the shots, but they were elite warriors that did the bidding of the calculating Triple Crown.

"What happens if we see one of them tonight?" he asked. He could feel his own anger stirring.

"We stick to the plan," Lenia said. "Our goal isn't to fight anyone in particular; it's to hold up a mirror to those we face. We show the Triple Crown what chaos looks like, so that they can see what they're doing to others."

"We dress like animals because they treat us like animals," Kase added. He and Lenia were repeating Cali's explanation to Dom.

"Our masks do more than send a message," Lenia said. "They allow us to be what we need to be, rather than who we are. As the Unicorn Knight and the Dandy Lion, we can do things that Lenia and Kase wouldn't normally do. We can be the same animal, but become a different beast." She squeezed Kase's hand again.

Kase wondered what it meant to be the same but different. He didn't know how to pretend to be something that he wasn't.

Lenia sighed. "It's so nice to have company on these missions, and experience these things together." She leant further into Kase. "I was so afraid to tell you about everything; I assumed I'd always walk this path alone. Now, I don't know how I could do it without you."

Kase felt his stomach drop. He was in the moment he wanted to be in, trying to understand Lenia's motivations and feelings. He appreciated her telling the truth, and felt the need to do the same.

"Can I be honest about something?" he asked. Lenia squeezed his hand again. "I'm not completely sold on the plan. I wish I had an alternative, but I can't shake the feeling that what we're doing is wrong. Life is valuable, and taking that away from those indirectly involved in the plans of the Triple Crown can't be the only solution."

"It might be wrong, but ..." Lenia paused. "But please keep believing in *me*. The farther we go down this dark path, the more I feel myself changing: this hole inside me expanding. I need you to keep being you, and challenging these plans, because if you don't … you might not be able to bring me back."

Kase closed his eyes. He could sense the battle going on inside Lenia. She might have been occupying herself with a war in the streets, but it was at the expense of her soul. He wanted to tell her everything would be okay. He wanted her struggle to disappear. He wanted to wrap his arms around her and tell her he loved her.

But was love enough?

If Lenia were changing, would she lose sight of her identity? Would she accept Kase's love if she became someone different? Would she still love Kase if he became someone different, too? Kase didn't enjoy the questions floating around in his mind, but he needed to remain patient if he was going to find the right answers; the answers they both needed to survive.

"Tell me more," he said. He nestled his helmet against hers, but paused for a second with his lips above her forehead. Mask kiss.

"Will you come with me the next time I see my parents?" Lenia asked.

"Do you mean visit them?" Kase asked. As a group, they still agreed not to visit anyone outside the Kingdom of Moiras, especially family members. If anyone knew that the group was alive, it would put everyone in jeopardy. Of all the questionable things that Lenia had done, he hoped she hadn't broken that rule.

"No, not visit them," Lenia said. "Cali assumes there are surveillance sage mirrors aimed at all of our family homes, so I've stayed clear of those hotspots. But sometimes I'll sit on rooftops like this one in Flonkertown, waiting for a glimpse of my mother, father, or brother running errands. I've only seen them a few times, but thinking about them gives me hope that I'll meet them again soon. I wonder if they think about me in the same way."

When Lenia had been murdered, her family blamed Kase. The Triple Crown had spread rumours that he was the one that held the knife, even though it was High Scholar Sheese who had actually killed her. He remembered the grief and disappointment in Mrs. Rie's eyes when he tried to explain the truth, but he didn't have any proof at the time. He wondered if they'd forgive him when they discovered he'd brought Lenia back.

"It might be painful for them to remember you, but you're impossible to forget," Kase said. He squeezed Lenia's hand.

"It goes both ways," Lenia said. "I used to feel the push from my parents to follow in their footsteps. I wanted to create my own identity instead. I'm on that path now, but I wish they were a part of my journey. I miss being a part of their lives, too."

"We'll make it happen," Kase said. He felt Lenia's vulnerability when she talked about her family, and he was grateful to learn more.

"It's been nice to have some time to reflect," Lenia said. "Maybe we'll both get a chance to build new relationships with our families, when the time comes."

Kase didn't want Lenia's beautiful thoughts to turn into a lecture about Dom. She was subtle about her suggestions to mend fences, but Kase didn't want to hear it while they were sharing this moment. Just thinking about Dom made his anger bubble up, but maybe he could use that emotion under the mask of the Dandy Lion.

"Do you think it's time?" Kase changed the subject.

"Let's check," Lenia said.

The duo peeked over the parapet again. A few more businesses had closed, and there were less horse-drawn carts travelling the road. No Guardians were posted anywhere, but that didn't matter right now. They needed to wait for the crowd to disperse before making their move.

Lenia and Kase went over their plan one last time. There were still a few unknowns, but they had done their best to mitigate the heavy risk. They were both confident that they'd be successful, as long as they followed three rules: don't talk, don't use magic, and don't get caught.

After one final look up and down the street, Kase and Lenia crept to the other side of the building. They peered over the edge. The only thing in the alley was their cart. Lenia stashed her trident in a safe spot against the edge of the parapet, and then teleported Kase down to ground level.

The alley was so dark, Kase could barely see. He felt the hay in the cart, and lifted some up for Lenia. He heard her climb in, but he didn't know if she was tucked away inside the nook they'd created. "Ready," she said. He lowered the hay, and felt his way to the front.

He pulled the cart to the end of the alley. The dim light from the main street guided his way, but he couldn't see where he was stepping. He didn't have far to go, since there was only one building between their lookout and the main strip.

The cart that Curtis had built had solid wheels, but Talen had stripped some of the unnecessary material to make it lighter. Some of the side panels were missing, and a few of the runners along the base were removed.

The cart wasn't built to last long: it just needed to hold together long enough to transport a hidden Lenia to the centre of the intersection. A warrior with a lion's helmet might get some odd looks, but a unicorn helmet would instantly cause a ruckus. They were counting on her notoriety to draw in some Guardians, but they needed to be in the perfect position before the mayhem could begin.

When Kase hit the street, he didn't stop to look around: he just headed straight for the stone fountain in the middle of the intersection. The fountain consisted of five giant fish holding fins, standing on their tails with water spouting from their mouths. It wasn't the prettiest fountain in Kimroad, in Kase's opinion, but it made for a nice centrepiece. The fountain would also provide cover for Kase and Lenia to be backed up against during their upcoming battle.

Kase wheeled the cart to the side of the fountain opposite their lookout, and then stopped. He finally looked up, and was relieved to see how much light the streetlamps gave off. He noticed a few odd looks, but still didn't see any Guardians.

Lenia burst from her hiding spot, spraying hay everywhere. She spread her arms wide, holding her bow in one hand, and stared at the sky.

"It's the Unicorn Knight!" someone shrieked.

Kase wondered what they would call him, since none of them likely knew of his clever Dandy Lion name. He grabbed his bow and quiver from the cart with one hand, and one of the potion bottles that Aura and Lenia had made with the other. He waited for the signal.

Lenia hopped out of the cart. She took a long look around, as more and more people gathered to point. Some of them held their sage mirrors, likely capturing a moving image of the scene. The clock had officially started.

The Unicorn Knight dropped her arms. Kase smashed the potion bottle into the cart, and then jumped away. Lenia lit an old and rusty fire starter, dangled it in the air for the crowd, and then tossed it into the cart. The potion flashed like a shooting star as flames engulfed the hay within. The crowd murmured louder.

Kase pulled an arrow from his quiver. The tip was covered in a flammable cloth that he lit using the spectacle beside him. He readied his bow, aimed at the closest building, pulled the arrow back slowly, and launched it towards the storefront sign.

All of the storefronts lining the intersection were owned and operated by Brothers' Inc. Since Mardious Hood still had influence over the Badlands, and his partners from the Badlands ran Brothers' Inc., any damage to the businesses would get the attention of the acting High Wizard.

It wasn't likely that a few arrows would burn down the buildings, but Kase enjoyed the message associated with it. He smiled as he watched the shop sign burn.

Lenia withdrew an arrow from her quiver, and began her own aerial attack. She and Kase both launched arrows at different buildings as the onlookers panicked. Both the Unicorn Knight and the Dandy Lion were careful not to hit any innocents, landing all of their arrows outside the buildings they were aiming at. Kase didn't want anyone else to get caught inside like Josephine's sister.

The first Guardians finally arrived on scene. There were three of them on foot. They had to fight against the panicked crowd to get through.

"Drop your weapons!" a Guardian yelled.

Kase lowered his bow, but kept the arrow pulled back. Lenia glanced at him, and then slapped her chest twice with an open palm. She dropped her bow, the steel clanging on the stone cobblestone, and walked towards the Guardians with open arms. Kase aimed his arrow in the opposite direction, and shot at another building.

He peered around the fountain to the street behind them, but didn't see any more Guardians. He glanced at the two open streets in his view, grabbed another arrow, and lit the arrowhead with the cart. He took aim at another building, and shot at another sign.

Kase looked back at Lenia. She had drawn her sword, and dragged the tip of it along the stone behind her. Two of the Guardians stood strong, with their own swords drawn, but the third one screamed and ran towards Lenia. She must have been the alpha.

The Guardian swung her sword down towards the unicorn helmet, but Lenia easily dodged the predictable, overhead strike. The Guardian's sword hit the pavement, and then redirected towards Lenia's side. The Unicorn Knight easily blocked the weak attack, and then stomped on the Guardian's boot. The Guardian lost focus, allowing Lenia to strike her wrist. The Guardian dropped her sword.

The way Lenia moved was impressive. Her steps were smooth, quick, and light, like a dancer. Her decision-making was confident, and her strikes were precise. As a professor he was proud. As a warrior, he was appalled that she was hurting those trying to protect their community. As her boyfriend, he wanted to stare and watch her all day.

He looked away to shake himself out of his daze, and noticed the crowd parting down the street to his left. Two High Guardians on horseback were racing towards them. Both were dressed in shiny battle armour.

Kase was at a disadvantage. If he were to fight two warriors on horseback, he'd lose. High Guardians on horseback had more leverage in combat, and the horses could trample Kase, among other things. With so much space around the fountain, the High Guardians could attack with speed, too.

Kase needed to level the playing field. The easiest way would be to control the horses, but he couldn't use magic. If the horses disobeyed their riders, it would be obvious that a wizard was influencing them. Kase grabbed an arrow instead.

He didn't need to light the arrow on fire. Although a single arrow wouldn't kill the horse, the sharp point would hurt it enough for the animal to panic.

If Kase could keep the horses away, the High Guardians would be forced to adjust their attack.

Kase glanced back to Lenia as he drew an arrow. Two of the Guardians were on the ground. One wasn't moving. Kase trusted Talen was watching the news reports, so he could find them again later. The final Guardian was defending well, but Lenia was clearly in control.

Kase pulled the arrow back, and aimed the tip just left of the closest horse's snout. He wanted to hit it in the chest so it would rear up. He waited a few more moments for the perfect angle, and then let his arrow fly.

As expected, the horse whinnied in pain when the arrow hit. The rider had difficulty controlling the animal, and slowed his charge. The other High Guardian also slowed down, and then dismounted quickly, about forty yards away from Kase.

The High Guardian disappeared from view for a second, and then came around his horse with his own arrow drawn. As the High Guardian fired, Kase ducked and rolled to avoid a direct hit.

Kase heard a snap, but it wasn't from the arrow. After bouncing back to his feet, he checked his bow. It had broken in half. Dom's poor craftsmanship angered Kase, but he didn't have time to understand why the bow was so weak. The High Guardian was loading another arrow, while the other had also dismounted and calmed his injured horse.

Kase was a sitting duck without his bow. He wished he had a shield. He should have prepared for this situation.

He thought about Lenia's analysis. If the High Guardians were more aggressive than regular Guardians, Kase wondered if he could bait them into a swordfight. He waved his broken bow in the air, and then tossed it to the ground. He drew his sword with his right hand, and then motioned with his left for the High Guardians to come at him.

Instead of firing, the High Guardian lowered his bow. The two High Guardians had a short discussion, and then took Kase's bait. They both drew their swords, and came rushing towards him.

Kase quickly checked on Lenia. She was fighting two new Guardians, but was still dancing like a seasoned veteran. He checked the other streets, and only noticed a few onlookers holding their sage mirrors high. No other Guardians were drawing near.

He didn't want to stray too far from the fire, so Kase stood his ground. He gripped his sword with both hands and studied the movements of the aggressive High Guardians. Lenia was right again: the High Guardians were working together. They approached Kase at a similar pace, splitting up so they could both attack Kase at the same time. Kase wasn't going to wait around to let them gain the advantage.

Kase lunged at the High Guardian to his right. He spun away from both of them as he landed a quick strike to the High Guardian's sword. His partner hollered, and ran at Kase with his sword held high.

Kase jumped out of the way, and quickly circled the duo. If he could use one High Guardian to block the other, he might have a chance at landing a few heavy blows. He swung a few more times while evaluating the weak points in his opponents' stance, defense, and armour. Nothing out of the ordinary stood out.

The High Guardians had open masks, which was good for communication, but it created a vulnerability at the neckline. Their body armour covered their shoulders, chest, and arms, but any strike to the armpits, inner elbows, or wrists would do damage. High boots protected their calves and feet, but the knees were exposed.

Kase remembered when he wore the High Guardian uniform, and had appreciated not having plates on the knees. It was beneficial for movement, especially when mounting and dismounting from a horse, but also in a fight.

Kase's priority was to expose this knee weakness.

He waited for the closest High Guardian to swing his sword. The blade came across the High Guardian's body, so Kase moved the opposite way. Kase swiped down with his own blade, catching the inside of the High Guardian's knee, which caused the High Guardian to fall away.

Unfortunately, the other High Guardian was already on the offensive. Kase didn't have time to get out of the way, but he was able to lift his sword to block the oncoming overhead strike. Being off-balance, he was forced to one knee due to the blow.

The High Guardian had all his weight on Kase's sword, so Kase couldn't do much except roll away. But not before he noticed the point of a black unicorn helmet over the High Guardian's shoulder.

The High Guardian's eyes widened. He spat some blood as he fell forwards. Kase shifted his weight, guiding the High Guardian away. Lenia followed him to the ground, unable to pull her sword from the crumbling warrior. Now she was exposed.

Kase noticed the High Guardian he'd struck realize the same thing. With a battle cry, the High Guardian limped forwards and made a high, arcing swing towards Lenia's head. Because Lenia's helmet was in the way, Kase wasn't able to meet the sword, so he pulled his hilt into his body to shorten his strike. He swiped right in front of Lenia's mask, hitting the High Guardian's exposed wrist before Lenia was struck. With their combined momentum, Kase's sword chopped right through.

The High Guardian screamed in pain and fell to the ground. "You monsters!" he yelled, clutching the fresh stub that Kase had given him.

Kase felt conflicted. His training had kicked in, and for a few minutes, he had thought about nothing but winning the battle. Now that he had a moment to reflect on the outcome, guilt crept into his stomach.

Lenia pulled her weapon from the dead High Guardian and looked behind Kase. She tapped him on the shoulder and pointed.

He turned, and felt relief to see horses galloping down the road. There were at least ten High Guardians, coming from the direction of the castle of the Triple Crown. That relief turned to anger when he noticed the High Wizard's golden carriage following the group.

Lenia pulled Kase by the arm towards their hay fire. They both grabbed their bows, and then huddled in the backseat of the cart, closest to the fountain. Kase didn't want to look at any of the mayhem they'd caused, but he couldn't help it. Seven bodies were sprawled on the pavement, and a few of the building signs were still on fire. It was all within the scope of their plan, but it was still a shock to see.

Lenia pulled a potion sac from her belt and tossed the contents onto the fire. The flames turned purple, and then a black cloud billowed from the centre of the cart. Kase held his breath, but he could sense the smoke get trapped inside his mask. He closed his eyes so he wouldn't start tearing up. He could hear the sparking fire, the cries of panic from the wounded High Warrior, and the galloping horses echoing down the street.

Then all he heard was silence.

He opened his eyes, but all he saw was smoke. He panicked and started coughing. He felt Lenia rub his arms.

"It's okay," she said. Her trident clanged on the floor. "Let it all out. We made it home."

Kase fumbled with the clasp on his helmet as he continued to cough, but then he finally got it off. He bent over and coughed a few more times, dropping his helmet to the floor. His coughing fit quickly ended.

He tried to forget the images: the darkness, the fire, and the blood. In the midst of battle, his training allowed him to survive. There were even times where he was almost having fun. But now, arguments of right and wrong flooded his mind, along with the stories, reasons, and excuses he was using to justify his actions.

He noticed they were alone in their room. Cali had mentioned that she'd be waiting to debrief them after the mission, but maybe they were to meet elsewhere. He wondered why Lenia didn't just teleport them directly to his sister.

Lenia shook her gloves off, and then snuck a hand underneath Kase's leather vest. "Is yours pounding as hard as mine?" She steadied her warm palm over his heart.

Kase had never taken the time to reflect right after a battle. His sparring sessions were not as intense as a real showdown. Each time he'd fought before, he'd always thought about what was next, not what had happened. His heart beat rapidly.

"I don't know," he said. He undid the clasp on Lenia's helmet, and lifted it off. Her hair was still tied up, but a few stray strands were stuck to her face with sweat. She looked fatigued, confident, and beautiful. He felt the need to kiss her, and succumbed to the feeling. He tilted his head forwards and met her lips passionately.

After a hot moment, Lenia pushed Kase away. "Let's examine further," she said. She undid the straps on Kase's vest, and pulled it over Kase's head. She tugged the vest so hard that he almost fell over.

When he regained his balance, Lenia was already ripping at her own straps. Kase helped her lift her chest plate over her head, which was a little more difficult with her cape attached, but they succeeded together. They both stood shirtless, wrapping their arms around each other, kissing again.

Their debrief with Cali could wait.

# CHAPTER 14

# Insanity Laughs Under Pressure
# We're Breaking

It was the third time Sheese had studied the moving image. He felt like he was missing something obvious. The Unicorn Knight had been doing well on his own. Why would he include the Lion Knight all of a sudden? How many other animal warriors was he recruiting? What was his motivation?

"Things have escalated since he got himself a partner," High Warrior Mac noted. "We've lost a lot of good men this week. None in this last encounter, but fifteen overall."

"Not all of them were good." Mardious chuckled. "Good one, babe," he mumbled.

"I hope the Unicorn Knight comes for you next." Mac sneered.

"Oh, I'll be safe," Mardious said. His leg dangled over the edge of the lounger as he watched the sage mirror above the fireplace. "He seems to enjoy the taste of warriors' blood." Mardious chuckled again. "Probably because it's foul, babe."

Mac scoffed. "A warrior—"

"He makes a good point," Sheese interrupted. He hadn't called this meeting for Mardious and Mac to bicker. He needed to guide their energy towards a viable solution. "Why does the Unicorn Knight target Guardians? Is he a criminal getting revenge? Or is he a former Guardian with resentment?"

"Maybe he just likes to watch the world burn," Mardious said.

Even though Mardious was having more audible conversations with the voices in his head lately, he still had a lot of good ideas to contribute. Was it that simple? Could the Unicorn Knight enjoy the chaos and destruction he caused, just for the pure pleasure of it? Did he have no remorse for his actions? Did he not care about anyone in the realm but himself?

Sheese had been in this position before, when he'd evaluated Money Jane. At first, he didn't know that Money Jane was a pair: Mardious and his late partner Amelia working together. Money had been their motivator, and they were successful in their elaborate plans to steal from the rich and give to the poor.

Well, until they were caught.

Sheese did not have a hand in catching them, or in Amelia's death, but he had followed their every move. When Mardious was caught, Sheese seized the opportunity to befriend the criminal. Sometimes the best relationships came from dark corners.

"Could they be more than friends?" Sheese asked.

"A father-son duo would make sense," Mac said. "They both move in similar ways."

"Possibly lovers?" Sheese wondered if they were around the same age. The Unicorn Knight was lithe, and the Lion Knight had youthful, well-defined arms.

"No one loves warriors more than other warriors," Mardious quipped.

"They're loyal to each other, nonetheless," Sheese said. "High Warrior Mac, I need you to look into the Guardian archives. Identify how many current and former warriors have sons, and which warriors are linked romantically. I'll check the prison archives for the same."

"That's a lot of work," Mac said. "Good to see the High Wizard contributing."

Sheese glanced at Mardious. As much as Mac was trying to get a rouse out of him, Mardious was still comfortably splayed across the lounger, giggling to himself.

"He's setting the trap," Sheese said. "Even when we find out who they are, we need to catch them. Sometimes you need a criminal to catch a criminal."

"How many of my men are going to die before you lay your trap?" Mac asked.

"Not enough." Mardious chuckled again.

Mac jumped up from his chair. He scowled at Mardious, and then at Sheese. "Are we done here?" As angry as he seemed, he still showed respect to the sanctity of the Triple Crown.

Sheese waved towards Mac's seat. "Almost," he said. Mac's scowl didn't leave as he cautiously sat back down. Sheese looked to Mardious. "Are you ready to show off your bait?"

Mardious brought his left hand to his chin. Strapped to the inside of his wrist was an Aileron-sized sage mirror. "Mirror, mirror, connect to Useless Warrior Number Three."

That earned another glare from Mac. Sheese didn't like the tension, but knew that creativity was sometimes born from stressful situations.

"We're ready," Mardious said.

The trio sat in silence for a few minutes. The moving image on the sage mirror above the fireplace still flashed, but the crackling of the fire drowned out the low sound. Sheese liked the ambiance of his office and the space his guests had to lounge about. It was a lot more comfortable than Mardious' secret room.

Two knocks on the door cut through the tense air, and then Jax entered, carrying a crate. He closed the door tightly before marching to the table in the middle of the three loungers. He was wearing a beige cape that covered his entire body. He placed the crate on the table, and then removed his cape, revealing a black uniform.

Mac's attention quickly turned to Jax, but Mardious still studied the moving image above the fireplace.

Jax removed the lid on the crate to expose a black helmet with a unicorn horn, purple visor, and purple plume. He flipped his hair back, and then slid the helmet on. He posed, but his shoulders drooped forwards, showing his reluctance to wear the costume.

"Where's your bow?" Mardious asked. He pointed to the sage mirror. "The Unicorn Knight and the Lion Knight each have one."

Three of the four times the Unicorn Knight and the Lion Knight had been together, they'd used the bow and arrow to their advantage. Although their locations and methods were difficult to predict, Sheese had also noted that they were both skilled archers.

"I don't have my permit," Jax admitted. He pulled his sword from his sheath, showing off his black-handled blade instead.

"So?" Mardious looked at Mac, but Mac was staring at the floor.

"All Guardians need to register for bows and arrows," Sheese said. "There's a yearly exam, to ensure that they meet the accuracy requirements. Plus, there's an aptitude test to remind them of their responsibility with ranged weapons. Most Guardians don't practice enough to keep up with their yearly review, so they opt not to carry a bow at all."

"It's also a little bulky," Jax said. He rotated his torso a few times, looking at each shoulder. "I don't know how the Unicorn Knight manages his quiver with this cape in the way."

"We should incentivise High Guardians to obtain their bow and arrow permits," Sheese said. "In order to get more archers ready against these vigilantes."

"Both knights are skilled," Mardious said. "If they're Guardians, or were, would they be on a permit list?"

Sheese smiled and clasped his hands in front of him. "Yes, they would," he said. "Mac, you have another list to reference."

Mac shook his head slowly. "Why wasn't I told about this?"

"If he was competent, you wouldn't have to do his job for him, babe," Mardious muttered.

Mac glared at Mardious. "I'm tired your games," he snarled. He clenched his fists. "Both you and your pathetic ghost."

Mardious finally turned to look at Mac. He didn't say anything, but lifted his gloved hand and twiddled his fingers.

"Enough!" Sheese yelled. With Mardious attempting to use his magic, and Mac with his fists ready, Sheese had to avoid a confrontation; they needed to continue without delay. "Mac, you have your orders. Leave us."

Mac smiled and stood. He pounded his heart when he faced Sheese, and headed for the door.

"You too, Jax," Sheese said. Jax fumbled with his helmet as he returned it to the crate. He covered himself with his robe once again and hustled for the door. Mac held the door open as they exited.

"Anytime, anywhere," Mac said before slamming the door behind him.

Mardious had already returned his attention to the sage mirror. The Unicorn Knight had just dropped his trademark smoke solution, covering the area completely. There were no other surveillance mirrors in the area, so it had been impossible to track the criminals from that point on.

"Did you discover anything from the residue?" Sheese asked.

"It's a common smoke screen," Mardious said. "Anyone can buy the solution at market, or make their own. There are only two ingredients: saltpeter and water. Even a warrior could figure it out."

"I'm glad Jax won't have trouble using it," Sheese said.

Mardious chuckled. "Mac was pretty agitated, wasn't he?"

Sheese was still displeased that Mardious was the reason for Mac's agitation, but he couldn't afford to make Mardious angry. He needed at least one of the members of the Triple Crown to remain calm if their plan was to succeed.

"He deserves it sometimes, but we don't really need him," Sheese lied. He forced a laugh. "Who is Jax's first target?"

One of the reasons that Sheese and Mardious were able to obtain power, and remain the leaders of the Triple Crown for so long, was because they eliminated their competition. Sometimes it involved a scandal, other times an arrest. Now, with the Unicorn Knight being a public vigilante, they were using his reputation for carnage to their advantage by killing a few high-ranking officials that were a threat to their crown. It would be even easier now that they had their look-alike.

Mardious stood from the lounger and paced in front of the fireplace. "The Goblin," he finally said.

The Goblin's name was Rafi Jabot, but he'd earned the nickname because of his appearance. He was a young healer that had initially been hired to join the Department of Health and Safety at the Triple Crown. Although his resume wasn't impressive, he'd gained a lot of favours from other wizards in power.

Rumours swirled that he'd be first in line to replace High Wizard Zuke one day.

"Good choice," Sheese said. The Goblin didn't seem to have a bad bone in his body. Sheese knew he'd be unable get the wizard's support if Mardious were to be replaced. "Location?"

"Home invasion." Mardious tickled the air and made the flames in the fireplace dance as he continued to pace. "He lives alone. Should be easy."

Sheese nodded. "Next?"

"Julissa Ripling," Mardious said.

Julissa was similar to Rafi in terms of favourites to challenge the crown, but she was on the scholar side. Although not a direct threat to Sheese's position in the short-term, she could be a strong candidate in a few years. She was smart, creative, and personable, and would make a good leader one day—but she was also unlikely to support Sheese's agenda.

"What about Karen Klump?" Sheese asked.

"The Minister of Finance?" Mardious replied. "When did she become a problem?"

Karen Klump had been in her role for the past twenty years. She rarely questioned the spending that Sheese had included in his proposals, which served Sheese well when he manipulated the numbers to serve his own personal ventures, but things had changed recently.

"She's become more frugal as of late," Sheese said. "In most cases, her keen eye helps save the Triple Crown money, but not for our planned increase in our … secret resources. She's also opposed to offering more of a reward for the capture of the Unicorn Knight."

"We don't need the public's help," Mardious said. "Our new plan will work."

Sheese smiled. He loved Mardious' confidence, but he wanted to use the opportunity to feed Mardious' ego. "I wanted to increase it, as a tribute to Money Jane."

Mardious stopped pacing. He stared at Sheese, but didn't respond.

"The reward for Money Jane is still the largest bounty in history," Sheese said. "If we offer a reward of one Aileron less than that amount, the public will be forced to make the comparison. They'll remember Money Jane, and the impact she had on the realm. At the same time, history will still note that she was a bigger threat than the Unicorn Knight, or any other criminal, for that matter."

Mardious smiled. He turned to the fire and mumbled something to himself. He started pacing again. "Karen is Julissa's mentor," he said. "We can probably get to them at the same time."

Sheese was pleased that Mardious could be more efficient with their kill list. Three targets seemed like a suitable starting point. "Have you considered what we're going to do with the Unicorn Knight when we catch him?" Sheese asked.

"We'll need to interrogate him first," Mardious said. "I don't like your idea of sending him to track down the doorway of life until we know who he is, and what he's about."

There were other powerful relics that Sheese needed to track down, but the ability to bring the dead back to life would make Sheese a god. He had fantasized about what it would feel like to have the ultimate power, and yearned for the opportunity to try.

"The Unicorn Knight's punishment will be death," Sheese said. "He won't have any other option than to help us."

Mardious paused again. His dark eyes stared through Sheese, seemingly through his soul. "You taught me that patience is a virtue. You should practice what you preach."

"Apologies." Sheese held his palms up. "I don't want us to lose sight of our ultimate goals."

"Mac has lost sight, but I haven't." Mardious sneered and twiddled his fingers. An illusion of Amelia appeared beside him. She wore a blue dress that matched her eyes, white gloves, and mean scowl.

"How dare you," Amelia said.

"Again, I apologize," Sheese said. It had been years since he'd seen Mardious' illusion, and he had still never witnessed another wizard create a person in such detail before. He knew how difficult it was, but Mardious clearly kept his priorities straight. He needed to change the subject to calm Mardious down.

"I wanted Porkchop to have all the support he needs."

"Porkchop is motivated to bring back J.R.," Mardious said.

"And me too, babe," Amelia added.

Mardious smiled. "Amelia too," he repeated.

"Wasn't he already on a mission of vengeance?" Sheese asked. After his son's death, Porkchop had vowed revenge on the killer, but multiple gangs had taken the credit. Last time Sheese was updated, it sounded like Porkchop was having difficulty tracking down all of the culprits. "What did you call it?"

"The Millennium Massacre," Mardious said. "It's done. Now he's motivated to bring J.R. back. He's ordered members of the Brotherhood to track down the Garrick crew, scour their last known whereabouts for clues, and keep watch on their families."

It had been months since Cali, her brother Kase, and their friends had stolen the doorway of life from Mardious and Sheese. It was surprising that they'd stayed underground for so long, but like Mardious had pointed out, patience was a virtue.

"I'm glad you have it all under control," Sheese said. He noticed Amelia soften. "I don't know what I'd do without you."

Amelia disappeared. Mardious stretched his arms and yawned. "Anything else?"

Sheese sighed. He felt tired too. He shook his head.

Mardious wasted no time leaving Sheese's office, but Sheese didn't follow. Instead, he went back to his desk. He sat down, reached underneath the desktop to flip a secret latch, and then pulled out an old journal from the secret compartment. He placed it neatly in front of him and turned to the first page.

'Kill or Be Killed' was the title of his personal journal.

He enjoyed writing creatively; it helped him reflect on his personal philosophies. His journal wasn't incriminating, like some of the other books he kept that held details of secret relics, logs of fallen mercenaries, or confidential profiles of those that threatened him. It was a reminder of where he started, and how far he'd come.

He noticed the moving image of the Unicorn Knight and Lion Knight start from the beginning on the sage mirror above the fireplace. Both knights fired arrows at nearby buildings, begging for the attention it drew. Mardious' words crept back into Sheese's thoughts: maybe they enjoyed watching the world burn.

Sheese knew what it was like to wear a mask. For too long, he'd played the role of politician. He smiled when he was in public. He courted other politicians to sway them to his council. He found solutions to the many problems that plagued the realm. His mask had helped him gain power, but he'd dreamt of having that power without having to play the game.

The doorway of life was his ticket to reaching those dreams.

Over the years, Sheese had been motivated by different means. He had yearned for popularity while attending the Academy, and thus became the most popular scholar in his senior year. He'd been motivated by money, and earned access to the richest lifestyle in the realm. But even though he'd been motivated by power, being the High Scholar didn't make him feel superior; he was still in the routine of fixing other people's problems.

He'd cut taxes to gain favour from the rich, who wanted to hold onto their wealth. He'd provided health care programs to help the sick, in return for their votes. He'd invested in technology to produce surveillance mirrors to keep the vulnerable safe. While some valued money, more valued health, and others valued security, there was one currency that surpassed all others: life.

With control over those that lived and those that perished, Sheese wouldn't have to trade favour for anything. The people in the realm would beg for him to bring back loved ones that they'd lost. They'd praise him for his mercy, and pay homage to his grace. They'd worship him like a god.

On the other hand, he'd get to watch people struggle when they were faced with death. He'd look into their eyes, and recognize the pain that he caused by not granting life. He'd already taken lives before, whether with a dagger, a sword, or a noose. Watching someone beg for their life was a simple pleasure that he wished he could do more of.

Over the fireplace, the Unicorn Knight moved closer to the surveillance mirror that had captured the latest attack. He hoped that the Unicorn Knight wouldn't fall to the sword of a Guardian. He wanted to look into the captured killer's eyes: to wait for the moment that a monster became fearful, because he held its life in his hands.

The Lion Knight flashed to the forefront of the image. As the follower, the Lion Knight was likely to compromise his own safety for the survival of the leader. Sheese was already thinking about what he could manipulate the Lion Knight to do, and maybe force him into joining the search for lost relics.

He couldn't wait for his chance to test his new theories. He picked up a quill, but didn't turn to a new page in his journal. He read the title again.

He would never be killed.

## CHAPTER 15

# How Ever Do You Want Me?

Eyes closed, Kase swayed his head with the wind, but his stress struggled to fly away. He noticed his stomach drop, which signalled Maxim's descent. Kase tried to enjoy the ride down, but his eyes were forced open when Dominic squeezed his ribs tighter.

"Are we there yet?" Dom yelled.

Kase thought about telling Maxim to do a loop the loop to scare Dom even more. In the best-case scenario, Dom might even let go of Kase and fall to his second death. As much as Kase would love to get a break from Dom for a few hours, the disappointment on Cali's face would last longer in Kase's memory.

Maxim had reached the treetops in the eastern part of the kingdom, where a wide river ran. After a few moments, she passed the top of the waterfall, and followed the flowing water to the nearest bank. Dom shrieked.

Aura and Talen were lying on the embankment: Talen scribbling notes in her book, and Aura basking in the sunshine. When Maxim landed, neither one of them moved, although Aura pointedly kept her eyes closed. Dom leapt from Maxim's back and knelt in the loose dirt. Kase petted his friend, and then slid casually off her back.

"Remind me never to do that again," Dom said. He took a few deep breaths, stood, and brushed his pants clean.

Maxim growled, which made Kase smile. He'd told her to growl at Dom whenever she was nearby, to scare him as a joke. Even though she didn't understand their human speech, her timing was perfect.

"I didn't mean it." Dom walked backwards, keeping a fearful eye on the friendly, but menacing, beast.

"I need to get back to the pack," Maxim told Kase.

"Thank you for the ride," Kase said. "I'll be gone for a few days, but I'll see you when I get back."

"You're not bringing more people back, are you?" Maxim asked.

"Maybe one," Kase said. "Is that a problem with your parents?" Maxim had expressed the concerns of her pack. They'd spent their entire lives without people in the Kingdom of Moiras. They were peaceful with Kase and his friends so far, but Kase had been obligated to make a promise not to overpopulate it.

"Not yet," Maxim said. "They just don't like surprises."

"I understand," Kase said. "I'll come for a hunt with the whole pack when I return, and answer any questions your parents might have about the safety of their kingdom."

"They'd like that." Maxim purred, flapped her wings, and then flew away.

"Hey, Aura," Dom said. "What did the river say to the riverbank?"

Kase looked to the sky. He imagined himself flying away with Maxim, getting away from Dom and his lame attempts to connect with everyone as fast as possible.

"What?" Aura asked. It didn't sound like a question, but more like Aura didn't hear him correctly.

"Nothing," Dom said. "It just waved."

Aura and Talen didn't respond. Kase closed his eyes and felt the soothing sunshine on his cheeks. He could sense a few animals scurrying about in the forest around him, but none of them were laughing either.

"Tough crowd," Dom said.

"Typically, when waves are mentioned, it's in reference to the sea," Talen said. "Waves are generated by the friction between wind and the water's surface, and are most noticeable when they crash against the shore of an ocean beach. But in rivers, water flows from higher elevation to lower elevation. When the water runs into the riverbank, it doesn't really crash against the shoreline, so your punch line is a little confusing."

Kase tried not to smile. Hearing Talen tear Dom's joke apart made his day.

"Well, I didn't mean to … uh …" Dom stopped.

The awkward silence made the morning even better. Kase turned to the group. Talen was still writing in her notebook; Aura basked in the sunshine; Dom was hunched over with his arms crossed, with his right fist under his chin. Kase let his broad smile flash.

"You should ask Kase to help you," Talen said. "He writes really original, well-thought-out material."

Kase's smile disappeared. Dom turned towards him and picked up the smile that Kase had dropped. "Is that so? I'd love to hear one of your jokes, son."

Talen turned towards Kase. She was grinning, which Kase hadn't seen on her before. It was like she recognized Kase's disgust to help Dom, and revelled in the awkwardness. If she was happy with her suggestion, it made her sense of humour pretty ruthless.

"Maybe later," Kase said.

"We should have a Jester Joust," Aura said. "Maybe the others would join in too? I've been wanting to write a few jokes myself, so a competition might motivate me to start on them."

"I love that idea," Talen said, which was odd because she hadn't been a fan of it when she studied with Kase.

"If you two need a competition to show off your sense of humour, then I'm in," Dom said. "I don't mind listening to jokes before or after the Jester Joust, though. Any time is a good time to laugh."

This wasn't a good time to laugh. Kase was interested in Aura's jokes, and wondered who else might enter the competition. Would Lenia tell jokes, or be a judge? Did Maxim have a few langara inspired one-liners?

A rustling from the bushes caught Kase's attention. Helena stepped towards Dom with her arms wide open. "I thought I heard your voice," she said.

Dom stood proud and slammed his fist into his chest. "Dragoon!"

Helena looked to Kase, then back at Dom. "We don't do that anymore, son," she said. "Come here." She wrapped her arms around Dom and lifted him up, like a toddler hugging a ragdoll. From Dom's expression, he hated hugs just as much as Lenia.

"It's good to see you, Mother," Dom gasped.

"You were a teenager the last time I saw you," Helena said. She lowered Dom back to the ground and put her hands on his shoulders. "You've grown into a distinguished young man." She combed her hand through his hair.

"I'm sure it's quite a shock," Dom said. "It must seem like only a few weeks since you've seen me last."

"We're blessed to have this time now to catch up," Helena said. She winked at Kase, and then put her arm around Dom's shoulder. "Come see our camp." She led Dom into the brush, and down a narrow pathway into the woods.

Instead of following right away, Kase held back and took a peek at Talen's notebook. "Do you really think my jokes are well thought out and funny?"

"I do," Talen said. She was shading in a new mask design. It was like Lenia's unicorn helmet, but with stripes and no horn. "I also think you could help your dad out."

"He needs all the help he can get," Aura said. "If he knew his jokes were bad, and he was saying them ironically, then that would be different. But they're just terrible."

"I think he might be trying too hard," Talen added.

"What are you working on?" Kase asked.

"It's Aura's A.K. design," Talen said. She shifted her notebook so Kase could see it better.

"Call me the Zebra Lily," Aura said. "I like how your name is both an animal and a flower, so I wanted something similar. The mask will be black with white stripes, and have a black mohawk and black visor. I don't know if my armour will match yet; we'll see how the mask turns out first."

"I love it," Kase admitted. He wished he were the Zebra Lily instead of the Dandy Lion.

"I have also been working on this one," Talen said. She flipped to a previous page in her book. She'd sketched out a black helmet with a golden beak around the visor, complete with a red mohawk. "For Dom," she said.

Kase chuckled. "Too bad I didn't win that bet," he said.

"If Dom sees how cool this design is, maybe he'll change his mind," Talen said. "We've already started working on his goat helmet, but we could build this one too, as a backup."

"I'd like that," Kase said. "Thank you, Tal. That almost makes up for you pressuring me into helping Dom write jokes."

Talen's uncharacteristic smile didn't return, but her eyes dazzled with wicked joy. "I'm testing your patience as king. So far, you've passed, but we'll see what happens during the competition."

With so much going on with his Dandy Lion duties, Kase had forgotten about his King Classes. He was glad Talen was on top of it. "Anything else you'd like to assign me?"

"I have an entire lesson plan ready," Talen said. "When are you available for class?"

"Would it be okay if I sat in too?" Aura asked. "With Curtis spending so much time here lately, I don't have much extra to do."

"So you haven't been monitoring him?" Kase asked. "What if he's drinking again?"

"He doesn't need my help anymore," Aura said. "Go see for yourself."

Talen returned to shading her designs while Aura rolled over to tan her back. Kase followed the path that his grandmother and Dom had taken, and soon heard someone chopping wood. When he found the group, he was surprised to see Curtis with his shirt off wielding an axe—mostly because Curtis didn't do that work at the castle.

"Two Gees!" Curtis shouted. He slammed the axe head into the stump in front of him, and attempted to hug Kase.

Kase took a step back from Curtis' grasp. "You could use a bath."

Curtis sniffed his left armpit, and then scrunched his nose. "You're not wrong," he said. "Guess I've lost track of time. It's been so fun here! Look at this." Curtis flashed his palms. There were multiple blisters on each hand; some of them were bleeding.

"Yikes," Kase said. "Aura isn't that far away, you know. I can heal them quickly for you while I'm here." Kase reached out, but Curtis yanks his hands away.

"No way," Curtis said. "Your grandfather calls these badges of honour, and I can see why. They make me proud of my work."

Kase placed the back of his hand over Curtis' forehead. "Are you feeling okay? I've never heard you talk about working hard before, let alone showing it off."

Curtis chuckled and swatted Kase's hand away. "Don't tease me, Two Gees," he said. He chuckled again. "Maybe it took a while for me to realize, but I can be pretty useful around here. I'm chopping wood, hauling things, hunting and fishing with your grandparents, and we've even been training together every morning. They even gave me the perfect Animal Kingdom nickname."

Curtis stood tall, puffed out his chest, and posed with his fists on his hips. "Kodiak Mountain."

Kase smiled. He was proud that Curtis was excited about his newfound identity. It was much better than the drunken mess that he'd been before. "I love it," Kase said. "Is Talen designing a helmet for you yet?"

"No, I'm designing it," Curtis said. "I like her ideas, but I feel like I need to do this on my own."

Kase almost took another step back. He was surprised at how much ownership Curtis was taking. "I can't wait to see what you come up with, Kodiak Mountain," he said.

Curtis smiled again. "This may sound stupid, but it feels like I have my confidence back," he said.

"It's not stupid," Kase said.

"It was a struggle for me to fit in with the Liberati," Curtis admitted. "You all had your own bond. But now that your grandparents are here, I feel closer to the group as a whole. The time we spend together, the guidance they give, and the tasks they assign me make me feel important again. They also make this kingdom feel more like home."

Kase smiled. "Sounds like you're part of the family," he said. "Maybe I should call you Uncle Kodiak Mountain?"

Curtis laughed. "That makes me sound old," he said. "I hope you get a chance to spend more time with your grandparents. They have a certain confidence about them: a deep understanding of what they're doing. Maybe we can all spend some family time together."

Curtis slapped Kase on the arm and then strode down the path towards the river. Kase went in the opposite direction, until he saw Helena with her arm around Dom, pointing at the trees above. When Kase was closer, he noticed Roman sitting on one of the branches, almost twenty feet up, his feet dangling over the ground below.

"Grandson Garrick!" Roman yelled. He shuffled across the branch to the trunk, where some planks were nailed into the tree like a ladder. He scaled the ladder to the ground as Helena and Dom turned towards Kase. Dom was the only one not smiling.

"Is this your camp?" Kase asked. He didn't see any tents anywhere, but there was a fire pit in a clearing beyond the trees with some stumps around it.

"We're building our dream home, up here in the trees," Helena said. "We've always wanted to construct our own, but never had the time. We're going to build a guest house in that tree over there." Helena squeezed Dom again, and then pointed to a tree to her right.

"Wonderful," Dom said with a sigh. His tone made it sound like he wasn't impressed.

"It really is," Kase admitted. He thought about the tree house event the Liberati had completed in their second Quest Series. "I want to build my own tree house someday too, but I don't know how. Would you construct it on the ground first and then move it up? Or do you just build it in the tree?"

"Each tree is a little different, so we're tailoring our design accordingly," Roman said. "It's not very efficient, but it's a lot more fun. Like on this one, there are a lot of branches on the left side, so we're going to build a staircase to the upper level."

"Upper level?" Kase craned his neck higher. "Are you building a tree castle?"

Roman chuckled. "I like the thought, but it will be pretty cozy. Just a place to sleep at night and not get bothered by little critters, trampled by the giant elk, or eaten by giant lions."

Kase knew that the tree houses would hide them from critters and elk, but nothing would stop them from being eaten by the langaras. The only reason the langaras hadn't killed them yet was because they had decided not to.

"What do you think, Dom?" Helena asked. "Any ideas?"

Dom cleared his throat. "We could build a pulley system first," he said. "That way, you could easily move lumber and other materials up the tree."

"We don't need anything to move materials up," Roman said. "Your mother has quite an arm. She's been throwing me logs all morning."

Dom noticeably slumped his shoulders.

"She throws logs all the way up there?" Kase was shocked. He doubted he could throw a log even halfway up the ladder that was built into the tree.

"Some are easier than others," Helena said. "But we have a good system. I like the pulley idea, though." She patted Dom on the back. He had to lunge forwards to stop from falling over.

"I guess we could—" Roman started, but a scream sounded from the riverfront.

Kase didn't hesitate to race back to his friends. He heard Roman follow him through the forest, but didn't need to check to see if the others were right behind. He leapt through the bushes at the riverfront and rushed to the edge of the water.

Aura was clutching her leg, while a wet Curtis and a dry Talen hunched over her.

"It stings!" Aura cried. She rocked back and forth, tears running down her face.

"What happened?" Kase asked. He knelt next to Aura. Her hand was pressed against her bare thigh, where the skin on her leg was discoloured. It looked like she'd squashed a purple octopus under her skin, with legs that sprawled beyond her fingers.

"We were swimming, splashing around," Curtis said. "Then—"

"Something bit me!" Aura sobbed. Her hand shook. "Make it stop."

"Can I take a look?" Kase asked. He placed his hand gently over Aura's, and she yanked hers away. Kase kept his hand cupped over her wound, sheltering it from her view. He could smell the puss pouring out.

Three small, circular puncture wounds were embedded in Aura's leg. The holes were white instead of bloody, but the edges of the wounds were dark purple. Kase didn't recognize what animal made the marks, but he could tell it was poisonous because of the discoloration of Aura's skin.

"I don't know if I can help you," Kase said. "Isn't an antidote the only way to heal a poisonous wound?"

"For other wizards, but not for you," Aura said. "Please just ..." she screamed.

The purple streaks extending from the bite marks seemed to get thicker. One streak even stretched to Aura's foot. It was only a matter of time before the poison took over her entire body, and she'd succumb to its effects. Kase could just wait until she died, but he'd already brought her back to life before. Solving a new healing problem seemed more intriguing, and may stop her pain faster.

"Stay with me," Kase said. He closed his eyes and pressed his palm to Aura's thigh. He felt the breeze flow across his skin, as if he were flying, but this time he was connected to his waterfront surroundings.

There were a lot more creatures near the river than he'd realized. A mix of sand flies, crabs, and bloodworms hid underneath the sand on the beachfront. A few different fish swam about downstream of where the group was, but Kase only recognized their difference in size. He didn't feel any predators lurking around, or anything with sharp enough teeth to cause the puncture wound in Aura's leg.

Aura's pain transferred to his leg as his healing ability took over. The sharpness of the bite was the focal point, but the spreading toxins were a completely different experience. It was like the bite was a scalp, and the strands of toxins were its hair.

He started pulling the strands one by one. He visualized each strand ending at the source of the bite, and once he was done tugging, he let it fall to the ground.

He continued pulling, one at a time, until every strand of toxin had exited the wound. Once he was finished, he absorbed the pain of the bite mark, and opened his eyes. The soft glow from his hand dimmed as he removed his palm from Aura's thigh. He didn't leave a scar.

Aura sighed. "Thank you," she said. She'd stopped quivering, and stretched out her leg.

Kase smiled. He couldn't wait to tell Lenia what he'd accomplished. He wondered if she'd be impressed with his poison-curing ability, since she was the one who'd taught him how to heal in the first place.

"What do you think it was, Kase?" Talen asked.

"Will it return?" Curtis added.

"I'm not sure," Kase said. He stood up, and then helped Aura to her feet. "I didn't feel any …" Kase stopped when he met Dom's surprised gaze.

"You're … a wizard?" Dom asked.

Kase didn't feel like explaining everything to Dom. He was enjoying his success, and focused on the unique experience he'd tell Lenia. He turned back to Talen and Curtis. "I'll walk the bank, and see if I can find it," Kase said. "Maybe we should avoid the water for a little while until I figure this out?"

"Works for me," Aura said. She hustled to her beach chair and started packing her things.

"Let's start a fire back at camp," Helena suggested. "We still have some rations that you brought from the castle, Aura. We can heat them up for lunch."

"I could eat," Curtis said.

"Good, let's get Kodiak Mountain some grub so he can keep up the good work." Roman slapped Curtis on the shoulder and they headed back down the path together, arm in arm.

Kase helped Talen gather her things, and then tried to walk to camp with her, but Dom stopped him.

"You saved Aura's life," Dom said. "I'm proud of you, son. You are a remarkable young man. Eowin and Anna did a great job of raising you."

Kase clenched his fists. Although his uncle and aunt had taken care of him, taught him important life lessons, and supported his warrior training at the Academy, Kase had relied on a lot more people to become who he was. His father wasn't one of them.

"He's saved us all," Talen said.

"I don't doubt it," Dom said. "Would you care to share your stories?"

Talen looked up to Kase. She gestured towards Dom, and then kept walking down the path. As reluctant as Kase had been in telling Dom the truth about his power, it seemed like now it was only a matter of time before Dom put the rest of the pieces together.

"You assumed that Lenia was the chosen wizard, but you're wrong," Kase said. "I hold the power of the doorway of life. I brought everyone here back, including you."

"Oh no." Dom put his palm over his mouth and stared at Kase. "The curse."

Kase tried not to roll his eyes. Dom's reaction was different when he thought Lenia had brought him back to life. Why wouldn't Dom be happy Kase had the power instead?

"Wait up, Tal," Kase called. He would help the others, then come back to look for the predator. He followed Talen along the path, leaving Dom behind.

After they were ten feet down the trail, Kase turned to look back. Dom was gazing at the river, still with his hand over his mouth, as if the water would give him the answers he was looking for.

Kase tried to feel if the animal that bit Aura was still nearby. Maybe it was ready for another snack.

# CHAPTER 16

# As An Old Memoria

The fur on the inside of the hat was soft and comfortable, but Kase now wished it would drown out sound as well. He hammered another nail into the sled.

"Can you shape-shift?" Dom asked.

"No." Kase wished he could transform into a bird and fly away.

"Too bad," Dom said. "If you could turn into a yak, we could ride you up to the mountain top much faster."

Kase wondered if Dom was joking, but since it wasn't blatantly unfunny, he assumed Dom was being serious. Dom's ignorance of Cali's meticulous plan made Kase appreciate his sister all the more. He wished the other members of their team would return soon.

Lenia and Cali were gathering the final supplies needed for their journey up Yeti Berry Mountain, while Kase and Dom were left to build the sled at its base. As much as Dom had bragged about being an excellent weapons craftsman, his construction knowledge didn't transfer to other areas. In the end, Kase had to build the sleds on his own, but he didn't mind.

The trip up the mountain was the same trek that Kase's mother had made years ago, but failed to return home from. Only half of her crew had survived the dangerous trip, and they had told Dom what they knew of Ashlyn's demise.

Since Lenia could only teleport to places she'd been before, the group had to spend time hiking up the mountain. With the changing seasons, the ice roads that led to the base of the mountain were finally thick enough to cross, which made their travel easier. But their trek was still going to take a lot of physical effort, careful planning, and a little perseverance.

To help carry the load, Cali suggested using horses. Since they didn't have any of their own, the group had brainstormed different ideas to obtain a few. The most obvious was to buy horses from the nearest town, but that would require a merchant and possibly some paperwork. They could search for wild horses, but Lenia didn't know if she could teleport a horse to their destination, because they were so heavy.

Kase's idea was to bring a few horses back from the dead, but he didn't know where to find suitable carcasses. Lenia knew of a specialty butcher shop that sold horsemeat, so she purchased a few T-bone steaks. She went on two separate occasions, to try to avoid buying meat from the same horse; Kase wouldn't be able to bring the same horse back from the dead twice.

"Maybe a yak isn't the best way to travel in the snow," Dom said. "What other animals can you control? A moose? A polar bear? Can you control a Yeti?"

"We could try flying up the mountain," Kase suggested, remembering Dom's fear of riding Maxim. Kase hammered another nail into the sled base.

"Can you fly?" Dom asked.

"No," Kase said. He slipped the hammer into his belt and grabbed the next plank, which was leaning against the sled. Dom pretended to help by grabbing one end, but the wood wasn't heavy.

"But you can control the elements, right?" Dom asked.

"Most wizards can," Kase said. After placing the plank next to the previous one, he took a nail out of his pouch and gripped his hammer again.

"If you're more powerful than other wizards, you can probably generate a bigger gust of air." Dom asked. "Have you ever seen the wreckage from a tornado?"

"No," Kase said. "Have you?"

"Once," Dom said. "It really blew me away!"

Kase didn't even flinch. He hammered his next nail.

Dom chuckled at his own joke. "I kid," he said. "But a tornado tore through your aunt and uncle's farm once. It wasn't near their house, but it uprooted some trees in one of the northern acres. If a tornado could rip a tree out of the ground, maybe it could help you, or us, fly?"

Kase wished he could make Dom fly away, even if the tornado idea wasn't all that bad. He thought about how he was able to control lightning, and if he could do the same with a windstorm. He'd have to do some research with Talen when he was back at the castle to see if King Michael ever wrote about controlling one.

"Maybe," Kase said. He hammered in another nail.

"Maybe what?" Lenia asked. She was holding a few blankets, while Cali held a basket of food. Her trident was strapped to her back, but it had a brown casing around it—Talen's idea, to make it look like a wooden pitchfork.

"Here, let me help," Dom said. He tripped over the last plank that was on the ground and stumbled towards Lenia.

Kase almost chuckled. "Dom thinks I should try to fly," he said.

"Fly how?" Cali handed her basket to Dom. He kept his head down.

"Like a tornado," Kase said. He hammered a nail into the plank, and then paused as he moved to the next spot. He expected Dom to speak up, but Dom remained silent.

"Great idea, Dad," Cali said. "I could see that."

"A flying Dandy Lion," Lenia said. She placed the blankets on the sled and wrapped her arms around Kase. "I'd make a wish."

"What would you wish for?" Kase asked.

"If I told you, it wouldn't come true," Lenia said.

"I wish I was better at tying ropes," Dom said. "But I'm just *knot* good at it." He grinned while twirling two open ends of the same rope.

Cali laughed. Kase couldn't see Lenia's reaction, since her furry hood was buried into his chest. "Good one, Dad," Cali said.

Kase finished building the sled, and then the group tied their supplies to the back of it. Dom got in the way at every turn, either by trying to help or cracking jokes.

The sled was wide enough for two of them to sit next to each other, but it wasn't very rugged. But the sled didn't need to get them all the way up the mountain, nor did it need to get back. The same theory applied to the horses.

After Lenia swept the area, Kase placed the first of four bones on the snow beside their sled. He hadn't brought a horse back to life yet, but in the end the experience was eerily similar to the elk he'd brought back in their kingdom. He didn't relive the horse's last moments, or feel that much pain. A little fire flash and some tingling, and the horse appeared in front of him.

The horse's brown coat was dull, and the animal was a little overweight, but it would be sufficient for their trip. Lenia quickly calmed the animal, connecting with their new friend to ensure it didn't run away. Kase reached into his pocket, but only felt one bone left. He was thankful that Lenia and Cali had the foresight to buy multiple steaks.

The second horse was like the first, but it had a black coat instead. While Kase controlled both animals, the rest of the group fastened the ready-made halters and leather straps to the horses. The group got comfortable on the sled, wrapping blankets around their shoulders and legs.

Kase and Lenia sat towards the front, huddled together under the same blanket. Cali and Dom were behind them; Dom was already telling stories of their mother's trip. Even though the sun was shining on this chilly winter day, the best part of the trip was that Dom wasn't allowed to break Kase's concentration. It was a little white lie that Lenia had encouraged Kase to tell.

As much as Kase found Dom's voice irritating, the stories of Ashlyn were heart-warming. Cali remembered little of their mother, but Kase didn't remember anything at all. The only things he knew about her were what their Auntie Anna told them, which didn't go into a lot of detail. It was difficult for Anna to talk about her sister without shedding a few tears.

Dom loved talking about the good times he'd had with Ashlyn, and told a story about how they'd first met. He'd first noticed her on an opposing Quest Series team, but didn't have the courage to approach her, since she wasn't a scholar.

During the volunteering event that year, he sat beside her as they made gift baskets for a service that sent food to poor communities. They started talking, and Ashlyn accidentally punctured an apple with her wand. She asked

Dom if it was still good, and he'd told her it was wand-erful.

Kase wondered if bringing his mother back would spawn even more of Dom's bad jokes. Despite that, the more he heard of her, the more excited he was to have her back in his life.

Ashlyn was an apothecary, but she didn't just make well-known medicines. She worked for an organization that funded the research and development of new remedies. She was one of the pioneers that experimented with new ingredients, and tried different combinations of powerful potions. The expedition for the Yeti Mountain Berry had intended to bring new insight into the delicate and mysterious fruit.

The ride up the mountain was less dangerous than Kase had thought. There weren't any heavy winds or snowstorms. The road was clear of debris, and they didn't meet any other travellers or predators. Dom even fell asleep because the ride was so smooth and boring.

As Kase was daydreaming about seeing a Yeti, one of the horses collapsed on the trail. Kase didn't have to wonder what had happened; he had felt the heartbeat of the horse slow to a halt. He bowed his head in a moment of silence.

"What's wrong?" Cali asked.

"He's gone," Kase said. Lenia rubbed his arm.

"Can't you bring him back again?" Dom asked. "Or does your ability only work once per creature?"

Kase sighed. "The power doesn't prolong life, it just renews someone's time when they've died too early," he said. "This horse was old, which is probably why it was turned for profit at the butcher shop."

"Interesting," Dom said. "Lucky we got some good use out of it."

"There's more to life than just function," Kase muttered.

"What?" Dom asked.

Lenia squeezed Kase's arm.

"We don't have much farther to go," Cali said. "According to my map, it's about a mile and a half to your coordinates, Dad. Should we keep moving with the single horse?"

"Of course!" Dom said. "We're almost there—then I … we can see your mother again."

"He's not that strong, either," Kase said. He didn't know how much longer the brown horse would last, but he didn't feel like testing it.

Dom looked like he was about to retort when Lenia threw off her blanket. "I could go for a hike," she said. She stood and stretched beside the sled.

Kase slid to the opposite side and shook his legs out. "Should we clean up first?"

"Definitely," Cali said. "We still have a few hours of daylight left. Maybe we can burn the sled, have some dinner, and teleport our supplies back before moving forwards?"

Dom didn't answer, looking down at the snow again.

"Works for me," Lenia said. She teleported away, but then returned a few seconds later with an axe. "Do you mind if I build the fire?"

Kase removed the rope and straps from the horses, and then released his control of the living one. It sped away, but then lingered in the distance. It was happy to be free, but also curious of the group it had travelled with.

Cali, Dom, and Lenia unpacked the sled. They set some blankets on the snow and placed their basket of food on it, and then tossed the sac of fire pit supplies next to it. The group didn't need to cook anything, since their snacks consisted of veggies, fruit, and cheese, but the fire would keep them warm.

Lenia chopped up the sled while Kase dug a pit in the snow. Once he hit the solid ground beneath the white powder, he placed some stones in a circle. He tossed the kindling into the centre, and then joined Cali and Dom on the blanket. Dom didn't wait for anyone before he started eating.

After placing a few of the chopped-up boards into the pit, Lenia aimed the head of her trident at the base of the pile. She'd removed the pitchfork casing around the prongs, so her trident wouldn't ruin the casing.

The fire was born. The flames danced around, but not by Kase's control. Lenia's smile gave away her influence over the fire.

The fire didn't end up producing a lot of warmth, but it was fun to watch it burn. Kase and Lenia huddled close for a few moments after they finished eating, and then the group cleaned everything up. Lenia teleported everything back to the kingdom. The dead horse was left on the trail; the living one had wandered off.

The break seemed to renew Dom's energy. He didn't stop talking during the hike, until they were almost to the spot where Ashlyn and her crew had tumbled off the mountain edge.

"They tried moving a carriage down this road?" Kase asked. The path here was noticeably skinnier. There wasn't much room for safe travel for even two horses; they would have been brushing against the rock.

"It's tight, but carriages have travelled this path before." Dom pointed down the road. "The first bend is where the accident happened."

Kase continued on, but he turned when he noticed no one was following him.

Dom was resting his hands on his knees while Cali consoled him. Lenia waved Kase to come back.

"Do we need a break?" Kase asked.

"I'm sorry, son." Dom sobbed. "I just need a moment. I've been waiting so long ..." he sobbed some more.

Kase leant against the mountain instead of comforting Dom like Cali. He enjoyed the view of the setting sun against the snowy mountaintops. It reminded him of the view from Skyland.

"I came here once before, after a conversation with Sheese," Dom said. He took a step forwards. Cali held his arm, but Lenia stayed back.

Kase hadn't heard Dom talk about their enemy. Cali spent more time with him, and had mentioned that Dom admitted Sheese had organized Dom's trip to Jenim Island. But she hadn't given all the details to the rest of the group yet.

Kase opened his mouth, but Cali made eye contact with him and shook her head. Kase and Lenia both clenched their fists.

"I knew Sheese's mission was dangerous, but everything just fell into place," Dom said. He didn't seem to notice Kase's glare. "We had support from a few High Guardians, I'd done enough research on the location, and your aunt and uncle had agreed to look after you while I was gone. The only thing that didn't fit was the nervousness that I felt in my gut."

Dom picked up his pace, but Kase and Lenia marched a few steps behind him. Kase could feel a different emotion stirring inside him, as if egged on by the breeze that had sprung up.

"I came here for solace, and in hopes I would see a sign to push me towards a better future," Dom said. "Your mother always talked about truth, and how it comes from within. I was searching for that feeling, hoping that her memory would somehow be stronger in this place."

The group stopped at the edge of the bend and looked over. Below the trail was a labyrinth of jagged rocks that looked like a shattered mirror. Deep crevices ran along the rocks, like long caverns that were too dark to see into. It was apparent that anything that fell from this height would be difficult to find, and impossible to survive.

"To die before you die." Dom looked at Kase, waiting for a reply.

"So you can live after you live," Kase said. The idiom was a philosophy created by the Chosen, and spoken by King Michael. The words promoted self-discovery as the key to controlling the power of the doorway of life.

"For me, it meant giving up everything I knew in order to get everything I wanted," Dom said.

Kase clenched his jaw and looked to Cali. It seemed like Dom had searched his soul for truth, and found the answer: to give up on the two of them in order to pursue his dreams. Cali didn't seem as insulted as Kase was.

"I believed that there was a reality where I could have it all," Dom continued. "Riches, family, and the woman that I loved more than anything: all existing together. And now, I finally have it."

Kase closed his eyes. He felt like screaming. How could Dom be so selfish? Was he taking credit for all the work and sacrifice of everyone else? Kase wanted to throw Dom off the edge of the cliff. He felt the wind rush past him, as if it would help.

Dom shrieked.

Kase opened his eyes. Dom had slipped and was falling, just as Kase had imagined. Cali reached out for him, but was too far away. Kase grabbed Cali's wrist, so she wouldn't fall too, and then watched the beautiful view of Dom falling into the crevasse below.

"Dad!" Cali yelled. She reached out, but was careful not to drop further.

"He said he had to let go of everything," Kase said. "Maybe we should let him go."

Cali stepped back and glared at Kase. "What's that supposed to mean?"

"You didn't force him off the cliff, did you?" Lenia asked. She must have noticed the unnatural breeze.

Kase realized how hard he was holding Cali's wrist, and immediately released his grip. His anger hadn't disappeared yet, though. "He was dead before, he's dead now: maybe he should stay dead," he said.

Cali softened. "But he's our father." She glanced back over the edge. "He's our blood. How can we abandon him?"

Kase scoffed. "He abandoned us."

Cali sulked down and sat on the edge of the mountain bend. She dangled her feet in the air, bowed her head, and started to sob.

Kase hadn't seen Cali sad in so long. It was like a dash of cold water on his face. His anger evaporated like steam. He sat in the snow beside her, but didn't put a consoling arm around her, even though he wanted to.

"I'm sorry, Cali," Kase said. "I didn't mean to—"

"I wanted what he wanted," Cali sobbed. "For us to be a family again; for us to be whole. Couldn't you see that? I know we can't capture what we've lost, but at least we could try to build something new. Don't you want the same thing?"

Kase looked to Lenia, but she looked to the ground.

"It's okay if we're broken," Kase said. "Some people still see beauty in that."

Lenia looked up. Her eyes started to water. She dropped to her knees and put her arms around Kase and Cali, but didn't say anything. The three of them huddled together for a sad moment.

"It's okay if you're broken too, Kase," Turanus said from behind them. "Sometimes it's easier to help others see the truth, but we must also learn to accept it for ourselves."

Kase peeked over his shoulder, past Lenia, and saw Turanus kneeling behind them. His wings were stretched wide.

"Turanus is here," Kase said.

Lenia turned. Cali sniffled.

"Why now?" Lenia asked.

"I know where your mother is; I witnessed her death," Turanus said. "I was too young and too weak to save her then, but I can take you to her now. And to your father."

"I guess he's going to help us find the bodies," Kase said. "I just … wish I had more time."

"More time for what?" Cali asked.

Kase thought about what Dom had said: that the memory of his mother was stronger in this spot. He reminded himself of the word carved into her wand, and how it might impact his road of self-discovery. "More time to heal," he admitted.

"You don't need to heal all at once," Lenia said while rubbing Kase's shoulder. She'd mentioned that sentiment before when trying to calm him. "It's terrible that Dom abandoned you, but your relationship doesn't need to be fixed immediately. With a little more time, maybe it could just be less broken?"

Kase sighed. Lenia's truth made him feel better, but he still wasn't sure if he'd ever feel less broken about how Dom had treated him and Cali. He looked out at the sunset and felt the breeze tickle his neck.

Cali began to sob harder. She covered her eyes and rested her elbows on her knees. "I'm so sorry, brother."

Kase reached over and rested his palm on Cali's shoulder. "It's not your fault, Cali," he said softly.

Cali sobbed some more. "I haven't treated you well either," she said. "How long before you push *me* off a cliff?"

"That's different," Kase said reassuringly. "As difficult as things have been, we've always stuck together. Growing up, you've been the only constant in my life, and that's never going to change. When things get hard, that's when we need each other the most. If you fall off a cliff, I won't be pushing you, because I'll be falling right alongside you."

Cali chuckled, but the tears kept flowing. She tried to wipe them away. "That's dark, but it makes me feel better."

Kase chuckled. "That's because my jokes are funny, unlike Dom's."

Lenia giggled. "His sense of humour is different, isn't it?"

"I don't get it," Kase admitted. "But it seems to make everyone here laugh."

"I laugh out of courtesy," Cali said. She sniffled and wiped her tears again. "He's trying really hard, brother. I know it's hard for you to see it, but he really does. It makes him smile when he has an audience."

Kase rolled his eyes, and glanced at Lenia. "Is that why you laugh, too?"

Lenia smiled. "No, I don't get his jokes either. I end up laughing at you." She started to chuckle. "The look on your face … you're just so disgusted. It's hilarious!" She laughed some more.

"Really?" Kase said with a smirk. "I didn't think it was that obvious."

Cali giggled again. "Now I can't wait for Dad to tell another joke." She rested her hand on Kase's. Her eyes softened. "I know his presence now doesn't change his absence in the past, but his life is a gift, just like ours. Maybe bringing him back changes our future."

Kase nodded, and appreciated Cali's honesty. Bringing Dom back again felt more like a choice they were both making this time, rather than him doing it for her. He didn't just want to make her happy now; he wanted a chance to change their future, even if it changed slowly.

He looked back to Turanus, who still waited behind them. Turanus was in a crouched position, which usually meant he was ready to take them for a ride. If he knew where Ashlyn and Dom's bodies were, Kase was willing to bring them both back.

"Okay, I'm ready," he said. "Let's go get Mom and Dad."

Kase and Lenia helped Cali up after she wiped away the last of her tears. They all hugged again, and then mounted Turanus. Cali was a little wobbly, since Turanus still hadn't revealed himself to her. From her perspective, it was like she was floating in midair.

Before they left, Kase wondered what his reaction would be the next time Dom told a joke. He knew he would be more appreciative of his girlfriend and his sister, since they'd likely be laughing at him instead of Dom. He thought about what Ashlyn might think of Dom's jokes: was she as annoyed as him, or as respectful as Cali? He wondered if her presence would make a difference.

He wondered if, next time, he might feel less broken.

CHAPTER 17

# I Won't Cross These Streets Until You Hold My Hand

The next few celebratory days in the Kingdom of Moiras were a flurry of activity. Gone were the mornings when Kase got up alone to meet the day, only to occasionally see the others throughout the afternoon as they went about their separate tasks. Now, their castle rang with the chatter of their expanding family.

Despite juggling their increased training regime, daily tasks, family gatherings, and Cali's latest missions for the Unicorn Knight and Dandy Lion, Kase was still the most excited for the one-on-one time that he got to spend with Lenia.

Even if she was winning more.

Lenia collapsed the moment she crossed the imaginary finish line. Kase jogged past a few seconds later, and then joined her on the ground. He was proud that she'd pushed the pace, but he was exhausted.

The rest of the group was enjoying their lunch outside. Talen mumbled something, to which Dom laughed out loud. Kase stared at the blue sky above, trying to catch his breath. He just wanted a few moments to himself before he had to get on with his day.

A shadow crept into view. "Lemonade?" Ashlyn asked.

Lenia sat up and wiped her brow, accepting the glass from Ashlyn. "Thank you, Mrs. Garrick. You're a life saver."

"You're welcome, Lenia." Ashlyn smiled and handed the other glass she was carrying to Kase. "I should be thanking you, though. You brought us the lemons."

Kase sat up and took a sip. He enjoyed how cold it was.

"Well, you should thank Kase," Lenia said. "He helped me choose all of our goods from the market. He's surprisingly good at buying the right ones."

Kase almost choked, and then giggled. "What's surprising about it?"

Lenia giggled too. "Right," she said sarcastically. "It's all in the fundamentals."

Kase tried to hide his smile behind his glass. He looked to Ashlyn so he wouldn't burst out laughing at his inside joke with Lenia.

Ashlyn was smiling, but didn't seem to know what was going on. "Okay, lovebirds," she said. "How about some lunch? We're making silly sandwiches."

Lenia spit out her lemonade and then chuckled some more. Kase giggled, but luckily hadn't taken another sip. "What's silly about them?"

"It's something we used to make when you were younger," Ashlyn said. "It was a way to trick Calista into eating her vegetables—although you never had that problem." Ashlyn's smile faded. "I guess neither of you remember eating silly sandwiches."

Kase didn't want to dampen the mood. "I'd love to try one." He jumped to his feet, slammed back some more lemonade, and felt his energy return. Lenia wiped her mouth and stumbled with Kase and Ashlyn to the table.

Kase slipped into a seat beside Talen, while Ashlyn stood next to him at the end of the table. Lenia sat across from Kase, beside Dom.

Before grabbing some much-needed nutrition, Kase examined Talen's plate. She had a piece of white bread with some lettuce at one end, jam in an arc at the bottom, two olives, and a cherry tomato. "Interesting combination," he said.

"It's a jester," Talen said. "Turned out more scary than silly."

Kase chuckled. "What?"

Ashlyn grabbed a few pieces of bread, placing one on Kase's plate, and one on Lenia's. "There are no rules when creating a silly sandwich," Ashlyn said. "Simply choose enough items to create a design on your bread. It can be a face, an animal—"

"Just be careful," Dom said. "I ended up pea-ing myself." He held up a couple of pea pods, and shook them while he grinned.

Kase quickly looked at Lenia. She squinted her eyes and then burst into laughter, which made Kase laugh too.

"Finally!" Dom smiled proudly at Kase.

"Even better the second time," Ashlyn said in support.

Kase ignored Dom's reaction. He grabbed a couple more slices of bread, and went to work creating his own silly sandwich masterpieces. There was a wide variety of ingredients available, including vegetables like carrots and celery that were good for eyes and eyebrows. There were walnuts and almonds, which were good for ears and noses. He even used some pineapple for blonde hair on one of his creations. He didn't care what it would taste like together, but he was excited to try.

"The copycat has struck again," Cali said. She sat at the opposite head of the table. She held her sage mirror up towards Lenia and tapped its face.

"Where?" Lenia asked. She took a bite of her creation, which looked like a red unicorn.

"The capital," Aura said. "The targets were political."

"It has to be the Triple Crown," Cali said. "They just—"

"Sorry to interrupt, Calista," Ashlyn said. "Do you need Kase for this conversation? I'd like to go for a walk with him, if that's fine with you … well, everyone." She giggled and curtsied, but it seemed forced and awkward.

Kase looked to Cali for permission, then wondered why he was waiting for her approval. "Fine with me," Cali said. She pointed to her sage mirror. "The main victims were promising scholars, and likely posed a direct threat to High Scholar Sheese."

Kase had finished making his silly sandwiches, and didn't mind eating away from the table. He stood and grabbed his plate. Talen pushed her sandwich towards him and nodded, so he tossed the jester onto his plate too, and then carried his lemonade in his free hand. He smiled at Lenia, but she was invested in Cali's revelation.

"Sheese had a mantra when I knew him," Dom said. He cleared his throat.

"The powerful strike first! The powerless don't strike at all!" Dom's impression of High Scholar Sheese was almost as bad as his jokes.

Ashlyn led Kase through the garden and into the castle. As they turned down the first hall, Ashlyn turned and walked backwards. "This castle is so pretty," she said. "Is it possible for you to share any of your favourite moments here? Something that made you really happy?"

Kase liked sharing stories with Ashlyn. While Dom's interest seemed to focus on what Kase could do, Ashlyn was more interested in how Kase felt. It was nice to share honest, tender-hearted moments with her.

"Aura used to organize craft nights," Kase said. "One time, we tried painting. Curtis built easels, Talen stretched canvass, and Aura developed the paint. It was all part of an instructional guide that Cali had found in the library."

Kase rounded a corner, entering the main hall. Ashlyn almost backed into the wall, but pivoted just in time and walked normally beside Kase.

"There was a basket of fruit in the middle of the room that was supposed to be our inspiration," Kase continued. "I couldn't tell what anyone else was doing, but my painting was terrible from the start. The shapes were off, and the colour wasn't right: it looked like a giant, rainbow puddle. The experience wasn't fun, until I accidentally spilled some red paint on my shirt. It made Lenia laugh."

Kase remembered feeling a little embarrassed, because everyone else's paintings were much more successful; although Curtis was too busy dancing to notice Kase's blunder. But Lenia saw Kase's distress, and spilled some paint on her shirt to match.

"To make me feel better, she painted 'klutz' on her shirt," Kase said. "I ended up painting 'thumbs for fingers,' and then the game was on. We took turns openly admitting our struggles on our clothes, which ended up being a lot more fun than trying to capture a bowl of fruit. Everyone else got in on the game once they realized how much fun it was to break the rules."

Ashlyn smiled. "It sounds like fun," she said. "I like those spontaneous nights. There's an innocence present, knowing that the only way to experience that feeling is to live in the moment."

"That's true," Kase said. "We tried recreating that night again, but it wasn't the same. I'm sure we'll come up with something new, though."

"I'd like to be a part of the next one," Ashlyn said.

"I'd like that too," Kase replied.

They had made it to the main entrance of the castle. There was a shady spot with a bench just outside, where they had a wonderful view of the kingdom. Beyond the courtyard and the surrounding perimeter wall, a few langaras rested in the grass.

Kase finally bit into his first silly sandwich. It wasn't as delicious as he'd hoped, but he didn't care. He was famished.

"How do you like your creation?" Ashlyn asked.

"It's interesting," Kase said around a mouthful. He chewed some more, and then swallowed after a little struggle. "Did I use the same ingredients as I did when I was younger?"

Ashlyn checked Kase's plate. "Not really," she said. "You definitely eat them differently now, though. Before, you'd pick off each part of the face and eat the ingredients one by one. Sometimes I'd sneak you extra toppings when you weren't looking."

"Thanks for helping me grow," Kase said. He took another bite.

Ashlyn chuckled. "Trust me, you didn't need help. You were one of the fattest babies I'd ever seen."

Kase almost choked on his food. He met his mother's grin and laughed with his mouth closed. He chewed some more and swallowed. "Do you mean chubby, but in a cute way?"

"That's exactly what I meant." Ashlyn laughed some more. "You should have seen my arms after carrying you around." She curled her forearm to her shoulder and flexed.

Kase laughed. "I guess I know where I got my warrior strength from," he said.

"Well, I don't want to take all the credit." Ashlyn dropped her arm. "It sounds like you worked very hard to become who you are. My friends used to praise me for having two children and continuing to work the way I did. I can't imagine how much effort it takes to continue with your warrior training in the morning, study in the afternoon to be a king, sneak around at night for the freedom of the realm, and still be a loving friend and family member. It's …"

"Incoming," Maxim called in warning.

Kase looked across the field, but he didn't see Maxim where the other langaras were resting.

"Heroic," Ashlyn finished.

Raiden landed on the ground in front of Kase and Ashlyn with a thundering crash. Her black wings stayed wide as she bared her giant fangs and roared. Ashlyn's hair drifted back from the mother langara's breath. Maxim landed behind her mother, but she didn't seem angry or distressed.

Ashlyn melted behind Kase's shoulder.

Kase took another bite of his sandwich. "What's going on?" He asked. He'd seen Raiden angry a few times before, but it never amounted to anything serious.

"You've brought more people here!" Raiden growled.

Ashlyn shrieked and stretched Kase's shirt over her face.

"It's okay," Kase said out loud to Ashlyn.

Raiden glared at Kase, so he put his silly sandwich back on his plate so he could give her his full attention.

"I thought they were friendly," Ashlyn whispered.

"This is my mother," Kase said to Raiden. "I thought we had an agreement that—"

"The agreement was for one, not two," Raiden said.

Kase hadn't meant to bring back an extra Garrick, but he thought he'd be able to buy some more time before they knew and he had to ask the langara pack for approval. They had a peaceful relationship built on respect, which made the langaras feel like family to Kase. They had all agreed that in order to keep the balance of the kingdom intact, and keep enough resources available for every living thing, all species had to live together in harmony.

"I'm sorry, I didn't know until she arrived," Kase explained. "Please forgive me. I promise, there won't be any more surprises. No more humans will come here without your blessing."

Raiden's fangs disappeared. "I believe you," she said. "But this is your only reminder. Control the size of your pack, or we'll control it for you." Raiden flapped her wings, rose up into the air, and then darted away.

Maxim didn't follow; she was facing the sunshine with her eyes closed. It seemed like she was working on her tan.

"Where'd it go?" Ashlyn asked. She peeked out from Kase's stretched sleeve, but was still huddled between his shoulder and the castle wall.

"She was just checking in," Kase said. "Her daughter is the white langara, who's much more pleasant to talk to. Would you like to meet her and go for a ride?"

"They talk?" Ashlyn said.

"Just with me so far," Kase said. "It's one of the benefits of having the power of the doorway of life. I can communicate with them in my mind. It's like how I talk with Turanus, except that the entire conversation is between our thoughts."

"A telepathic bond." Ashlyn released Kase's shirt and slid back to her normal seat. "The mother seemed protective … or was she mad that we didn't invite her to the silly sandwich party?"

Kase hadn't wanted to bring it up before, hoping that Ashlyn was saving the news for a special occasion. "They're the rulers of this kingdom," he said. "They've allowed us to live in the castle, but they don't want our numbers to get any higher and impact the balance of life in their territory."

Ashlyn nodded. "I pushed us over the limit."

"No," Kase said. "It was my little brother or sister that did."

Ashlyn hugged her belly. "You know," she said.

"I felt something when I brought you back," Kase said. He'd also felt Ashlyn's worry for her unborn child when he lived through her last moments of life. "I assumed it was a secret; if Dom knew, I'm sure he wouldn't have shut up about it."

Ashlyn chuckled. "He is a proud father," she said. She rubbed her belly. "I was waiting for the right moment to tell him before the accident, but now … everything is so different." Her smile quickly faded, and water pooled in her eyes. "I don't even know if I can be a good mother." Her shoulders started to shake.

Kase set his plate beside him and put an arm around Ashlyn. "Different isn't bad," he said.

Ashlyn cleared her throat and wiped her tears. "I know, I know," she said. "I just … one minute you're two, the next I'm barely older than Calista. You both grew up without me, and are so much wiser and stronger than I am. I should be the one giving advice and guiding you, not the other way around. I … it's so … messed up." She groaned and wiped her tears again.

Kase rubbed Ashlyn's shoulder. He thought about how Lenia felt she was missing out on being with her family, and understood what she and her parents were going through a little better. He felt sad at the missed opportunities, and angry that the opportunities had been taken away.

"It's not your fault," Kase said.

"Maybe not, but what happens now?" Ashlyn asked. "I don't know how to be your mother, because I didn't get a chance to grow as one. How am I supposed to be there for you and Calista, *and* take care of a newborn? How do I care for our family?"

Kase rubbed Ashlyn's shoulder again. She might have missed out on his past, but she was now part of his future. "You're not alone," he said. "You asked how I have the energy to do so much around here? It's not just something that comes from within; it's supported by everyone and everything in this kingdom."

Kase looked again at Maxim. She was still basking in the sunlight, as if she didn't have a care in the world. She was one of the deadliest creatures in the realm.

"I didn't become a wizard in one day," he continued. "Lenia taught me how to break boundaries with my limited power, and she gives me confidence with my new power. I taught her how to hone her warrior skills and create good habits to increase her strength and technique. We work through our struggles together, and it hasn't been perfect, but we persevere because we're in it together."

"She's a special one," Ashlyn said. "I can see why fate brought you together."

"Fate brought us all together," Kase said. "We wouldn't be here without the sacrifices that Curtis and Aura have made. We wouldn't be moving forwards without the innovations that Cali and Talen create. We're continuing to grow as a group, and just because we haven't had motherly guidance up to this point doesn't mean we don't need it now. We need you."

Ashlyn wiped her face again. "Aura did ask me to help her make some new potions this afternoon."

"I wish Aura would invite me for potion-making," Kase said. He'd wanted to improve his apothecary knowledge ever since he'd found out about Aura's sleeping tea. "Do you think you could use your motherly persuasion to get me in?"

"I've got your back." Ashlyn rested her head on Kase's shoulder and sighed. "Thank you for listening. I feel more accepted here."

"Thank you for your honesty," Kase said.

Maxim yawned. It was like she felt him looking at her, because her eyes popped open and stared back. "Would you like to go for a ride now?" Kase asked.

"I'm ready," Ashlyn said.

Kase picked up his plate and led Ashlyn across the courtyard to Maxim. After introducing herself, Ashlyn scratched Maxim behind the ear with Kase's guidance. Kase helped her mount Maxim, and then tried giving his last silly sandwich to the langara for a quick snack. She spit it out and told him it was awful.

Kase sat behind Ashlyn, so he could keep her steady. They both gripped a tuft of fur as Maxim took flight. Kase was able to catch Maxim up on his talk with Raiden, give updates on what was happening at the castle, and share more about his mother. Ashlyn spent most of the ride screaming and laughing.

Maxim took Kase and Ashlyn over most of the kingdom, but needed to report back to the pack. She returned them to the garden, where the rest of the group was still sitting around the table. Cali stood at the head, pointing to a string diagram she'd created.

"In one way or another, we can connect all of these events to High Scholar Sheese," Cali said. She gestured to encompass the diagram as a whole. "He should be our main target now. If we take him out, all the violence stops."

Kase took a seat beside Talen, but noticed that Ashlyn remained standing.

"I feel really good right now," Ashlyn said with a smile for Kase. She looked to the group. "I have an announcement."

"Not now, Mother," said Cali. "We need to make a decision so that we can plan accordingly. Otherwise, more innocents might lose their lives."

Ashlyn closed her eyes and took a few long breaths.

"I still think we should focus on the copycat," Lenia said. "If we take away the Triple Crown's weapon, we'll buy ourselves more time to calculate our next move."

"I agree with Lenia," Talen said.

"If we want to take out a weapon, we should target Mardious Hood," Dom said. "He's much more dangerous than—"

"I said I have an announcement!" Ashlyn yelled.

The entire group went silent and stared at her.

She winked at Kase. "I learned that from Raiden," she said softly.

Kase couldn't hide his smile. He liked the impact that his short time with Ashlyn had on her, but he liked the surprised look on Cali's face more.

"I realize that I'm interrupting an important conversation, and we're facing a lot of obstacles ahead, but we still need to find ways to celebrate." Ashlyn hugged her belly. "I'm pregnant."

"What?" Dom said.

"Really!" Aura jumped from her chair. She clasped her hands together in front of her mouth, but they couldn't hide her wide smile.

"That was fast." Cali looked to Dom, then back at Ashlyn. "Congratulations!"

"I was with child before the accident," Ashlyn said. She looked down to her belly. "I'm sorry I didn't tell you sooner." She looked to Dom.

Dom stood. He walked around Lenia and hugged Ashlyn. A few tears fell down his cheek. "It's wonderful news."

"We should have a baby shower," Talen said.

"Yes!" Aura hopped excitedly. "We could have games, make—"

"We should focus on the Triple Crown," Cali said. "Then save the party for after."

"C'mon, Calista," Kase said. He noticed Cali smirk. "We can plan both at the same time, right?"

Ashlyn and Dom both looked to Cali, who was leaning on the table. "Okay," she said slowly. "Let's plan a party too."

Cali then walked around the table and hugged Ashlyn. Aura followed, and then Lenia and Talen gave their congratulations. Ashlyn was crying again, but this time Kase knew they were tears of joy.

Kase was happy for his mother and his new younger sibling. He wondered what it would be like to be the middle child.

# CHAPTER 18

# You Can't Hide, Going To Find You

Kase popped another grape into his mouth. He thought about throwing it at one of the local Guardians patrolling the streets, but when he looked, there wasn't one in view. Best not to waste a good bunch, anyway.

"Is Kase short for something?" Lenia asked. She stole a grape from Kase's stash.

"My real name is Kase-tholomew McCormick Tallion von Garrick the First," Kase said without missing a beat. He purposefully avoided Lenia's gaze, trying to stay composed.

Lenia giggled and leant her head on his arm. "You're such a dork," she said.

Kase broke, and rested his head on hers with a laugh. "Is Lenia short for anything?" he asked. It hadn't occurred to him to ask before.

"No," Lenia said. "I've never told you this, but I was named after my dad's family dog. She was a border collie, so I guess you can tell what he thought I looked like when I was born."

Kase felt like she wasn't joking. Based on her tone, she sounded remorseful. "Do you know where she's buried?" he asked.

"No, but it doesn't matter," Lenia said. "I think she died of old age."

"Too bad," Kase said. "The world could use more Lenias."

Lenia giggled. "Well, I'm glad there's only one Kase-tholomew," she said. "And I get him all to myself."

Kase grabbed Lenia's hand and looked up to the dark sky. The light rain was relaxing. He wished they could simply enjoy another date night. He felt Lenia lean forwards.

"Looks like he's on the move," Lenia said.

Kase and Lenia were sitting on the roof of a three-storey townhouse, located on a small hill in the richer side of Kimroad. It was an area that they weren't as familiar with, but it was quiet, private, and peaceful. Most importantly, they had a clear view of the entrance to the stables of the Triple Crown.

They were a few blocks away from the gate, but the golden carriage that exited the castle stables was distinct even at this distance. Only Mardious Hood rode such a pompous mode of transport, even though it could seat more than a dozen. The High Wizard wasn't their only target this night though. In fact, they were more interested in the driver.

In order for Cali and Dom to plan the A.K.'s next move, they needed information on the habits of their enemies. Where did they like to go? What times did they normally travel at? Ultimately, what patterns provided the opportunity for an easier ambush?

For the driver, it was important to recognize which route they chose, how the carriage would turn, and what could cause them to make an unanticipated stop. With Kase's ability to control multiple animals at the same time, he could easily create a situation where the driver's quick decisions might lead to an accident.

The six horses that pulled the carriage headed east. Since Kase and Lenia were to the south, they stayed in their position. Luckily, the golden carriage was easy to see from a distance, so they didn't have to make a move yet.

Kase pulled out a tiny notebook and quill from his pocket. He noted the direction of the carriage and the relative time. Lenia was looking at her map, which noted the familiar rooftops she knew were safe for travel. She'd already done a sweep of surveillance mirrors at each location, and de-risked any chance of interaction with a commoner.

The golden carriage travelled five blocks before turning south. The higher it climbed into the hills, the more difficult it became for Kase and Lenia to see. Kase tried to sneak a peek at Lenia's map.

"We should move," Lenia said, noticing Kase's attention change.

Kase adjusted the cloth he wore to make sure it covered his mouth and nose. It was nice to have a stakeout without their Animal Kingdom masks. It was easier to see and breathe, especially in the rain.

"Ready." Kase stood with Lenia, and then she teleported them to her target.

The rooftop they teleported to was shorter than the last, but they had a clear view of the carriage. After a few more turns from the driver, Lenia needed to teleport again. They followed this pattern as the carriage weaved its way through one of the richest parts of town.

The carriage finally stopped.

The driver didn't move, but a door opened near the rear of the carriage. A broad figure exited, closed the door, and walked in the opposite direction of where the carriage was heading. The figure had his hair tied into a bun, and was wearing a cape that fluttered just below his knees.

"That looks like Jax," Kase noted. He wondered why one of the Triple Crown's secret task force was out alone, instead of with his murderous team. Did he live in the area? Kase made a note in his book.

"He's the copycat," Lenia said.

Kase looked up from his notes. Jax was carrying something; it was difficult to see through the rain and darkness, but something thin protruded from it. The shape was suggestive of a unicorn helmet, so Lenia's conclusion made sense, even if it was a quick assumption.

The driver flicked the reins, and the horse and carriage carried on.

"Who do we follow now?" Kase asked. Their plan had been to gather information about the high level members of the Triple Crown, but they might learn more from following the direct threat to the Unicorn Knight.

Lenia clutched Kase's wrist and teleported back to their room at the castle.

"We don't follow: we hunt," she said. Her unicorn helmet rested on a chair, along with her cape and belt of potions. She quickly removed her cloth mask and dressed up as her vigilante alter ego. She armed herself with a sword and her bow and arrows.

Kase removed his cloth mask and changed into his Dandy Lion outfit. He armed himself with a sword and shield. He liked the idea of stopping Jax from killing more political leaders, but he wondered if they were rushing into an emotional decision.

Lenia teleported them back to the rooftop. Jax had turned the closest corner, but was still in view.

"I'll leave my trident here, where it's safe," Lenia said. "Stick close to walls and trees. Closed fist to stop, one finger for quick steps, two fingers for a sprint."

Kase felt thunder in the distance; their light rainfall was going to get heavier. But he stayed focused on their prey. They'd gotten pretty efficient at sneaking around, with Lenia taking the lead and him following. He'd match her going forwards, but always protect her back.

Lenia teleported them to street level. They crept along a corner townhouse, and then stayed as close as possible to the rest of the row while following Jax down the street. The rain helped to shield the sound of their steps through the neighbourhood's manicured grass.

Jax didn't seem like he was in much of a hurry. Since it was so late, everyone in this part of town was likely asleep. There wasn't light in any of the windows either, which added some eeriness, but helped their cause.

Lenia raised her fist. Jax stopped in front of his destination, put his helmet on, and then proceeded to the door. He pulled something out of his pocket, but then dropped it. As he picked it back up, they heard the jangle of keys.

Kase wondered if this was Jax's home. Normally, High Guardians wouldn't be able to afford a house in this part of town, but corrupt High Guardians might earn more. But then why would Jax be dressed in a unicorn helmet, and why wouldn't Mardious Hood drop him off directly in front?

It didn't seem like Lenia was going to wait to find out.

Lenia raced to the centre of the street, drew an arrow back, and fired it at Jax. She stood poised as the arrow struck Jax to the left of his spine. It wasn't an honourable attack, but it was effective. Unfortunately, Jax didn't seem hurt by it; he hardly even stumbled forwards from the force. He turned slowly to face the true Unicorn Knight and her loyal sidekick.

Kase trusted his peripheral vision, and knew they were alone. He kept his shield in front of him, but had his free hand on his hilt.

Jax also gripped his sword handle, but slowly crept down the steps of the townhouse. Instead of drawing his weapon, he pointed to the sky, and then slammed a potion bottle to the ground. The glass shattered, and the pathway to the house filled with smoke.

Kase and Lenia both drew their swords, and then slowly moved in opposite directions while facing their enemy. They didn't want to give away their position, but they each tried to anticipate what Jax would do next.

The copycat didn't have many escape options, because there wasn't any room to sneak between the townhouses. He could either return to the house, or try to flee down the street. If he could teleport like the real Unicorn Knight, then he'd already be gone.

Another option was to face Kase and Lenia in battle, which wouldn't be a wise choice for Jax. Kase had fought Jax once before, when he had tried to rescue Cali from the Triple Crown's clutches. It was a quick fight, that ended in Kase standing over an unconscious High Guardian.

Kase glanced up and down the street again. No one else had appeared, and no lanterns were lit during the commotion outside. The rain had picked up, but it didn't have any effect on the smoke potion. Kase was tempted to use his power to blow the smoke away, but he didn't know if there were any surveillance mirrors in the area that would record his use of magic.

Jax exploded through the smoke cloud down the street, closer to Lenia, and sprinted away. He'd made the right choice, but Lenia slammed her sword back in her sheath and took off after him.

Kase checked behind him first while sheathing his own weapon, and then raced after Lenia. He was disappointed that he'd brought along his shield this time. It wasn't all that light, so he had to waste more energy holding it as he ran. In hindsight, he should have picked a smaller shield that he could have strapped to his back.

Jax didn't look back. He was faster than Kase remembered. Perhaps Jax had changed his training techniques to gain more speed, or maybe the adrenaline was making him perform better. He rounded the corner, and kept racing down the next street.

Lenia wasn't too far behind, but it didn't seem like she'd gained any ground.

When Kase finally rounded the corner, Jax had veered off the road into a park halfway down the block. Kase wanted to shout to Lenia to slow down, but she had already followed Jax into the darkness. Kase tried to sprint faster.

At the park's edge, a path led down a long hill. There was thick brush on either side, but the path itself was clear. The decline seemed to make Jax run even faster, because he'd already made it to the bottom. With Lenia halfway down, Kase focused on not tripping over his feet as he sped after them.

In the middle of the park was a giant stone gazebo. Cylindrical pillars held up a domed roof, but instead of spiralling up, the steps went down to the centre. Jax had reached the edge of the gazebo, and didn't hesitate to descend into the depths of the artistic, structural masterpiece. Luckily, Lenia stopped and waited for Kase before making her next move.

Jax had stopped in the circular centre, which was about twenty-five steps down from the park level. Rows of seats surrounded the centre on all sides, making the structure suitable for musical or dramatic performances. The domed roof had arches that reached from one pillar to its opposite, but the inner covering was painted. A realistic-looking, jovial crowd of angels looked down from the rafters.

Kase didn't like the situation. Jax didn't have anywhere to go. The open gazebo left little room for a surprise attack, and there didn't seem to be any other High Guardians lurking in the shadows, but it still felt like a trap. He held up two fingers to Lenia and then pointed in the direction they'd come from.

Lenia shook her head. She pointed to herself, held up one finger, and then pointed at Jax. She pointed at Kase, then poked at her eyes. She drew a circle in the air with her index finger and mimed shooting an arrow.

Kase nodded. He understood what Lenia wanted, and would cover her from above. He wasn't worried about her fighting Jax, because she was a tremendous warrior in comparison, no matter that Jax had the size advantage. With them so far away from Lenia's trident, he hoped she would finish Jax off quickly so they could escape.

Lenia removed her bow and quiver from her shoulders. Kase rested his shield against the closest pillar, and then secured the quiver to his back. As Lenia descended the stairs, Kase loaded her bow and circled the perimeter.

He didn't see any moving shadows at ground level. The park appeared deserted. Although it was still lightly raining, Kase could see across the landscape in every direction. Whenever he came to a pillar, he hustled around so it didn't block his view for long. He checked each one as best he could for surveillance mirrors, but he didn't spot any. He made it three-quarters of the way around the gazebo by the time Lenia hit the centre platform.

Jax had poured a potion around the edge of the platform while Lenia approached. He ignited it, creating a ring of fire with a small gap for Lenia to enter. The flames rose to shoulder height, providing ample light for the battle.

"You're shorter than I expected." Jax's voice echoed around the dome of the gazebo. He removed his helmet, tossed it flippantly, and then unsheathed his sword. The helmet clanged to the ground with the sound of steel on stone.

Lenia drew her sword, but kept it pointed down. She casually touched the surrounding ring of fire, igniting the blade.

"Even with gloves on, I find fire weapons too hot," Jax said. "And don't even get me started on how difficult it is to see through that stupid mask. Why have a mask at all?"

Jax was trying to bait Lenia into a conversation, and Kase was glad she didn't fall for it. She knew that even though there might not be any visible surveillance mirrors, a slip-up could provide their enemy a wealth of information.

Lenia raised her sword and readied herself in her battle stance.

"Before we get started, I'd like to make you an offer." Jax took a few steps closer, his sword dangling at his side. "Let's join forces, and we can cause more carnage together. Me, you, and the lion." Jax pointed his sword in Kase's direction.

Kase checked the park behind him. There still wasn't any noticeable movement. He decided to continue his patrol, rather than stay in one spot.

Lenia shook her head and took a step forwards.

"Hold on," Jax said. He stuck his palm out. "I understand that you might be hesitant, but let me explain what I have to offer. Not only am I a gifted warrior, but I also have connections within the Triple Crown. The leaders look to me for guidance, courage, and action. I can be a valuable asset if you're looking to infiltrate their circle and strike from an unexpected angle."

Kase huffed under his helmet. Not only was Jax embellishing his warrior skills, but it was highly unlikely that he'd turn on the Triple Crown. Talen argued that nothing was one hundred percent certain, so Kase would give Jax's statement a ninety-nine percent change of being a lie.

Lenia shook her head, and took another step forwards.

"Five seconds, Green Dragon," a new voice said.

Kase recognized the code, but not the voice. 'Green Dragon' was Jax's code name on the task force; Kase had worked as Blue Dragon. They had kept sage mirrors on their wrists to communicate during an operation. Kase hadn't noticed if Jax was talking to his wrist, but it didn't matter now. Kase's head swivelled as he tried to pinpoint an ambush.

The park was still quiet.

"Word of advice," Jax said. "Don't wait for your opponent to attack first. Always lead with your strongest move." He tossed his sword at Lenia point-first. "Fire, Gold Dragon."

Lenia easily sidestepped the sword, but Jax had reached down and opened a trap door on his side of the platform. He waved goodbye, and then jumped down the hole. He slammed the door shut, and a locking mechanism clicked.

Lenia sprinted to the door. Kase followed here with his arrow, making sure he covered any potential attackers. Lenia yanked on the hidden handle, but failed to open the passageway.

Kase wondered where the Gold Dragon was. Was it Mac? No, Mac was King Dragon. Shay was Red. Josephine was Yellow. Was it a new task force member? Were they going to have to face them in combat?

A few clinking sounds on the roof were all the warning he received: like a ball bouncing on the stone structure. Then an explosion split the quiet night.

The first caused dust to fall from the roof. A quick follow-up sent a piece of stone to the ground. A third explosion forced one of the pillars to buckle.

Lenia hesitated. Kase fired his arrow at the trap door, hoping that it would stick into the panel. The arrow embedded itself in the floor, its tail pointing exactly where Lenia needed to go.

Her flaming sword lit her climb up the stairs. Multiple explosions sent rocks everywhere. Two pillars tipped over, one heading outwards, the other towards Lenia. She wasn't going to make it to the top before the entire structure crumbled. Kase thought about racing towards her, but getting crushed wouldn't help.

Another pillar tumbled after more explosions. The golden carriage came into view, soaring overhead. It was now horseless, and moved like the levitation container that Lenia had helped the Triple Crown to develop. The High Wizard must have added the magic magma mix to his carriage, saving it for the perfect opportunity.

The explosions stopped.

Kase slid to the base of the closest broken pillar. He didn't have time to appreciate the High Wizard' innovation. He pulled an arrow from his quiver, but couldn't get a good line of sight on the driver.

Since the roof of the gazebo was completely destroyed, the carriage had to circle over the grass northeast of where Kase was positioned before slowly landing. Rain splattered on the red tint of Kase's mask.

Kase could take a shot at the driver, and engage the High Wizard in battle, or he could search for Lenia. The pillar that had fallen next to Kase provided perfect cover from the carriage. Beside the pillar, about halfway down the gazebo seats, was a flaming sword. Kase rushed down the steps towards the fire.

The dust was still settling, helped along by the rain. Kase dropped his bow when he reached Lenia. He patted down the sword with his gloves and extinguished the flames. Kase checked her vitals. Nothing. The Triple Crown had been successful in defeating the Unicorn Knight.

"I've been trying to reach him, but he doesn't answer!" Mardious yelled. "If you'd given me control of the patrols like I asked, we wouldn't be in this mess."

Kase peeked over the fallen pillar. There was rubble everywhere, and part of the ring of fire in the centre of the destroyed gazebo was still burning. The brightest light came from the inside of the carriage. The door closest to the driver was wide open. Mardious stood there with his sage mirror in front of him.

"Here, take a look," he said.

Before Mardious could turn the sage mirror, Kase ducked behind the pillar. He wondered how much time he had before he was found.

A door closed. "Get back in the air," Mardious said. "See if the lion is out there."

It was obvious that Kase had missed a surveillance mirror, unless Jax's wristband had captured Kase's location. It didn't matter at this point, because Kase needed to stay hidden. He thought about the rain, and how a harder downpour might extinguish the fire. It also might cause Mardious and his driver to take cover.

Kase heard the carriage take off with a clatter of its wheels. The driver must have been a wizard to control the levitation potion.

"That's a historical landmark you destroyed," High Scholar Sheese said. "How are we going to spin this?"

"Easy," Mardious said. "We just blame the Unicorn Knight. We'll make a plea for heightened security, and continue to do what we do."

Kase focused on the rain. He wasn't supposed to use his power, especially around other wizards, but no other wizard could control the weather. The risk of Mardious noticing Kase using his power was likely low.

"And rebuild it?" High Scholar Sheese asked. "It was one of my favourite landmarks."

"Of course," Mardious said. "It will bring the community together."

Kase felt the storm clouds high in the sky, and assumed that moving more to the area would cause a greater downpour. In the meantime, he tried to funnel the water that was falling over the entire park directly over the gazebo area. He felt the rain hit harder.

"Draw up a plan, I'll visit you when I'm finished here," Mardious said.

"I'll have drinks ready," Sheese said. "We need to celebrate this victory."

Kase felt the rain pour over his bare arms. He looked up to the sky, and couldn't see anything but falling water. The carriage must have been circling the other side of the park.

"End," Mardious said. "Mirror, mirror, connect with Geoffrey."

Kase rested his hand on Lenia's shoulder. It was soft where it was supposed to be hard.

"Get back here," Mardious said. "I'm soaked."

"Yes, sir," Geoffrey said.

Kase rested for a few moments. He didn't want to make a noise and give away his position. His plan had worked, and he needed Mardious and his driver to leave him so he could get Lenia out from the rubble. She only had one free arm; her other limbs were trapped under rocks.

"Accept," Mardious said. "Where are you?"

"The tunnel caved in," Jax said. "I'm trapped. I can't breathe down here."

Kase didn't know where the trap door was anymore. He studied the stones around Lenia. There were some smaller boulders around her shoulders and waist, but large pieces of the ceiling covered her legs. Hopefully there was a bit of a gap, and he could slide her out from underneath them.

"You'll be fine." Mardious' voice was calm and reassuring. "Relax and focus on your breathing. We'll get you out of there soon enough."

"Hurry," Jax said. "I don't like—"

"End. Accept," Mardious said. "Finally! Where have you been?" His tone had changed back to anger.

"I was sleeping," High Warrior Mac said.

The carriage landed, which sounded similar to when the langaras hit the ground with their paws. Kase wanted to peek out from his hiding spot, but was it too risky? The rubble was almost completely black, and the only way he'd be discovered is if someone was looking at his exact spot.

"Well, I'm so sorry for waking you," Mardious said sarcastically.

"What do you need?" Mac said. He seemed annoyed.

"I need every available High Guardian to come to the Red Camellia Odeum," Mardious said.

The carriage door opened with a click. Kase decided to peek over the fallen pillar. Geoffrey was holding the door open for Mardious, and followed the High Wizard into the carriage.

"I caught him, you pompous—" The door closed behind them.

Kase hopped to Lenia's torso and tossed the loose rocks away as quickly as he could. He felt around the large stones that blocked her legs, but they were crushing her. He jumped back to her free arm, grabbed her wrist, leant back, and pulled.

His grip slipped, and he fell back to the stairs behind him.

He couldn't waste any time. He grabbed Lenia's hand and tried again, gripping her so tightly he could feel the ring she wore beneath her gloves. She didn't budge. The rain fell harder. Tears began to cloud his vision. He wanted to scream, but he couldn't give himself away.

What else could he do? Should he try cutting her up? Did he have time to get her trident and teleport them to safety? Could he stand his ground and take on Mardious, the High Warrior, and the entire High Guardian army?

Leaving Lenia was not an option. Getting captured was out of the question. Giving up seemed impossible because of what he and his friends had already lived through.

His grip started to slip again, which gave him the idea he needed.

Kase focused his power on the rain once more. Instead of allowing it to fall where it pleased, he focused the droplets where Lenia was trapped. The raindrops crept around edges, slithering their way between Lenia's body and the surrounding rock. Controlling the water reminded Kase of when he had manipulated an ocean whirlpool with the help of the mermaids. This was a much smaller scale, but the circumstances were just as dire.

He adjusted his grip, leant back again, and felt Lenia budge.

Raindrops filled the passages that opened with Lenia's movement. Kase kept tugging. More tears fell down his cheeks.

Lenia's body inched forwards, and then burst from the rubble. Kase landed on his back, with Lenia covering his legs.

The rain began to let up.

Kase felt across Lenia's body, and noticed that her left hip was mushy, her right leg was facing the wrong way, and her boot was missing. At least while dead she couldn't feel any pain.

Kase dragged Lenia up the stairs, trying to keep as low to the fallen pillar as possible. His head pivoted back and forth, on the lookout for any Guardians. He reached the top of the odeum, but didn't stop there.

He dropped Lenia, then grabbed her around her chest instead of dragging her by her wrist. He stood up taller and backpedalled across the park. Lenia's head bounced, but her helmet remained on. Kase dodged a few trees, but his goal was to get to the brush on the hill they'd ran down. He'd be able to rest under the cover of the foliage there.

When Kase and Lenia were halfway across the park, Kase noticed a few High Guardians on horseback enter the area from the opposite direction. They held torches, the light rain not doing anything to hinder the flames. The warriors headed straight for the golden carriage.

Kase focused on his steps, and the park behind him. There weren't any torches near his escape route, and no High Guardians approached from that direction. He made it to the brush without getting caught, and found a spot just inside the edge. He rested Lenia against a tree, and then watched the mayhem around the odeum.

They were safe.

More High Guardians had shown up. Some of them were setting up torches around the perimeter of the odeum, while others headed down into the rubble. Mardious stood on top of the carriage, where the driver would normally sit, pointing and shouting orders.

Kase felt the irony of the situation. There was a time when the Triple Crown had thought they'd had the doorway of life erected correctly, but Kase and his friends had foiled their plans. Much like Mardious thought he'd completed the doorway, he now thought he'd captured the Unicorn Knight. Kase had plucked her out of the Triple Crown's grasp, too.

Like when they'd escaped to the Kingdom of Moiras, the Triple Crown didn't know where Kase and Lenia were. This time, it might be easier for the High Guardians to follow the trail; it wasn't like the Kingdom was impossible to find. It was just a matter of time before someone or something stumbled upon its hiding spot.

One of the things that the Triple Crown did have control over was the story. They'd caused destruction, pain, and misery, but the rest of the world didn't know what had happened. Kase couldn't tell his side of the story, so High Scholar Sheese could spin past and present details any way he wanted to. Kase and Lenia would be vilified by the very villains they were trying to defeat.

Kase wondered what would happen if he took things into his own hands. Even though the storm was dying down, he could bring lightning to the area. If Mardious were to get hit by a bolt, no one would be able to explain it beyond an accident. Kase could have a tornado cross paths with Sheese on his next excursion, or maybe the sea would get the best of a Triple Crown ship.

More High Guardians had shown up around the odeum. They all obeyed Mardious, whom they believed to be High Wizard Zuke, without question or conflict. They all respected him and his position of power. If the leaders of the Triple Crown were killed, would the High Guardians accept whoever next came into power?

Kase thought about his conversation with Ashlyn, and how she'd missed out on growing as a mother. She didn't know how to act with Kase and Cali now because she'd been gone for so long. In the same way, how could Kase and his friends take over the realm if nobody knew of what they'd experienced? The Triple Crown leaders had been in power for so long, would anyone respect something new?

Kase felt restless. He had more planning to do. He rested his hand on Lenia's shoulder. She'd sacrificed everything, and there was hope that she could still do more.

It was time for the world to know the truth.

# CHAPTER 19

# Everybody Wants To Live Together

**M**axim was as still as a statue. Her front paw hovered just above the ground as she stared through the trees. Her wings were drawn back, her mouth was closed, and her claws were retracted, but she was ready to strike at a moment's notice.

Kase leant against the tree. He gripped the arrow against his loose bowstring, but he had no intention of using his weapon. As much as he wanted to prove himself to the langaras as a hunter, he was distracted by the events of last night. It was difficult for him to appreciate what he had when he was so close to having it all come to an end.

The langaras were targeting a herd of water buffalo. Their strategy was different than when hunting elk, because the water buffalo acted together as a mob. Instead of stalking a single prey, the langaras needed to manipulate the entire herd.

But water buffalo herds didn't like to be manipulated.

If any of the water buffalo became threatened, the entire herd would work together to stampede the attacker. Since the herd outnumbered the langaras, it was possible that one of the langaras could be injured or killed.

To the east of Kase and Maxim was a river. The langaras planned to surprise the water buffalo and scare them into fleeing towards the water. Once in the water, the water buffalo would slow down and be vulnerable to an attack, because they wouldn't be able to charge through the river with any force. The langaras would pick the weakest member, and peel it away from the herd.

Kase liked learning the langaras' strategy, proving even the strongest, fastest, and most ruthless killers used their surroundings to their advantage rather than just attacking straight on. He didn't know how he could help with his little bow and arrow, but in order for him to help feed his friends and family, he had to join the hunt.

"Get ready to move," Maxim said.

A water buffalo bellowed. A few hooves trampled the ground, and then the entire herd took off. Kase felt the anger and panic of the herd without even trying to connect with them.

"Go!" Maxim ordered. She lunged past Kase and headed with the herd towards the river.

Kase was surprised how fast the water buffalo could move through the trees. Branches broke and trees shook, but the water buffalo focused on their escape with grunts and bellows.

The herding reminded Kase of his work on the farm. Although his aunt and uncle could control cattle with their wizard power, they couldn't control many at once. They had to be precise with which animal they controlled, so that those cows or bulls could lead the rest of the herd. Sometimes Kase would have to stand in harm's way and wave his arms so that the cattle could see him clearly and avoid him; at the time he didn't have his own wizard powers, so his actions were the only way to manipulate the herd.

It wasn't always perfect, but it was effective.

Kase and Maxim were at the far end of where the langaras were set up, closest to the water. The buffalo were charging fast, but Kase was able to make it to the edge of the trees before the herd. Maxim was already in position, ensuring that the buffalo headed into the water and didn't turn to run down the embankment.

Maxim's father Chance roared from deep in the forest. Kase felt the herd shift. Instead of heading directly towards the river, they curled towards where Maxim and Kase were stationed.

"Something's wrong," Kase warned Maxim.

"I see it." Maxim crept towards the water, but stayed on the edge of the trees. She let out a low growl.

It was too late. Kase felt the leaders of the herd turn down the shoreline instead of crossing the water. He jumped forwards and stood in their path, waving his arms frantically. He felt their anger increase as the leader focused in on him.

Maxim jumped beside Kase and roared.

The water buffalo were undeterred; they simply sped faster towards them. Kase knew that the buffalo couldn't be turned towards the water at this point. There was no way for them to escape—but he didn't feel like getting trampled today.

Kase quickly used his power to connect with each one of the water buffalo, and helped them feel peaceful instead of panicked. They all dug their hooves into the riverbank simultaneously, and ground to a halt. They all stared at Kase and Maxim, now quiet and calm.

Maxim lowered her wings. "Strange," she said.

Kase stepped towards the herd, and manipulated the leader to lower his head. Kase rested his palm on the snout of the massive beast, and felt the calm take over his entire body.

Chance landed with a thud behind Kase, along with Raiden and the three other langaras that were hunting with them today. "What's going on?" Chance asked.

"I'm using my power to control them," Kase said. "Don't worry, we're all safe."

"How?" Raiden asked.

"As a wizard, I can connect with other animals," Kase explained. "I can feel their emotions, and manipulate their movements to a certain extent. In this case, the water buffalo are calm and content, so they feel no need to defend themselves or cause any destruction."

"Do you control us?" Chance asked.

Kase felt the worry creep in. Luckily, he was able to separate his emotions from the water buffalo, so everything remained safe. "I can't," Kase said. "You're too complex, unlike the water buffalo. They're simple-minded."

Maxim grumbled, but that's how langaras laughed. Chance didn't stop staring at Kase.

"Can all of your kind do this?" Raiden asked.

"Not to this extent," Kase answered. "I'm controlling all fifty-six of these water buffalo at once. Normally, a wizard might be able to control only a few at a time."

"You're able to do this, yet you let us carry on with our hunt?" Chance asked.

Kase sighed. He wondered how his relationship with the langaras might change if they felt threatened by his power. But he couldn't lie to them. "I wanted to hunt with you, and earn my first kill the way a new member of your pride does," Kase said. "This feels like cheating, because it's different than your tradition."

Chance purred. "Thank you for respecting our customs," he said. "But you don't have to hide who you are. Your talents are unique, and can help us in new ways while protecting us from making poor judgements. If Maxim knew of your ability, she might not have risked her life by jumping to your side."

Maxim bowed. Kase took the moment to appreciate that Maxim had his back, and would have been trampled with Kase under normal circumstances. Maxim might have known that Kase would bring her back to life, but she would have felt the pain of death nonetheless.

"You will never be one of us," Chance continued. "But that doesn't mean we can't live in harmony. We will continue to hunt to the best of our ability, but when you join the hunt, we have more advantages. You've earned the right to fight by our side. Now, it's finally your turn to make the kill. Which one will you choose?"

Kase looked back to the water buffalo herd. He understood the need for the langaras to eat, and he was honoured by Chance's respectful gesture of welcoming Kase as a hunter. There was nothing ceremonious about the end of today's hunt: just the need for predators to satisfy their hunger.

Remembering what his uncle had taught him about livestock, Kase sifted through the water buffalo herd. He waved his hand towards the river, and controlled which animals would cross to safety. All of the buffalo remained calm as he guided them along.

The first to cross were the biggest water buffalo. They were the leaders of the herd, and would offer protection so that their numbers could remain strong. He also guided the females across the water, since they could give birth to new calves.

He focused on an older male, who had enough meat to feed all the langaras, but was past his prime compared to the younger, stronger males. Kase guided the older male forwards. The rest of the herd finally regrouped on the other side of the river. He released his power over the herd, and they quickly moved away to a new pasture.

"Good choice," Raiden said.

Standing in front of the single water buffalo made Kase realize how weak his choice of weapon was for the hunt. A single arrow might penetrate the rough skin of the water buffalo, but it wouldn't reach any vital organs.

Kase drew his sword, but didn't know if he had the strength to drive the blade through the muscular frame of the giant beast. Instead he set it into the ground, with the tip of the blade facing the bottom of water buffalo's neck.

Kase closed his eyes and felt the water buffalo drop to the ground.

Just before its neck hit the tip of Kase's sword, Kase lunged backwards, letting go of the handle. The weight of the beast was enough to cause the sword to penetrate its neck and head, delivering a single, deadly blow that was nearly painless. Kase felt his power diminish as the water buffalo's life came to an end.

Chance crept towards the head of the water buffalo, while all the other langaras surrounded the carcass. Chance purred again. "Killers eat first," he said. He bit the horn of the water buffalo and lifted its head so Kase could grab his sword.

The other langaras roared in support.

Kase puffed his chest out. He hoped he'd be able to pull his sword out easily, to show his strength.

It wasn't like sliding through butter, but he managed to retrieve his weapon without embarrassing himself. He moved to the buffalo's flank and carved out his portion. He wrapped the meat to take back to the castle.

While the rest of the langaras feasted, Kase walked home alone. The hunt was supposed to be an escape from his responsibilities, but the events hadn't provide any relief. His fear of disrespecting the langaras had lifted, and he was grateful that his relationship with them had grown in unforeseen ways. He wondered why he had been so worried of hiding his power from the langaras in the first place. Although things had changed, they had adapted to it and then continued on as if that were normal.

Did that mean change was inevitable?

Kase felt his confidence build. He needed to speak with Lenia, Aura, and Cali. Their strategy of striking fear into the Triple Crown had failed—so now they needed to adapt, and change their plans. Would Kase's power be more useful now that the Unicorn Knight had lost? Could his talents be shared with the world? If truth had gained the respect of the langaras, could it also earn the respect of the entire realm?

Blood from Kase's kill dripped from his carry sac, and ran down his arm. He wiped it away, smearing it over his mermaid design. The octopus ink permanently outlined the symbols of a sword, fire, and quill. When he'd gotten the ink design, he wanted a reminder of the strength in unity between warriors, wizards, and scholars. It paralleled the bond he felt between his wizard and scholar friends.

His bond with his surroundings had grown beyond his friendships. With his advanced power, he was connected to the langaras, other animals, the weather—even life and death. Even though he was still discovering the benefits of those bonds, the drawbacks also humbled him. There was strength in working through his weaknesses.

He enjoyed the walk back to the castle, and was happy to find everyone gathered in the kitchen. He put his sac of meat on the counter, sat down beside Lenia, and grabbed some fruit. He was starving.

"Go wash up first, Kase," Ashlyn said. She nibbled on some bread. There was nothing silly about her brunch.

Kase stood and went to the washbasin. Cali, Dom, and Aura sipped their tea. Each of them seemed deep in thought. Talen was scribbling something in her notebook. Lenia stared at Kase, as if mesmerized by his presence.

Kase smiled at Lenia as he scrubbed his arms. She pointed to her cheek, so Kase did the same. He hadn't realized he had some blood spatter on his face. He dipped his hands into the water, and then gave his face a quick scrub too. He returned to the table refreshed.

"How's the hunter?" Cali asked.

"Hunt her, he barely knows her!" Dom said.

Kase ignored the comment, which didn't get any laughs. "I made my first kill," Kase admitted. He wasn't looking for praise, but he did want to lighten the mood. Only Dom seemed upbeat.

Lenia leant on Kase's shoulder and hugged his arm.

"What did we get?" Aura asked.

"Buffalo," Kase said. "I was hoping we could have a feast tonight. Invite Roman, Helena, and Curtis, and take some time to celebrate."

"Celebrate what?" Cali scorned. "We've lost. There's uproar in the capital about the Unicorn Knight destroying landmarks. You and Lenia used to be wanted dead or alive, but now it's just dead. People were cheering the High Scholar this morning when he made his address."

Cali passed her sage mirror to Aura, who bypassed Lenia and gave it directly to Kase.

Kase didn't look at the sage mirror. "Things have changed, but that's okay," he said. "We'll just adapt our plans, and move forwards. I have an idea—"

"We've already discussed it," Cali said. "We're going to lie low for a while and let the heat die down a little bit. We're trying to decide on a vacation spot, since Jenim Island seems to be too dangerous." Jenim Island was a good place to escape to, since Guardians didn't patrol it; the only other place in the realm without Guardians was under the sea in the City of the Mermaids, but only those with a mermaid trident like Lenia would be able to breathe.

"It's just a little too soon for me," Dom said. He lowered his head. "The birds …"

Lenia squeezed Kase's arm tighter.

Kase tried to understand where his friends and family were coming from, but he was also tired of them making all the decisions. "It's time for us to unmask ourselves," he said bluntly.

"No, brother," Cali said. "We've already discussed this, and we're not even close to—"

"I understand how careful you've been with your planning," Kase said. "And I appreciate everything you, Aura, and Lenia have done as leaders. But you don't have to make all the important decisions alone. Is it reasonable to consider something new? Since we are stronger together?" Kase lifted his left arm and pointed at his mermaid design.

Cali leant forwards. "What did you have in mind?"

"When Lenia was trapped, Mardious spoke about controlling the story," Kase said. "Even though he had destroyed the landmark, he could blame it on the Unicorn Knight. His title gives him credibility, but we have something more powerful. The truth."

Ashlyn perked up and smiled. Talen also stopped writing and looked up from her notes.

"Our actions have given us a voice, but our masks don't define us," Kase continued. "We aren't different beasts as the A.K., because they're only a part of who we are. We're the same animal and the same beast, and we're connected to the entire realm. We need to build that connection stronger by spreading the truth, rather than hiding from the Triple Crown and their lies."

Dom leant forwards. "This reminds me of Money Jane," he said. "Nobody knew her identity, so she was feared by the realm because she was unknown. Compare her rebellion to Mardious Hood: because he was more of a real person in the eyes of the public, it gave substance to his cause. He was able to recruit an army from the Badlands because they knew him, and thus he represented a formidable foe against the Triple Crown. Unmasking makes you a target for your enemies, but it also attracts others who feel the same."

"But in our instance, it's not just Kase and Lenia who would be unmasked," Cali said. "It's all of us. Those who are here now, our extended families that are currently safe in the realm, and … this changes our future."

"Change isn't easy, but it is inevitable," Kase said. "And we don't have to sacrifice what we're afraid of losing in order to gain what we're missing. We can still keep our new home in this kingdom, but stretch our services to others in the realm. Aura can meet new people. Lenia can spend time with her family. Dom and Ashlyn can vacation in places besides the island of the giants."

"Same animals, same beasts," Lenia said, rubbing Kase's arm.

"It's not just about punishing the Triple Crown, and exposing them for the vindictive leaders that they are." Kase looked at his mother. "It's about giving people a chance to grow together. We can't become powerful on our own, overtake the Triple Crown as leaders, and expect the realm to adapt to our new and wonderful leadership. We need to share the power of the doorway of life. We need to show others that it's not necessarily a superior gift, but a part of an evolving and beautiful world. The Triple Crown's answer is death. Our truth is life."

"Is the world ready for this?" Aura asked.

"I can draft some articles about our journey," Talen said. "Explain what the doorway of life is, the Triple Crown's attempt to piece it together, and the unruly ways they tried to steal the power for themselves."

"I don't think that will be enough," Cali said. "Once we give this information to the world, it's a new beginning. But it's not an end to the Triple Crown."

"There will be some growing pains, but we can come up with different strategies to mitigate the fallout," Lenia said. She squeezed Kase's arm again. "As long as we make those plans together."

Cali stood and leant on the table. "Okay," she said with a smile. "We have a lot of planning to do, but we have time to make sure we consider all the factors before moving forwards. Thank you, brother, for speaking up. Maybe we should take some time to reflect on and celebrate this new idea."

Dom stood and smiled at Kase. "I second that notion," he said. "I'm proud of you, son. I wonder where you got those good, scholarly ideas from."

"From my mother, obviously," Kase said. Everyone chuckled, except for Talen and Dom. Talen was back to scribbling notes in her notebook, more furiously than before.

# CHAPTER 20

# Freaking My Mind Out

Kase slowed his breathing. The horse-drawn cart he was lying in bounced as it travelled down the cobblestone lanes of Kimroad. The motion was soothing, as if his back was getting treated to a massage.

Curtis, Helena, and Talen had modified the cart to look like a circus cage, with bars on one side and wood covering the rest. Black linens covered the bars, so the only light was whatever crept in through the cracks.

The red tint of Kase's helmet dimmed the late afternoon sunshine further. He felt Lenia nestle against him, but they didn't need to be relaxed; they needed to be ready. They were riding into the belly of the beast.

They had decided to confront their enemies head-on, instead of drawing them out into the open. The Triple Crown leaders would not expect such a bold attack; plus, they couldn't hide behind the walls of their castle if the A.K. infiltrated their stronghold.

Escape wasn't an issue, since the Triple Crown already knew of Lenia's abilities: once she was unmasked, she didn't need to create a smokescreen to teleport away. They just needed to keep it simple: get in, make a statement, and get out.

The A.K. was a force to be reckoned with.

The horse-drawn cart slowed to a stop. Kase and Lenia sat up, but were careful not to lean against any of the walls.

"State your business," an authoritative voice said.

"I've captured the Unicorn Knight," Curtis grumbled. He kept his voice low as part of his disguise. Even so, it was unlikely that any guards at the Triple

218

Crown castle would recognize him, since his previous experience working as a Guardian had limited him to street duty.

"Unicorn Knight capture claims are taken to the warrior stables," the guard said. He seemed unimpressed. "Go five blocks east, make a left, and enter the last gate on that side of the castle perimeter."

"I haven't been to the capital in a while, but I'm familiar," Curtis said. "Isn't Paula's Deli down that way? I could go for a peanut butter and jelly sandwich."

"I don't think so," the guard said. "Do you need the directions again?"

"No, no, I remember," said Curtis. "Thank you, sir."

Kase wasn't aware of any delis in the area, but Curtis had done well to integrate the code word on the spot. Roman had advised the team that no plans were perfect, so they'd created phrases to signal any pivots to their strategy. 'Peanut butter and jelly' meant to trust each other and continue as planned. 'Bacon and eggs' meant proceed with caution. 'Tea time' meant abort the plan and retreat.

Kase wondered what the phrases would have been if they hadn't been decided over brunch. Considering they spent weeks planning their attack, the code words themselves weren't that important. It was the message that was key: create chaos in front of as many witnesses as possible, stand up to the leaders of the Triple Crown, and take ownership of the destruction.

Curtis led the horses down the correct path, and was stopped by the High Guardian at the warrior stable gate. After stating his intentions again, he received the response they were looking for.

"Show me," the High Guardian ordered.

A thud signalled Curtis' dismount. A few steps later, the cover of the cage slowly peeled open. Kase and Lenia both stared at the High Warrior peeking in, but didn't make any sort of acknowledgement.

"Nice costumes, but the lion looks a little dull," he said. He made a signal to someone out of view. "Good luck," he said.

"Good luck?" Curtis let the cover drop.

"Go left of the entrance and join the line close to the wall," the Guardian said. "There are only four ahead of you right now, so you came at a good time."

Curtis climbed back onto the cart and set the wheels in motion. Kase slid to the side with the bars. He pulled the cover to one side while Lenia hovered over him. Their view was met with a shaded castle wall.

Lenia spun to the other side and gently pressed her hands against the wall to peer through a crack between the slats. Kase crawled beside her, and found an opening closer to the floor.

The entrance to the stables was halfway in the courtyard of the castle. Kase recognized it from when they had first tried to unmask Zuke as Mardious Hood.

The short path and the surrounding grassy area that led to the stables was empty. Chariots were parked on the far side of the area, but the only one Kase recognized was Mardious' golden carriage. He tried to tilt his head, but he couldn't see where Curtis was taking them.

"What do you think?" Lenia asked.

"Bacon and scrambled eggs," Kase said.

The cart stopped. A louder thud soon sounded on the carriage's barred side. Kase slid back to Curtis as he peeled the cover open.

"We can't see anything," Kase said.

"There are two riders in front of us, each with two dead bodies dragged behind the horses," Curtis said. He was bobbing his head to get a better look. "Someone is talking to a High Guardian, who is holding a boot in one hand and a leash in the other. There are two hounds, but they're not doing anything."

Lenia rushed over. "They must be using the scent from my boot left at the odeum to identify the real Unicorn Knight," she said.

"So if we make it to the front, we'll be caught," Kase said.

"It's time, Kodiak Mountain," Lenia said. "Park us between the stables and the gate, so we have a good view of anyone joining our party."

Curtis tapped his chest twice, kissed his fingers, and pointed to the sky. He grabbed his helmet and war axe from a compartment under his seat.

Kase stood and opened a panel they had installed to access the compartment from inside the cage. The compartment was as long as the seat, and had ample room for all their swords, arrows, and potions. He grabbed his quiver and swung it over his shoulder, and then gripped his bow. Lenia grabbed her sword and a potion bottle.

"Hiyah!" Curtis yelled.

The carriage pivoted quickly. Kase peered out the corner of the cover. Jax was staring at the cart, holding the leash of two hounds as Curtis had described. Two other warriors stood next to him, each holding a sage mirror.

"Rematch," Lenia said. She ran to back of the carriage and grabbed the wooden pin that held the far corner together.

"Same animal, same beast," Kase said. The new mantra was a reminder for both of them to be the complete version of themselves, rather than being too aggressive or too conservative.

The rumbling carriage stopped. Kase grabbed the wooden pin above his head, at the front of the carriage. He connected with the two horses pulling their cart, so they wouldn't panic at the loud noises they were about to make. He waited for Lenia's signal.

Lenia nodded. They both pulled their pins at the same time.

Kase stomped the barred wall to their right, while Lenia kicked the slatted wall to their left. Both sides fell open, with the roof going down with the barred wall. The back panel fell forwards, creating a ramp. The walls flopping down created three sides for them to escape down.

The courtyard they revealed was wider than it was long. Behind them was the castle gate, flanked by guard towers. Halfway down was the Guardian stables, followed by the outdoor sparring ring.

Hardly any Guardians were in attendance. Only those that guarded the castle entrance and overhanging balconies at the courtyard's far side were a direct threat, but plenty of support was available within the castle walls.

The clock was ticking.

Lenia slammed her potion bottle to the ground in front of the ramp. The glass exploded, and the potion burst to flames. It created a nice fireball, with flames that lingered on the doused grass.

Kase spun towards the gate and drew an arrow. He manipulated the fire Lenia had created so that a spark travelled to his arrow tip and ignited.

He didn't need to hide his magic anymore. He aimed at the guard tower and fired.

He discovered that he could control an arrow a little better when it was lit. Since he had power over the flame, he could ensure that it stayed on course. He'd practiced his warrior techniques for years, so he was more than capable of making a shot without his wizard power, but the fire manipulation added precision. Plus, he was quickly able to make the flame spread upon impact.

The lone High Guardian in the perch of the gate tower ducked. When Kase made the flame spread, the warrior headed for the stairs. Kase quickly pivoted and shot another arrow towards the carriages. He didn't necessarily want the magma solution in Mardious' carriage to ignite, but he wanted fire in that corner of the yard to give him the option just in case.

Curtis spun and faced the stables, from which a lone High Guardian charged with her sword held high. He gripped his war axe and got into a battle stance.

With his brown, open-faced helmet, the shaggy fur around his armour, and the scruffy beard he now sported, Curtis looked the part of the Kodiak Mountain. He screamed and engaged the High Guardian.

Barking turned Kase's attention back to Lenia. The hounds were off their leash and raced towards her. She had dipped her sword into the fire, and gripped the weapon as she readied for the attack.

To help Lenia out, Kase gained control over the angry dogs. They still charged forwards, but he made them split well in advance of attacking Lenia. They ran right around her and carried on to the two High Guardians charging Kase from the gate. The hounds leapt onto the warriors, biting and snarling. Kase was happy to have bought himself a little more time from that direction.

He also used his power to move their two horses, now unhitched from their cart, into the stables. They didn't block the entire walkway, but it would be more difficult for a charging Triple Crown army to enter the battleground.

Now they just had to worry about those already in the courtyard. Two mercenaries trying to cash in on fake Unicorn Knight and Dandy Lion bodies drew their swords and stepped towards Lenia.

Kase was about to fire a warning shot, but Jax stretched his hand out. "He's mine!" Jax shouted. He dropped the boot he was holding and drew his weapon.

One High Guardian was speaking into a sage mirror, but another accompanied Jax as he stalked forwards. It seemed like Jax and Lenia were destined for their rematch, but the additional High Guardian was worrisome.

The High Guardian that Curtis was fighting screamed. Kase checked to see what the Kodiak Mountain had accomplished: he stood over his enemy's corpse. He pulled his axe from the warrior and looked to Lenia. He seemed to have the same concern that Kase had, and headed to her side.

Kase turned his attention back to the mercenaries and shot flaming arrows in succession. He wasn't targeting individuals, but rather trying to set their possessions on fire. He purposefully didn't control their horses, so that the mercenaries' energy would need to be focused on calming them down.

A hound yelped. One of the High Guardians behind him had stabbed it in the leg. Kase fired an arrow at that warrior, impaling his side. The High Guardian rolled in pain as he tried to put the fire out. The other High Guardian was on the ground, curled up as the second hound tore at his shoulder plate.

Kase changed his strategy. He reached into the hidden compartment and grabbed his second quiver. Tiny surveillance mirrors, which they had purchased from a shop in Kimroad, hung from pendants attached to the arrows. He brought the quiver below his chin.

"Mirror, mirror, capture surveillance," he said, activating all of the mirrors at once. He pulled the first arrow and slammed it into the cart.

He then turned towards the stables and fired a couple surveillance arrows into the wooden posts on either side of the entrance. Others he tried to stick to the high points. He hoped Talen would get the info she needed from the battle, so she could share it with more witnesses before the Triple Crown inevitably put their own spin on what had happened. He didn't know how it was set up on the back end, but trusted Talen to collect the right moving images.

Lenia and Curtis had engaged with Jax and the High Guardian. Kase wanted to watch, but the other hound yelped. The warrior that had fled from the gate tower helped the cowering warrior stand. Their comrade wasn't on fire anymore, and limped to his sword.

Kase fired a few more surveillance arrows before dropping his bow. He reached into the weapons compartment and grabbed two swords. He stood at the edge of the cart, with one sword held defensively and the other pointed at the three High Guardians from the gate. He kept his higher position, hoping the Guardians would try to fight him from the ramp. They didn't even consider other possibilities, and rushed him together.

Kase swiped at the first two Guardians with his left, forcing them to block his attack together. He slammed the sword in his right down onto the lone Guardian on the edge, who had hobbled up with his wounded leg. The warrior crumbled and left himself vulnerable. Kase quickly stabbed him in the neck.

One down.

One of the remaining Guardians sliced across his midsection, which Kase blocked with his right sword. With his left, Kase slashed at the other Guardian, who defended against Kase's attack again. Kase kicked the attacking Guardian in the chest, knocking him back, and then with the added room followed through by stabbing the defending Guardian in the side with his right weapon. That Guardian crumpled and rolled down the ramp.

Two down.

The now-lone Guardian grabbed his first comrade's sword to charge at Kase with two weapons. Kase swung down at the warrior's head with one blade. The Guardian used both of his swords to block the attack, showing his inexperience with handling an enemy with two weapons. Kase stabbed him in the gut with his free blade, and then kicked him back down the ramp.

"Get these horses out of the way!" High Warrior Mac yelled.

Kase spun. The High Warrior had made it past the two carriage horses, and was pointing at some High Guardians behind him. He carried a shield in his left hand, and the purple hilt of his sword was clearly visible from his beltline. Kase recognized the hilt immediately. Mac's sword handle was made from the purple scales of a dragon Kase had killed.

Kase remembered the story Mac had told him, after Mardious Hood had pressed that sword against Kase's neck. Memories flooded Kase's mind of that day, of Mac and the task force betraying him, High Scholar Sheese killing Lenia, and Mardious Hood proposing Kase retrieve all the pieces of the doorway of life to bring her back.

Kase wondered if the scales would allow him to bring back the dragon, so that it could fight the three-headed monster of the Triple Crown. "Peanut butter and jelly," he mumbled.

Mac was focused on Lenia. He pointed at her while giving orders to Shay and Josephine. A couple other High Guardians with shields entered the stable.

Kase needed to draw the High Warrior away from Lenia. He dropped his swords, and snatched up his bow and an arrow. He fired and hit Mac's shield.

The High Warrior moved his guard up and stared at Kase over the rim. He drew his sword and pointed in Lenia's direction. He marched towards Kase, followed by Josephine. Shay and the rest of the High Guardians rushed towards Lenia and Curtis.

Jax needed the reinforcements. He was on the ground, favouring his leg. Lenia must have landed a deep cut, but she was now fighting the mercenaries. Curtis pulled his axe from another freshly-defeated High Guardian, and waited for the onrushing Shay.

Kase drew another arrow. He could have aimed for Mac's helmet or legs, but instead he focused over Mac's right shoulder at Josephine. She didn't have a shield, and was instead crouching behind the High Warrior for cover. If Kase took her out, it would be much easier to face Mac one-on-one.

Kase fired, but as soon as he let go of the bowstring, Josephine jumped behind Mac's opposite shoulder. She had a much better strategy compared to the other warriors in the battle. Kase fired again, but her anticipation was on point. She bobbed back to her original position.

Instead of staying on the ramp, Kase ditched his bow and picked his swords back up. He leapt off the cart and charged at the High Warrior. Before he could get to him, Josephine sprinted in front of Mac to defend him from the first attack.

Kase swung both swords down at Josephine, forcing her to block them with her own. He remembered sparring with her once during his short duty with the task force, and remembered that her strength was her speed and defense, but not her balance. He kicked her in the chest plate, forcing her to the ground.

High Warrior Mac charged overtop her, protecting his comrade. Kase side-stepped left, and blocked Mac's strike, forcing both tips towards the ground. Josephine had already bounced to her feet, but had backed up to give Mac space to swing. Kase spun so that he was in between Josephine and Mac, holding a sword high at each of them.

If Kase were trying to win the fight, he'd focus on Josephine first. She was the greater threat, since Mac was already sweating profusely. Kase could dance around with Josephine, tiring Mac out more with the chase. As imposing as Mac was, he didn't seem to have much endurance.

A door opened high on the parapet of the outer wall to Kase's right, beyond where Lenia and Curtis were fighting. Sheese stepped through first, followed by High Guardian archers. The archers spread out about five feet apart.

"Finally," High Warrior Mac said.

The A.K. was running out of time.

A door opened on the other side of the upper wall to Kase's left. Instead of waiting for more archers to march out, Kase swung again at Josephine. He telegraphed his attack, going high with his left sword in a backhanded attack, and then following with his right aimed at Josephine's midsection. He hoped Mac was paying attention.

Josephine blocked both attacks easily. High Warrior Mac stepped forwards, and Kase was happy to see Mac take advantage of his high swing to dip low and lunge forwards. Kase braced for the painful impact.

High Warrior Mac stabbed Kase through the side and into his stomach.

The sword was so sharp it cut through Kase's leather vest like butter. It hurt more than Kase thought it would, and he let out a scream. He dropped his weapons, grabbed the hilt so Mac couldn't rip it out, and fell backwards. The High Warrior let Kase fall.

The High Guardians cheered as Mac spread his arms in triumph. Shay had backed off from fighting Lenia, supporting Jax, and the High Guardians took a step away from Curtis.

"Dragoon!" Mac shouted as he slammed his fist into his chest.

"Dragoon!" High Guardians shouted back.

The blow wasn't a kill shot, so Kase lay on the ground thinking about his next move. Josephine stood, but didn't try to finish the job. She let Kase writhe in pain, but Kase was starting to feel tingly on the inside. Instead of dying, it was as if his body was already beginning to heal itself. All he had to do was pull the sword from his gut.

"It's over!" High Warrior Mac shouted at Lenia and Curtis. "Surrender now, or suffer the same fate as your partner."

Mardious Hood crept from the stables. He cautiously peered at Lenia and Curtis, but didn't seem as happy as the surrounding Guardians.

All three High Authority members of the Triple Crown were present. It was time for Kase to make his statement.

Kase stood without struggle. He could feel the magic flow through him, and the pain had disappeared. Josephine took a step back as Mac turned back towards Kase.

"Unlike you, we never surrender," Kase said.

"What?" High Warrior Mac said.

Kase undid his chinstrap, and let it dangle for a second. He removed his helmet and held it by the red mane. Shock crossed High Warrior Mac's face. The High Guardians looked confused. Mardious Hood grinned wickedly.

Using the flame from his burning arrows, Kase created a ring of fire around him, and then slowly expanded it. Josephine quickly retreated from the flames, while High Warrior Mac stumbled back. Mardious took a step forwards, studying Kase's moves but not trying to counter his element control.

Lenia teleported with Curtis, placing him on Kase's right. She disappeared for a second, but returned on his left with her trident in hand. The head of the trident burst into flames.

High Warrior Mac looked up towards Sheese. Mardious smiled brighter.

"Aim!" Sheese shouted. The archers readied their bows, all pointing arrows at Kase, Lenia, and Curtis. None of the Guardians on the ground moved. "Fire!" Sheese yelled.

Kase manipulated the fire into a dome. Once the arrows hit the flame, he ignited their tips and forced them to the ground. It felt like controlling the herd of water buffalo: like he was connected to each individual arrow. But dropping arrows was a lot easier than stopping a stampede. He pulled the flames back down, to prove that the onslaught had failed.

The High Guardians and the Triple Crown Authority were all silent.

Kase grabbed the blade sticking out of his stomach, and pulled it out. Each tug hurt, but his body was already primed up for healing. Once the sword was completely out, he slammed it into the ground and pulled off his vest. Blood oozed from his wound.

Everyone in the stable area stared at Kase. The surveillance mirrors still dangled from their arrows. He concentrated, and a bright light shone from his wound. After a few seconds, his body was completely healed.

"We are the Animal Kingdom!" Kase said.

Lenia disappeared again. She reappeared with Roman and Helena, placing them beside Curtis. Roman wore a new bull-horned helmet, while Helena had a similar one with curved horns, like a ram. They earned a few confused mutterings from the Guardian crowd. Lenia left again, and brought back Dom and Ashlyn. Dom wore a rooster helmet, while Ashlyn sported the goat.

Lenia made a final trip, bringing back Cali in her open-faced wolverine helmet. Kase took a deep breath, and began the speech that he and Cali had practiced.

"I am Kase Garrick," he said. "I was proud to serve the realm as a High Guardian, until the leaders of the Triple Crown murdered someone I love. They forced me to hunt for a relic that grants life, but they had no intention of bringing back those closest to me. They wanted the power for themselves."

Kase pointed to Mardious. "They are all criminals, led by none other than the infamous Mardious Hood. For years he's masqueraded as High Wizard Zuke, and used his influence for personal gain. Not only did he send warriors like me to their death in pursuit of powerful magic, but he also used government resources to improve his personal wealth. He's worked with High Scholar Sheese and High Warrior Mac to build a criminal empire."

The High Guardians looked around, but many of them didn't seem as shocked as Kase had anticipated. He wondered how many of them were already part of the Triple Crown's Shadow Army.

"We have proof," Cali said. "We'll release it to the public, so everyone can see the lies, scandals, and crimes that all three leaders have committed. We will also rectify our own crimes, and bring back those that were lost in our war with the Triple Crown. Our goal wasn't to take away the lives of the innocent, but to show the Triple Crown how valuable life is; it's the most valuable thing that we have."

"Your accusations have no merit," High Warrior Mac said. "And your promises have no substance. We will defend the realm from your tyranny and lies, and we will use the power you discovered for the greater good."

"That choice isn't up to you," Cali said. "It's not even up to us. What we present to you, your comrades, and the rest of the realm is that we all have a voice in this matter. The tools we need to make the best decision for all come in the form of truth, respect, and freedom."

Mardious stepped forwards, and waved his fingers through the flaming circle, but only enough to see the group clearly; he didn't try to cross the barrier. "You're willing to bring back everyone, regardless of their transgressions?"

"Life deserves a chance," Kase said. "Some lives need more chances than others. It might be scary, but we must support each other as we grow, regardless of our fears."

Kase spun High Warrior Mac's sword and pointed the hilt to the sky. "Years ago, I killed a dragon," he said. "It may have been in defense of my life, but death wasn't the only option. Hopefully, we can all learn from a past mistake."

Kase gripped the handle with both hands. He didn't know how his next move would play out, but if it did, it would gain attention from the entire realm.

His companions glanced sidelong at him. "Bacon and eggs," he muttered, and they crouched, ready. His hands glowed.

"Stop him!" Sheese yelled.

Instead of living the last moments of the dragon's life, Kase immediately felt the pain of the lava. The fire melted his skin, tore through his body, and curled down his throat. As the pain became unbearable, the fire seemed to change course, like a swirling wind. Instead of it flowing inward, it began to explode out from his core. He felt a grumbling in his stomach, and then fire poured from his screaming mouth.

When he came back to reality, a fight had broken out. Roman was occupying three High Guardians. Dom was firing arrows at Mac, who was backing up to the stables. Mardious was hiding against a post, but looking up in wonder.

The A.K. stood together under the belly of the resurrected dragon. The dragon's head coiled into view, dipping low to study Kase. Both its eyes glared at him as it growled. Steam escaped its nostrils. Kase wondered if he could communicate with it like he did with the langaras.

"Hi," Kase thought.

The dragon stopped growling, but didn't offer a response.

"Fire!" Sheese shouted.

Arrows rained down on the dragon, but they bounced off its scales. The dragon winced, but didn't cry out in pain. It raised its head in Sheese's direction with a roar. It opened its wings, and its throat glowed orange. Fire shot at the balcony where Sheese stood.

The High Scholar dove back into the castle just before the flame destroyed the parapet. Some archers fell to the ground, while others were ablaze. A few, like Sheese, had managed to escape the dragon's attack.

Lenia appeared beside Kase and grabbed his arm.

She teleported them back to their new safe haven in the gold mines of Jenim Island, where the rest of the A.K. was waiting. He hadn't realized that she'd already teleported the rest of the team. Roman was pacing, Ashlyn was rubbing Dom's shoulder, and Cali was writing notes in her journal.

Talen sat at a large desk with three large sage mirrors. Aura stood behind her, studying and pointing to the moving images. Two of the sage mirrors showed the action at the castle, while the middle one was used to put together a sequence of the moving images.

"Is everyone okay?" Kase asked.

Kase felt a slap on the shoulder. "That was crazy, Two Times!" Curtis exclaimed. "But we did it! We won!"

"We accomplished what we set out to do, but time will prove our success," Cali said. "We can't wait for the chaos to end on its own, though. It's time to start phase two."

Kase nodded. He didn't want to slow down. He felt the need to reflect on his positive emotions, so he turned to Lenia. She disappeared before he could reach out to her.

The rest of the team took off their outfits, and got to work on organizing the room. Lenia returned with a few dead bodies, and Curtis and Roman helped organize them into manageable piles. Helena, Ashlyn, and Dom took an inventory count.

It was difficult to celebrate how far they'd come in that moment. After weeks of planning, they had succeeded in getting the attention of the Triple Crown and the rest of the realm. However, it was difficult for them to feel like all their hard work had paid off. Their battle with the leaders of the Triple Crown wasn't ending; it was only the beginning.

"We haven't won yet," Cali said. She leant beside Talen and studied the moving images while Talen made a few notes.

"What's happening?" Kase asked. He rushed over to view the images that his special arrows were capturing. He hoped he had all angles covered.

"The dragon is perched on the castle wall," Aura said. "It's not concerned with the High Guardians, but High Warrior Mac is panicking."

"With everyone preoccupied by the dragon, it's the perfect time to go after the High Authority," Cali said.

"The High Warrior is the only one in the courtyard," Lenia said from behind them. She dragged a High Guardian body neatly beside her pile. "But I think we should go after the High Scholar."

"Capturing the High Scholar is ideal for our plan, but not until we're ready for phase three," Cali said. "Remember that we can't bring him here alive, in case he recognizes where we're hiding."

Kase shook his head. "You agreed that revenge isn't the answer," he said to Lenia.

Lenia removed her helmet, then put on a High Guardian one instead. "It's not," she said. "Peanut butter and jelly."

"Do you know where he is?" Roman asked.

"He likely retreated to his office," Cali said. She flipped to the back of her journal, and pointed to one of the maps she'd created of the castle.

"We'll take on his army together," Helena said. She tapped her chest twice, kissed her fingers, and pointed to the sky.

"Thank you, Mrs. Garrick," Lenia said. She removed another High Guardian helmet from one of the bodies. "But a smaller team will work better; just the Unicorn Knight and the Dandy Lion."

Kase smirked. His nickname had grown on him, especially when Lenia didn't say it to tease him. "I'll need a sword," he said. He dropped the scaleless, damaged hilt he was still holding, took a weapon from one of the dead warriors, and also put on a chest plate.

Lenia also wore a chest plate, but looked out of place with her black pants and trident. Neither of them looked like proper High Guardians, but their disguise attempt would likely work in a castle full of mayhem.

Instead of teleporting back to the stable yard, Lenia took Kase to a stairwell outside a secret room in the castle of the Triple Crown. They were alone, but they could hear screams from inside the castle, and roars from outside. They hustled up the stairs, turned a few corners, and jogged down the hallways until they met five High Guardians guarding Sheese's office.

Instead of engaging in combat, Lenia teleported each Guardian away; Kase didn't know where.

When the entrance was clear, they burst into the office to find Sheese sitting at his desk. The High Scholar didn't even look up from his book.

Kase jammed his sword into the handles of the double doors so they couldn't swing open. He walked cautiously with Lenia, until they stood in front of the desk. The High Scholar was unarmed.

"Did you come here to share your power with me?" Sheese asked. He continued to stare at his book.

"You couldn't handle it," Lenia said.

Sheese looked up with a smile. "So what you promised isn't true then, is it?"

"The time for talking is over," Lenia said. "It's time for action." She unsheathed her sword and slammed the tip into Sheese's desk. She was a little off-balance because she kept her other hand behind her back.

"I didn't realize you were calling the shots, Unicorn Knight," Sheese snickered. "I should have recognized the plan of a wizard. So naïve. I know I trained Cali better than this."

"We're in this together," Kase said. He didn't know what Lenia's plan was, but he could tell she was facing her demons as she glared at her killer. She needed this moment, and could handle it on her own, but he wanted to show her that he had her back no matter what.

"And it is due to that none of you know what it is like to be a leader," Sheese said. "The masses don't know what they want. They lead lives of satisfaction, not of glory. Your pursuit is too ambitious for the general public, which is why you've already failed."

"Failing isn't a bad thing," Lenia said. "We've failed many times, including paying the ultimate price." She pointed her sword at the High Scholar. "As wise as you claim to be as a leader, you don't know what it's like to die, do you?" She rested her blade on his shoulder close enough to shave his stubble.

Sheese's eyes grew wide, and he remained silent.

"Why me?" Lenia asked. Her lip quivered. "Why did you kill *me*?"

Sheese raised an eyebrow. "It worked, didn't it?" He nodded at Kase. "Death is a powerful motivator. It gave us—"

"So you didn't even consider the heartbreak that others would feel?" Lenia asked. "My friends? My family?"

"Sacrificing one life for thousands is noble," Sheese asked. "Wouldn't you agree?"

"You didn't give me that choice." A tear ran down Lenia's cheek. She pressed her sword into Sheese's neck.

The office doors jerked. "It's locked!" Someone grunted.

Sheese smiled. "Your time is up," he said. "I killed you once, and I'll do it again. My armies won't stop until they take back what I've given you."

"Knock it down!" Mardious shouted.

Lenia raised her sword, but didn't follow through. Instead she smiled, and brought her other hand up. Dangling from an arrow was a surveillance pendant.

"We have something greater," she said proudly, looking over her shoulder at Kase. "The truth."

Kase smiled back. Lenia had captured Sheese's entire confession. His words would damage his reputation beyond any evidence that the A.K. had on him.

"No," Sheese said. His chair ground back, but before he could lunge forwards, Lenia teleported to Kase's side. "No!" Sheese shouted.

Lenia teleported Kase back to their hiding post on Jenim Island. The rest of the A.K. were huddled around Talen's desk, looked over expectantly, and cheered.

Lenia raised the surveillance mirror in triumph. "Now, we've won!" she exclaimed.

Kase beamed. Lenia had faced her demons and won. They had compelling evidence against the mastermind of the Triple Crown. They had made their first moves to announce themselves to the realm. Yes, that put them, and their families, in danger, but it also opened the eyes of the people. If they acted fast, they could get everyone to safety before combating the lies of the Triple Crown with their truth.

The A.K. had so much to do.

As Talen and Aura prepared the moving images and other evidence to broadcast to the rest of the realm, Lenia kept watch over the mayhem and destruction. She teleported a few more bodies to the Jenim Island gold mine while Roman, Curtis, and Helena restrained the dead with rope and shackles. Lenia would then teleport the dead bodies to an abandoned warehouse in Kimroad, where Kase would bring the High Guardians back to life.

Kase was proud that the A.K.'s bold, unorthodox, and risky plan had succeeded, because it meant they were taking their first steps to change the realm. They all understood and anticipated the uncertainty that now lay ahead of them, but they were ready to ride that path together. They were free from the confines of their hidden kingdom, passionate about their cause, and courageous enough to speak their truth, even though the Triple Crown had tried to bury them.

From The Wolverine to Kodiak Mountain, they were all doing their part for the greater good; the burden didn't lie solely on the shoulders of the Unicorn Knight or the Dandy Lion, because each member of the Animal Kingdom had their job to do. They had all grown so much individually that Kase trusted they'd evolve even more.

It might take years for the realm to heal from the destruction caused by the leaders of the Triple Crown, but truth was on their side. Change would happen eventually, but it didn't have to be all at once. Like the Animal Kingdom, it was time for the rest of the realm to be a little less broken.